T0244695

SERPENT'S FURY

DAVID BRUNS

CHRIS POURTEAU

SEVERN RIVER PUBLISHING

Severn River Publishing
www.SevernRiverBooks.com

ISBN: 978-1-64875-548-4 (Paperback)

ALSO BY BRUNS AND POURTEAU

The SynCorp Saga

The Lazarus Protocol

Cassandra's War

Hostile Takeover

Valhalla Station

Masada's Gate

Serpent's Fury

Never miss a new release! Sign up to receive exclusive updates from authors Bruns and Pourteau!

severnriverbooks.com/series/the-syncorp-saga

1

STACKS FISCHER • EN ROUTE TO THE MOON

I'd always wanted eyes in the back of my head. They'd come in right handy in my line of work. The way the g-forces were pulling on us, I wouldn't have to wait for Christmas.

The *Coyote* cut through space like one of Minnie the Mouth's Darkside customers on the lam from a jealous wife. Gregor Erkennen assured us the discomfort would be temporary as the ship got up to cruising speed, a small price to pay as his hypercharged Frater Drive, that miracle of modern magic, sped us to the Moon in half the time it should've taken. But I'd forgotten to check the fine print: he hadn't promised anything about us making it alive or even remaining three dimensional.

Four days to get there? Sure. And conveniently flattened for easy burial. No extra charge.

I sure missed the close comforts of the Hearse.

On my right sat my co-decedent—er, co-pilot—Bekah Franklin. Couldn't see her facial expressions side-on through my vac-suit helmet and hers, but I didn't need to. Her gloves gripped the chair hard, like maybe that'd help make us safer.

"Mandatory backup caution," Erkennen said when I'd asked about the need for the suits. I felt like an old-timey astronaut in mine. "You know, just in case."

"Just in case what?" I asked. But he'd just smiled and clapped me on the shoulder. Now I thought I knew. Just in case the ship ripped apart? Just in case the atmosphere vented?

The real reason was less humorous and more fundamental, pun intended—there was no getting up and retiring to the onboard toilet to tend to the mechanics of nature. Hell, blinking was a challenge, even with the anti-stroke drugs we had bolstering our bloodstreams. But sure, it'd all be fine as soon as the *Coyote* got up to speed.

Flying wasn't Bekah Franklin's thing. She seemed to be a fan of the sedate life one finds living on solid ground, even when that ground is an asteroid orbiting Titan. Come to think of it, so was I.

"How are you doing over there?" I asked through comms. I kind of had to push the words out of my mouth. Even speech felt restrained by the g's we were pulling.

Before she could answer, the *Coyote* began to vibrate like we'd just hit turbulence. Only there isn't air in space. So whatever turbulence there was came from the ship itself. Have I ever mentioned how much I absolutely despise new tech?

"Fiii-ii-iiiine," Bekah answered. I was unconvinced. For one thing, her grip on her seat arms disagreed. And I couldn't tell if it was the ship's shaking apart or her own clearly unfounded concerns that had put the tremolo into her voice. I thought she might be trying out for the opera soon.

The *Coyote*'s course had been pre-programmed on Masada Station, which was good considering our lack of mobility. I'd advised a shadowing of the Frater Lanes connecting the outer system to the inner, which would give us the best of both worlds—routes pre-screened for safety but far enough out of the mainlanes so no one would see us. Even the satellite system that lined the route with overlapping lidar to keep ships from crashing into each other didn't ping this far off the main routes. We should be damned near invisible. Then again, if anyone had seen us, I doubt they could catch us. So: upside.

"Approaching optimal acceleration," the *Coyote* said. Its emulator was robotic and eerie, like an old text-to-speech device. The lifeless tone didn't help reassure me of the ship's care for its passengers. Again, I missed the

Hearse—she loved me, and the feeling was mutual. "Inertial dampeners engaging in five, four, three, two, one..."

The force pulling my eyeballs against the back of my skull dropped a bit. I think I actually felt my brain expand forward again. The pressure on my spine decreased, and a part of me, specifically my bladder now that it was freely suspended in my innards, regretted slugging back the scotch and beer with Daisy Brace on the station before we'd left. Well, that's what the vac-suit was for. In a minute or two, I'd pass on my regret and only be left with the good memory of our parting.

Daisy had told me the story of Admiral Matthias Galatz finding her on Pallas when he'd landed, hoping to arrest a few space pirates. He'd mistaken her for one of those, she said, until she supplied him with some bona fides about Adriana Rabh. Only Rabh's own right hand would know the secrets of the double-bar-R clan that Daisy knew, and so Galatz had transferred her to his ship, the *SCS Sovereign*—to sickbay instead of the brig.

Staring into her mug of Masada's finest hoppy brew, she said, "They called it stunner sickness. Heard of frayed nerves? This was the definition of that. More like *fried* nerves."

I let her sit with that for a minute. The somewhat misnamed "stunner" tech—most people don't bother using the lower setting when it's so much more fun to electrocute someone—catalyzes a person's electromagnetic field and shocks them. Daisy had caught a glancing shot on Pallas, so I'd grabbed the intel we'd come for and left Daisy on the flight deck of the pirates' cove to take her own life—her choice to avoid a doom worse than death for people like us. But when she'd tried to embrace Mother Universe, her own stunner had misfired. By the time we were reunited on Masada Station, Gregor Erkennen and his medical wizards had already had her working back from paraplegia with something called neurological reconstitution therapy—aided physically by an exosuit specially designed to rehabilitate wounded soldiers.

I still didn't quite believe I was sitting in a bar orbiting Titan with Daisy next to me, alive and semi-well. I don't get sentimental. I don't get attached. But Daisy Brace and her give-as-good-as-you-get smartassery had wormed their way into my affections, something I hadn't even noticed consciously until I thought she was gone forever.

I took my time with my own beer. No sense rushing that, and no need to speed the conversation along. Gregor Erkennen might be anxious to get me gone, but he couldn't launch his Moon mission without me. And while saving Tony and the Company were top priority, I had other, more immediate concerns. One, anyway.

"Adriana know you're alive yet?" I asked.

"Nope." Daisy took another draw on her mug. The rehab suit helped her lift it to her lips. I wondered if the suit was permanent or if she was just renting. "Nobody knows what's happened to her. Not even Galatz. All he knows is she ordered him here instead of Callisto." The suit lowered the mug, and it clunked, empty. "Adriana is sometimes too smart for her own good by half."

I nodded, hearing what sounded like a daughter's concern for a mother's boldness. Adriana Rabh had lost her regency but placed the Company above that by sending Galatz to defend Masada Station. You had to admire the sand in that decision.

"Barkeep," I said, "two more." I drained my stein so he only had to make one trip because I'm considerate like that. My thinking then: I had four days of sitting in a chair to sleep off the hangover. Little did I know...

"I can't feel a damned thing," Daisy complained, as if reading my mind. She turned to look at me, and she was stiff in the suit. Like a crash victim whose neck decides it can only turn halfway. I hung on to her eyes for a little longer, or she hung on to mine. She broke the awkwardness when the barkeep replaced our empty mugs. She nodded her thanks, and he returned to his other customers. "Regent Erkennen's healing nanobugs are making it harder to get drunk," she observed.

"You should've had him fast-track brain cell repair," I said. "So, you could kill 'em proper."

Daisy smirked. "*Now* you tell me."

"Barkeep!" I said. He'd have to make a second trip after all. "Add two more scotches. Make hers a double."

The Draft King grunted acknowledgment.

"Thanks," Daisy said, friendly and meaning it. "So, you don't look so good yourself. I heard you took out an entire SSR strike force singlehanded."

I watched the Draft King place four shot glasses on the bar.

"That's an overstatement," I said, leering at Daisy in my peripheral. Her eyes were alive with humor and curiosity. "I used both hands."

She smiled.

The Draft King poured the shots, sloppy so the scotch spilled over. That's how you know it's not the good stuff. No one cares if they waste it.

"How long till you're not walking like Frankenstein's monster again?" I asked.

Daisy had to turn her body to get a better angle on me. "You think I'm a monster?"

I wasn't falling for the diversion. "How long?"

Daisy shrugged.

The barkeep placed two shots in front of each of us. "Anything else?"

"Sure, in five minutes," I said, dismissing him. I wagged a finger across the two mugs and four shot glasses. "All that, again."

He raised his eyebrows like he wasn't sure they'd let me back in the home if I came back staggering. I just stared at him until he remembered he had other customers.

There was a whir and click I hadn't noticed before. Daisy's suit, picking up one of the shot glasses for her. She downed it. The gasp and grimace were all her own.

Out of courtesy, I didn't press my question. Instead, I shot my own scotch. Once we'd both downed the second round, she cleared her throat.

"Erkennen says he doesn't know for sure, but it shouldn't be too much longer. We're working on it."

That surprised me, in a good way. I'd been prepping my gut to hear the suit was permanent.

"Well ... that's good," I eloquized. Mr. Clever Conversation, that's me.

"But," she said, and my gut perked up its ears, reluctantly, "he's not sure I'll ever have full functionality again."

I rolled that around in my head a minute, then decided, nope, I had no idea what that actually meant.

"Define 'full functionality.'"

"You know," she said taking a sip of the beer, "be on top."

The Draft King had wandered back to our end of the bar. He literally stopped toweling out the glass he'd been drying. His eyes found mine and read something like, *Old man, your drinks are free here from now on.*

I caught his innuendo like a springtime cold.

"She and I aren't..." I started to say.

"Uh-huh," the Draft King winked.

Daisy could barely repress a giggle.

"You've got three more minutes," I said to him. "Why don't you spend that time finding the bottle you *haven't* watered down?" He hardened his eyes but moved off again.

I said to Daisy, "Enjoying yourself?"

"Immensely!"

"Good," I said, meaning it. Having Daisy back—the *real* Daisy, with her smartass module powered up again—was worth a little public humiliation. "Another round?"

She took another, longer draught from the mug. "At least."

"And that's the last you heard?" Bekah Franklin asked.

I'd been telling her my barstool story for something to do while the *Coyote* nominalized the thrust gravity after the engine shut down. My eyes had started edging back toward their old place in the front of my skull.

"More or less," I said. "We finished our drinks. Then some of Erkennen's muscle came to remind me I had a mission. Which is what, by the way? What's so important on the Moon?"

Bekah went quiet. The *Coyote* shook a little as the perennial tension of inertia versus momentum was only slightly mollified by the prototype inertial dampeners in the prototype ship we occupied.

"The key to stopping Cassandra," she said.

A question struck me, then. It was one of those staring-you-in-the-face moments.

"Why all this high-tech mumbo-jumbo? Why can't we just shoot her?"

Bekah sighed. "That's the backup plan, of course. But Gregor is convinced that if we don't end the genomic programming, *undo* the tech that created Cassandra in the first place, we risk someone resurrecting her —or another like her—in the future. That's why we're headed to the Moon."

"And a lab no one's been in for thirty years?" It was getting easier to talk. My sarcasm flew its flag freely.

"How much do you know about Cassandra?" she said. "Her history, I mean."

"I know she's—it's—the hybrid human-AI daughter of Elise Kisaan— former Regent of Earth whose head adorns the end of a pike—and a merc Kisaan shacked up with. I know she's alive because I missed my target when she—it—was still a baby called Cassie Kisaan."

That last bit I'm not proud of. In a way, taking the contract to kill an infant from Adriana Rabh when I was young and looking to make my bones ruled my life ever since. But history is immutable. All you can do is live forward.

Bekah paused as she took in what I'd said, took a moment to digest it. Then she seemed to take it in stride with recent events, none of which made anyone involved smell like a white-hat-wearing hero from a storybook.

"And what about the Cassandra before her? Cassandra-Prime."

I only half understood the question. Before Elise Kisaan got knocked up with the cyborg baby, when the Syndicate Corporation was still a glimmer in Tony Taulke's eye, there'd been another Cassandra: a mainframe artificial intelligence that achieved pathological self-awareness. It had infected Elise Kisaan with DNA-level, mind-altering bugs that Kisaan passed along to her daughter when she got knocked up. I'd never heard the supersmart computer called Cassandra-Prime before, but it fit. I told Bekah all that.

"The base keys underlying Cassandra-Prime's programming," Bekah said. "They're in the abandoned lab."

"Okay," I said, doing my best Sherlock Holmes impression with the puzzle pieces I had. I'm not a good impressionist, by the way. "So—what?"

The thrust gravity had really let up. Bekah turned so she could see me through her vac-suit's visor. I accommodated as best I could likewise.

"Daniel's Cassandra-killer code is brilliant, but it has to get past her defenses to be effective," Bekah said. "Its entire mission is to penetrate Cassandra at the cellular level and break the enzyme bridge that made the human-AI hybridization possible. Gregor calls it Project Jericho."

"How biblical. I won't ask how all that works, kid. You've already lost me."

"But you asked ... I have to explain about that to—"

"The base keys?" I said hopefully.

Her eyes grew serious. I imagined her when she'd be my age, lecturing to wide-eyed, geeky students trying to soak up her knowledge.

"Imagine the most adaptive, resilient antibody defense system ever designed—*designed*—by natural law and machine learning, combined. That's what we're facing. Daniel figured out how to penetrate the cells. What he couldn't figure out is how to outwit Cassandra's defense system. Gregor is convinced the old code keys can help us do that."

It was hard to believe. Not Daniel Tripp's brilliance—Gregor Erkennen had risked everything believing in that. But even I know, tech has a half-life exactly equal to the next discovery that makes it obsolete. That can be days, even hours after it's born, depending on the innovation cycle. What was hard to believe was that tech we'd think of as ancient today—thirty years after it was cutting edge—could be the key to defeating the most advanced synthetic life form in history.

That would require a hell of a lot of faith from me. I don't do faith. Still, I said, "I'll trust you to know your business."

"Thanks." She let herself relax again and faced forward. Fighting gravity was possible with the help of the dampeners, but it still wasn't easy. "I've got to take this thing off," she said, her hand moving to the base of her helmet.

"Sure that's wise?"

She unsnapped the release, and I heard her suit air mixing with the ship's. A half turn, and the helmet came off. Bekah inhaled deeply.

"Seems fine," she said.

Points for chutzpah. I reached up to release my own helmet, remembering one reason I liked Bekah Franklin so much. She reminded me a lot of Daisy—sans smartass module.

"We've got a little while before the flip and decel burn," she said. "I think I can better sync the inertial dampeners with the thrust. Make the second half of the trip a little more pleasant."

The idea of her playing around with the code keeping us alive creeped me out, even if she was a savant. "You sure you know what you're doing?"

One glove off, Bekah flexed her fingers. "I cut my programming teeth on ship's systems."

"You're not using your teeth."

"You worry too much." The screen in front of her came alive. Her fingers typed faster than I could see them move. Menus turned to coded gobbledygook. Her fingers seemed to pick up speed as she dug in. "We'll be fine."

The *Coyote* shook harder around us. Whether from her massaging of the gobbledygook or just another round of the space shakes, I had no idea. And I wasn't sure I wanted to know.

As if reading my mind, Daisy—I mean, Bekah—turned and said, "I know my business, remember? We'll be fine."

2

ADRIANA RABH • SUSPENDED IN JUPITER'S ATMOSPHERE

Adriana Rabh held on as the winds of Jupiter's lower atmosphere buffeted the scoopship. The crude handholds she'd adapted in the vessel's interior were better than nothing—barely.

The ship hung on its tether from an orbital facility like a net trawled behind a fishing boat. Only instead of fish, the ship's job was to collect Jupiter's raw deuterium and helium-3 and deliver them for hypercompression in one of Callisto's orbital-ring refineries before gashaulers carried them to the inner system for distribution. Or that would have been the ship's job on a regular day devoted to mining instead of keeping Callisto's deposed regent alive and out of reach of the SSR's prowling sensors. The interference resulting from Jupiter's lightning storms had proven quite effective at that, Adriana had to admit. She was also quite sure the unpredictable atmosphere had loosened most of her internal organs from their moorings of ninety-odd years.

A new shockwave thrummed through the hull until her teeth hummed. Long and jagged lightning arced across the sky over the pilot's canopy.

Adriana wrapped her bony hands with excruciating desperation around the plastisteel grips. "*Goddamn.*" Bile welled up in her throat, and she clenched her teeth against the counter-cyclone forcing the Tin Can down again toward Jupiter's surface. She'd named their vessel that apparent misnomer, despite its behemoth-like main body below their tiny pilothouse. When you shared space in an oversized cockpit designed for a single pilot, everything became close quarters.

"Do you want me to explain again what causes the downward thrust?" Edith Birch asked from the one and only pilot's seat. She offered Adriana an infuriatingly indulgent smile. "It's a perfectly natural result of moisture and the movement of air and heat—"

"Please, for the love of fucking God, *don't*." Adriana bounced against the inner hull as a short, bone-rattling wave of turbulence shook them again. "If I hear one more scientific explanation of why this fucking monster planet does what it does, I'll kill myself."

Edith's smile faded. After a moment of quiet consideration, she said, "That would defeat our whole reason for being here, now wouldn't it?" Before Adriana could reply, Edith motioned with her finger upward. It took a moment for Adriana to realize what she meant. The shaking from the storms was suddenly, eerily absent for the first time in what felt like hours. The only feeling of motion was the slow, almost imperceptible swinging of the ship on its tether. The sudden calm was almost soothing and perversely uncomfortable.

"How long this time?" Adriana asked.

Gazing again through the canopy at the hazy atmosphere beyond, Edith said, "Maybe minutes. Maybe days?"

Adriana blew out displeasure with her breath. "And when I *need* scientific precision..."

She focused on making her hands relinquish their hold on the ship. They'd held their arthritic death grip for so long, her flesh felt one with the cold metal. Finally they began to uncurl, and the pain shooting through her joints made her regret the decision to pull them loose. She massaged the palm of her left hand with the thumb of her right. Blood began to flow again, and with it came the old, dull ache.

"Any of that liqueur left, Ms. Birch?" Adriana asked, beckoning with her stiff fingers.

"Sure, I think so," Edith said, feeling around below the pilot's seat where she'd secured it in the storm. "Why do they call it Absinthe of the Garden Green, by the way?"

Adriana sighed. It felt good to be asked a normal question again. "Its target market is expats from Earth. It's supposed to make you nostalgic for the homeworld."

"Oh," Edith said, locating the bottle. "I guess I can see that."

"Well, you be nostalgic for both of us, then." With difficulty, Adriana opened her hand. "I'm thirsty."

Edith passed the liqueur over with that same wan, patient smile from earlier. Removing the stopper from the carafe, Adriana took a drink. As the green liqueur washed the bile back down her throat, she took a moment to appreciate her own history with the sweet drink. People had wondered for years how a woman in her ninth decade could remain so vital and vigorous of body, so keen of mind. And the simple answer was that it was all thanks to this particular deal-making lubricant. It'd been over a second bottle of Green that Adriana had cut the deal that made being a nonagenarian feel like a new retiree of sixty-five. Achy, yes, especially in the mornings. But her skin? Perfect, like ivory. Her mind? Sharp as it had ever been.

The Wellspring: Gregor Erkennen's personalized, DNA-specific stem-cell therapy that introduced a proactive protocol via SynCorp's medical implant, the SCI. A unique sub-program that worked with the host's body and brain to retard cellular degradation and revitalize synaptic function. When Adriana suggested Gregor should call it "the goddamned Fountain of Youth," he'd made a face that—now that she thought about it— reminded her of Edith Birch–level judgment. He'd admonished her not to think in such clichéd terms.

Sometimes Adriana simply liked staring down at it, the amber liquid, losing herself in its dancing color—a reminder of Callisto, of home, even inside this godforsaken pilothouse with its dull, panel-fed lighting. The moon didn't look like much from space, just a pitted sphere of craters and cracks, the boxer's face of the solar system, pummeled with asteroids and other space debris for billions of years. But from the surface, Jupiter's ever-present bourbon light made Callistans feel wrapped in a warmth that other outer system settlements couldn't match—not even Gregor Erkennen's own Prometheus Colony on Titan, with its carnival-like distractions to attract settlers. Despite its frightening displays and heart-dropping updrafts, Adriana had to acknowledge that Jupiter had saved them. Obfuscated their sensor-scent from Cassandra's bloodhounds with its random, arcing lightning storms. In quiet moments like this, she could appreciate that fact without sarcasm or anger.

"Everything okay?" Edith asked. "Reconsidering your decision to send Admiral Galatz to Titan again?"

Not for the first time on their adventure together, Adriana looked up and found that Edith had a concerned puppy-dog expression. She took a swig from the carafe.

"Well, I *wasn't*," Adriana said sharply. A small tremor through the Tin Can made her reach out with a hand to steady herself. Wouldn't want to spill the Green. No alcohol abuse here. "But now I am."

Lightning bloomed, illuminating Jupiter's clouds from beneath. It made Edith, if only for a moment, appear as a gargoyle with an angel's face. Adriana put the stopper back in the carafe and handed it over.

"Better re-secure this, Ms. Birch," Adriana said.

Edith replaced the Green beneath the pilot's chair, then checked the harness holding her firmly in the seat. The Tin Can's shaking became constant. "I should probably say thanks again for giving me the seat. It makes things ... easier."

"Fuck off," Adriana said, though without any real rancor. Her hands found their metal handholds again. Her feet found the straps she'd rigged up on the deck.

"Hey, it could be worse," Edith said, her voice rising as the updraft of the cyclone lifted them high, then dropped them hard.

"And how, my dear, might you imagine that could be the case?" Adriana asked, her voice rising as the ship dropped. "Short of death, I mean."

Edith regarded her, her grip tight around the pilot's harness. Her smile was also tight and aimed at Adriana. "You could be two months pregnant."

———

When the Tin Can settled down again into a kind of steady state, Adriana motioned at Edith. "Hand it over. I want to take advantage of the quiet while I've got it."

"Oh, of course." Edith reached beneath her seat for the Green. "I wish I could take a drink myself."

"No, not that," Adriana said. "The other thing."

Edith hesitated for a moment, clearly still uncomfortable with the procedure and its necessities. Then, measured and matter of fact, she unrolled a tube from its hook on the side of the pilot's seat.

Whoever had last piloted the Tin Can had taken their emergency vac-suit and its built-in waste reclamation system with them. Both women were forced to share the backup—a long plastic tube with a vacuum-sealed cup on one end. Sharing it in such close quarters had forced an intimacy on the women neither would have accepted in easier circumstances.

Adriana turned away from Edith as far as she could in the tight quarters. For her part, Edith offered her the courtesy of looking away, ostensibly to study the intermittent silver lightning still painting Jupiter's golden-clouded sky. With a *shump* the cup attached itself to Adriana.

"Ah, that's better," she said. Then there was only the vigorous, slightly hollow *shushing* of transferring the contents of Adriana's bladder.

"To your earlier question—sometimes I wish I hadn't diverted Galatz to Titan," Adriana said, realizing she was making conversation to cover the sound. "I could've been pissing in luxury aboard a corporate warship right now."

Edith muttered something as she watched the lightning outside the ship.

"I didn't quite catch that, my dear," Adriana said in her most delicate hostess voice.

"Nothing." Edith continued to study the Jovian lightshow rather than look at Callisto's regent while she voided her urine.

"No, you said something." Adriana twisted the small butterfly release valve. Its seal broken, the cup detached. She held up the tube, and the vacuum sucked the last of her contribution to their future water supply into the recycler housed behind the pilot's seat. In four hours, it'd be potable. Which is one reason Adriana preferred the Green. She couldn't abide the idea of drinking her own purified urine. Or worse somehow, Edith's. "What was it you said?"

Clearing her throat, Edith turned to her. There was something in her unblinking stare Adriana hadn't seen before. "I simply asked, do you do *anything* but complain? I've spent days in this ship with you, and all you seem to do is nitpick. You're *alive*, aren't you?"

Full of her own frustration, Adriana had the sudden, perverse impulse to reach out and slap Edith Birch across the face. Then, recalling the circumstances of Edith's entry into her service, Adriana experienced a rare and unfamiliar emotion. Shame warmed her neck from her shoulders to her hairline.

Edith had reddened as well. "I'm sorry," she said, returning her gaze to Jupiter's sky. "It's just that we've been cooped up in here for several days, hiding and—"

"Don't apologize." Adriana's eyes were stoic and unyielding, demanding Edith meet them. "Never apologize when you're in the right. Else, you'll never earn a person's respect. Especially your own."

Without answering, Edith wrapped up the seal-and-vac and replaced it on its hook beside her seat.

"You know, in all the time we've been in this ... Tin Can ... I don't believe I've taken a moment to thank you," Adriana said. Did she need to do penance for the impulse she'd had to strike Edith? Would this spontaneous act of gratitude make up for that? "I mean, for making it possible for me—for us—to escape."

Edith smiled a small acknowledgment. "It was your piloting that got us here," she said. It sounded obligatory but sincere.

"Piloting a ship is like riding a bike," Adriana said. "The controls might be flashier these days, but the feel for the air—or lack of it—is the same."

"Like riding a what?"

Adriana exhaled. What these days *didn't* make her feel like she'd outlived her own time? She could almost feel Erkennen's Wellspring microbes, or whatever the fuck they were, hauling the skin tight over her cheekbones like sails on a clipper ship.

"How did you know where the scoopships were docked?" Adriana asked, turning the conversation back to Edith—more penance, less feeling older than dirt.

"As you know, my husband Luther was an atmo-miner," Edith said simply, her voice holding something dangerous and soft at the same time.

"He used to talk all the time about 'riding the lightning.' I'd sometimes meet him on the ring when he returned. He used to love sitting in a seat just like this one, monitoring the scoop. He said it was like getting paid to do nothing but ride a rollercoaster."

Adriana made a disgusted sound. "Just one more reason to hate that sonofabitch. Not that selling those hauler routes to the pirates wasn't enough. But Galatz did for those fuckers. *Dead* fuckers, now."

Edith said nothing. The Tin Can thumped with an updraft of turbulence, then settled on its tether again. Adriana observed her for a moment as they waited out the possibility of another sudden updraft.

"Luther Birch really did a number on you, didn't he, my dear?"

A nervous smile spread across Edith's face, reminding Adriana of Jupiter's lightning. Quick and almost pretty, but with a powerful, dark odor about it.

"Please don't call me that, Regent. It's condescending."

Adriana opened her mouth in indignation. Then she closed it again.

"It makes me feel *less-than*." Edith's eyes darted around the small cabin, as if she might find a secret escape hatch. "I don't want to feel that way anymore." Her eyes flitted across Adriana, then came back and stuck there. "Not even around you."

Adriana opened her mouth, indignation in her eyes. Then her gaze softened. "Very well ... Edith. Might I assume it's acceptable that I call you Edith?"

"Of course, Regent."

"Oh, let's not stand on ceremony, *now*. Decorum never survives long in revolutions," she said. "You may call me Adriana."

"I could never do that," Edith said. "I—even thinking it makes me uncomfortable."

"More uncomfortable than watching the richest woman in the known universe pee into a plastic tube?"

Edith worked hard to repress her laughter. "Yes," she said, "even more uncomfortable than that." Her eyes shifted, looking for something else to talk about. "Do you really regret sending the admiral away?"

"No," Adriana replied. "Erkennen tech has always been the secret weapon of SynCorp's success. If Masada Station falls, everything else follows like dominoes." She looked down her nose at Edith with a haughty air. "My pissing in comfort pales in comparison. And if you ask me what dominoes are, I swear to God—"

This time, Edith gave in to her laughter.

"What's so funny?" Adriana demanded. In truth, she'd intended to *be* funny to relieve some of the tension between them. But now that Edith *found* her funny, Adriana had lost all confidence in how she'd *been* funny.

"Piss ... pales," Edith said. The hilarity rolled out of her now.

"Yes?"

But Edith's laughter wouldn't stop. It seemed to feed on itself.

"Oh, yes, I see," Adriana said. Then, again affecting her voice-of-the-privileged, "I'm apparently becoming adept at scatological humor. You really can teach an old bitch new tricks."

Edith's laughter tapered off. Then, "Usually, that kind of humor—"

"I know what scatological *means*, Edith," Adriana said. "Even the rich have to shit."

The Tin Can vibrated. Adriana felt the waves striking sympathetic resonance in her bones.

"Here we go again," she said. Both women put away their good humor.

The ship shook again, harder.

Edith brought up the external view onscreen, catching the tail end of a bright flash. Another of Jupiter's tantrums.

"I've had just about enough of this," Adriana said. "My insides feel like a tornado's rearranged them."

Edith held on to the pilot's harness as the cyclone swept them upward, then the counter-cyclone pushed them down again. Adriana clenched her teeth so hard she wondered if they'd shatter in her mouth.

All Gregor's microbes and all Gregor's men...

The downdraft dropped the ship, and after one more bone-jarring moment, the ship became a pendulum again, snapping taut on the tether and swinging gently as the cyclone passed.

"We can't stay here forever, hiding," Edith said. There was hope in her voice.

It infected Adriana like a hypo shot of adrenaline. She let go her hand-holds as the Tin Can steadied its drifting arc.

"I'm tired of pissing into a cup. And you're right—I'm tired of hiding," she said. "I'd rather die at home than live here."

Edith gave her a smile without a whit of sympathy in it at all.

How refreshing.

"Me, too," Edith said, unbuckling her harness. "Here, you'll need this seat."

"Are you sure?" Adriana said, nodding to Edith's mid-section.

"Yes," Edith answered, lifting herself from the seat. "We'll fight for our home. Both of us."

Adriana winced as she released her handholds. "You'll have to give Junior my apologies later," she said as they exchanged places.

Edith hooked her feet into the jury-rigged straps and grabbed the plas-tisteel rings above her head. "Take us home, Adriana."

3

RUBEN QINLAO • DARKSIDE, THE MOON

"Hey, Boss Man. Wake up."

Ruben Qinlao swam upward toward consciousness and Richard Strunk's voice. He'd been dreaming of making love to Mai Pang, Tony Taulke's personal assistant. Tony had sent her to Mars as Helena Telemachus's shadow. Ruben and Mai had grown close quickly, and though he half-suspected early on she'd gotten close to him as Tony's spy, Ruben was later sure her affection was genuine—their passion hot and real in the way of new lovers, delighting in the discovery of one another. In the dream, he'd just risen from the bed to use the bathroom. When he'd returned, he'd found Mai's mutilated body with Elinda Kisaan standing over her, Mai's blood dripping onto the floor from the blades of her katara knives.

"You okay?" Strunk asked, lighting a tallow candle.

Sitting up on the crude bed, Ruben centered himself. The Moon. Darkside. The old church they'd taken refuge in from Elissa Kisaan's manhunt.

"Yeah," Ruben said. "Yeah. Bad dreams."

"Bad dreams are all there are these days," Strunk said. "Speaking of which..."

"Yeah?"

"The kid bolted again."

"What?"

"Junior. He snuck out again."

Closing his eyes, Ruben tried to remain calm. They were doing every-thing they could to lay low long enough to figure out how to break Tony Taulke out of Darkside's Marshals Complex. And for the second time, Tony's son had stolen away in the middle of the night. Was he *trying* to get them caught?

Ruben lifted himself off the bedding. His muscles ached after sleeping on the hard floor. "I thought you were on the door after the last time."

"I was," Strunk said. "But I feel asleep. No excuses."

But that wasn't true, exactly. Strunk had one very big excuse, or reason rather, for his lack of fortitude. Alone, he'd held off an entire platoon of SSR troopers and made it possible for Ruben to escape with an uncon-scious Tony Taulke and Isaac Brackin, the Darkside doctor treating Tony, from their hiding place in Point Bravo. Before that firefight, Strunk had been a massive man with an attitude as big and broad as his shoulders. Now, he seemed to have trouble taking a deep breath.

"The boy's sneaking out isn't your fault," Ruben said generously. "I'll go."

Strunk murmured something. The words were obscure, but the tone was clear. Ruben Qinlao was about to have to do Strunk's job for him. That didn't sit well with Strunk.

Ruben rose as Strunk lit another candle. They'd found several monks' robes in the back of the old church. Ruben sorted through them.

"I see one of them is missing," he said.

Grunting, Strunk said, "At least he had the brains to put that on before going out in public."

Ruben donned a set of robes that fit him best, cinching up the waist with a rope belt. Whoever had run this church in the past had gone for authenticity with the costumes, he had to give them that.

"How do I look?"

Strunk winced, the vertebrae of his back popping as he stood up semi-straight. "Like someone asking to be heckled every step he takes outside that door."

A wry smile ticked up one of Ruben's cheeks. Darkside was a cesspool with a whorehouse on every corner and sticky fingers constantly probing pockets that didn't belong to them. In his monk robes Ruben wouldn't be popular, but he'd likely be left alone.

"Any ideas where he went?" Ruben asked. He secreted one of his katara knives taken from Elinda Kisaan on Mars into each of his long sleeves. Then he dropped the magazine from the butt of the 11-millimeter pistol Brackin had given him and counted the bullets left. Five. A last resort in a colony where everyone was looking to collect a reward for turning them in. Too much noise. He reloaded the pistol and slipped it into a front pocket.

"Is that a serious question?" Strunk asked, trying to sound light. From his wheezy lungs, it was a hard sell. "He's a teenage boy."

"The Fleshway, then?"

"The Fleshway."

Ruben made for the front door.

"Watch your back, Boss Man. Remember the bounty. Anyone recognizes you..."

Ruben pulled up the hood of his robes. Tony's capture in Brackin's clinic had confirmed what had, to that point, been informed speculation—that Tony Taulke and Ruben Qinlao were indeed holed up in Darkside. By now, every bounty hunter with a transport pass would be crawling through the city, turning over every lunar rock they could find.

"Yeah, I know," Ruben said, cracking the door. All clear. "Hold the fort."

"Bring the shitbag home, Boss Man."

Stepping onto the circular walkway of the barrio rotunda, Ruben estimated it must be after midnight. He saw a few lights burning in windows. Not much foot traffic.

Folding his hands into the woolen arms of his robes, Ruben struck off for the Fleshway. Darkside's doublewide street of brothels and gambling dens wasn't far. He could already hear the din of humanity humming like bees around a flesh-peddling hive.

Standing at the mouth of the corridor that opened onto the Fleshway, Ruben surveyed the thick crowd. They seemed more like ants than bees, he thought, stirred up in their after-hours pursuits. Where to begin? Spotting anyone among everyone would be difficult if not impossible, even if his target was still wearing monk's robes like his own. Knowing Junior, he'd probably already ditched them.

Ruben began his reconnoiter, favoring the nearest side of the corridor. The volume of faces combined with his need to avoid attracting attention made progress slow. He paused in alleyways between businesses to glance into storefronts. He'd passed half an hour and was beginning to despair of ever finding the teenager when he spotted him almost by accident. And he wasn't alone.

Three figures surrounded him, leading Junior from a bar and brothel called the Arms of Artemis. An older woman pursued them, apparently expressing her displeasure at having her customer shanghaied. One of the three, also a woman, turned back to deal with her. Junior seemed to be going willingly, but Ruben chalked that up to fear. The three looked like lowlifes. Most likely bounty hunters, given the constant barrage of postings on *The Real Story*. The woman's partners—a man of medium build and another who could have graduated from Strunk's school for oversized bodyguards—hemmed in close to Junior while she dealt with the Arms' madam. The older woman made a rude hand gesture at the three and turned to reenter her establishment. The three began to hustle Junior away.

It was remarkable to Ruben that no one seemed to care about a straight-up kidnapping. Then again, it was the Fleshway. Hauling drunks and hack-heads and other unwilling sorts out of local businesses probably happened dozens of times a day.

The trio diverted the kid into an alleyway and disappeared. Ruben backtracked, then double-timed it down the alley he'd been observing them from, paralleling their path. He picked up the pace and was in position and observing them as they emerged onto the nearly deserted back alley that ran behind the Fleshway's main thoroughfare. The two men moved Junior along, not sparing his comfort, the woman leading them by several steps.

"Hey now!" Junior protested.

"This way," the woman said.

They were headed right for Ruben's position. The woman passed, glancing straight down the alley where Ruben hid in the shadows.

"—sack of shit," the bigger man whispered as they passed, giving Junior's shoulder a push. "This payday better happen, kid."

"Rayes, I swear," the smaller man said, "all you know how to do is bitch."

Ruben stepped out behind them. The smaller man heard him and turned.

"Shit!"

Ruben's katara dagger was already flying through the air. The man dodged, and the blade caught him in the upper thigh. Crying out, he lost his hold on Junior, and the bigger man, Rayes, pushed the teen hard. Junior stumbled into a trash heap. The woman drew a stunner.

Ruben dived forward toward his target, tumbling and cursing at the robes hindering him.

The woman fired her stunner twice.

Punk! Punk!

Rayes gathered himself to charge. Ruben tumbled back into the dark alley while the first man lay in the grime, gasping, his hand wrapped around the knife. Rayes bellowed, his thick boots smacking as he charged into the alleyway, and Ruben scrambled behind a pair of refuse bins. He loosened the rope and began shuffling off the robes.

"Get out of the way!" the woman yelled. "Rayes, I can't get a shot!"

"You ain't no monk!" Rayes said, ignoring her.

Opting for the pistol over the second dagger, Ruben tossed his robes aside and rolled up to one knee. But Rayes had seen Ruben go behind the bins, and he moved in, batting the gun aside and bringing his other hand around in a massive fist.

Ruben pulled away and twisted in the tight space, bringing his foot around like a tenterhook, sweeping behind Rayes's knee. It was like trying to topple a pillar, but Rayes was off-balance, and Ruben's leverage sent him sprawling.

That cleared the kill zone for the woman, who'd followed her partner into the alley. She slowed, taking the time to aim her stunner more carefully for her second shot.

Ruben rolled again, using Rayes's bulk for a semi-shield. The woman fired anyway.

Punk! Punk! Punk!

Rayes grunted with the impact of the stunner's catalyst slugs hitting him. "Watch that El!" he shouted.

MESH, Ruben realized. It was the only reason Rayes was still alive. The slugs had hit, but his MESH clothing had negated their deadly effect.

Ruben abandoned the bins' cover and crab-crawled deeper into the alley, turning and twisting to keep the woman, El, from getting another clean shot. Ruben pulled a large refuse bin in front of him. He could hear El pausing to help Rayes to his feet.

Smart. They weren't amateurs. They were taking their time. They had it to take. He didn't.

"Stop now, Qinlao, and we'll let you live," El said. "You're worth more alive than dead—it'd work out for all of us."

Ruben moved silently, carefully to the other end of the bin and took aim from the darkness. A pistol shot might bring the marshals running. Then again, he thought, recalling it was the Fleshway—as lightly as most marshals took their duties, the sound of gunfire might actually keep them away.

Crack!

The bullet hit El and she spun around with the force of it, the stunner flying from her hand. Curses fired from Rayes like machine-gun bullets. He charged the bin hiding Ruben and, as Ruben drew a bead on him, jogged left.

Crack!

The shot missed, and Rayes's momentum carried him forward like a stampeding rhino. Rayes rammed the bin, slamming Ruben hard against a wall.

Rayes dragged the bin aside with a roar. As the bounty hunter closed the space between them, Ruben dove forward, getting inside the big man's defenses as Rayes had Ruben's before. Making a split-V with the fingers of his right hand, he gouged the hunter's eyes, then hammered his crotch with a knee strike.

Rayes cratered, howling, one hand flying upward to protect his blinded eyes, the other lower. Ruben struck three times quickly, and Rayes went down. He made a wet, smacking sound as his cheek hit the alley floor.

Ruben turned to El. The shot had taken her high in the shoulder, and she was scuttling across the alley, trying to reach her stunner. Three quick leaps and Ruben stood over her, the 11-millimeter pistol pointed at the back of her head.

"Stop now," he said, "and I'll let you live."

El ceased moving and turned to glare at him. Pain was sketched across her face. The wound in her left shoulder soaked through her shirt. In the back alley beyond, he could hear the second man, still cursing from the knife wound.

"Why?" she spat. "We'll just keep coming. You're worth too much, Qinlao. There's a new regime now, and we—"

Ruben clocked her across the forehead with the pistol barrel. She slumped unconscious onto her side.

"Because I don't kill people in cold blood," he said.

Behind him, he could hear Rayes trying to wake. If he didn't collect the kid and get moving, Ruben feared he'd have to forego the luxury of principle after all.

He found the second man standing, favoring his good leg, waiting for Ruben as he exited the alley. One hand clutched his thigh. The other held a stunner pointed straight at Ruben's chest.

"Well, well," the man said through his pain. "Payday just got bigger."

There was movement, and a pipe cracked the back of the man's skull. He went down, revealing Junior as the wielder of the pipe.

"Take that!" Tony Junior shouted. "Sonofabitch! Treat me like—"

"Quiet! You'll have the whole Fleshway after you looking for a payday," Ruben hissed. "Stay right there. Don't move!"

He returned to the dark alley where he'd dropped his robes. El was still out cold. Rayes was moving, moaning. Ruben rendered him unconscious again with a quick strike to the back of his thick skull. He slipped the robes back on, cinching them up with the rope belt.

"We should kill these fuckers," Junior said when Ruben approached. The kid was irritated, agitated, sweating like hell. Maybe this experience would teach him a lesson in prudence. "They'll just come after us, right?"

"Maybe," Ruben said. He considered removing his katara from the thigh of the third bounty hunter but figured the man would bleed out if he did. So, he was down one knife—he had another. "But that's not how I do things."

"Then you do things stupid!"

"Stupidly."

"What?"

"The word you're looking for is 'stupidly,'" Ruben said, grabbing Junior by the arm and taking him back toward the Arms of Artemis. Any way but the way the three bounty hunters had been headed. "As in, 'I stupidly put us all at risk looking for a little fun.'"

Junior clucked his tongue. "You shouldn't talk to me that way," he said. "I was just trying to help Pop."

"I told you the first time you snuck out," Ruben continued with a glance behind them, "you're risking everything when you do that—including your pop." He turned them back toward the Fleshway and its sea of human camouflage. "Pick up the pace."

"I was headed to the Marshals Complex," Junior said, shrugging off Ruben's grip. Somewhere in that half explanation lurked a teen's logic.

"The Arms of Artemis isn't the Marshals Complex."

Junior flashed him a wicked grin. "I was stopping off for a quick—"

"Just shut up," Ruben said. The sights and sounds and smells of the bustling Fleshway were only a few steps away. "It's a wonder you're even still alive to *get* captured."

"You should have more respect. I'm technically your boss in the business now, y'know."

Ruben regarded him with cold eyes. "All you are is an idiot. Your only 'business' lately consists of brothels and bad decisions. Now, put your hood up, boy. It's time you went back to church."

4

BENJY ANDERSON • NORTHEASTERN FARMING COLLECTIVE, BETHLEHEM, PENNSYLVANIA, EARTH

Benjy Anderson pulled the weed stalk from his mouth and adjusted his sitting position. The root pressing into his back had become a more-than-mild irritant. Now it was just painful. He paused the display of *The Adventures of Huckleberry Finn* projecting onto his retina. The words halted their scrolling.

Reading had become a favorite pastime, a privilege of circumstance in a late spring marked by inactivity. Their farming clique should have moved on by now, following the auto-threshers and reaping combines as they harvested crops across the collective.

Begun the day after his twelfth birthday, his internship studying at his mother Anne's right hand was less than a year old. But that, like everything else, had come to a screeching halt when Elise Kisaan died. The last few weeks had seen the clique's routine of monitoring, maintaining, and moving with the machines from one plat to the next disrupted by revolution. Not just disrupted—halted. Their clique languished as the machines they were charged with maintaining stood motionless, supposedly felled by a virus. Rows of cabbages sat unharvested, ripening in the ground. The sweet corn plucked in the previous rotation was rotting in the silos.

Without direction from the Kisaan Faction or a remedy to fix the machines, cliques all over North America had fallen into idleness. Many of the adults and even some of his teenaged friends had become hackheads addicted to Dreamscape. Other kids had turned to more traditional diversions and simply passed the days in play, looking for anything to push off boredom. Benjy's choice was reading, a pastime he'd enjoyed from early childhood, when his mother would read him to sleep in the flickering solitude of their clique's tent. *Huckleberry Finn* was a challenge with its ancient Southern dialects, but that's why Benjy had chosen to read it again. He hated being bored, and these days boredom was as much a plague as the reports of blight from the Midwestern Collective to the west.

Even his mother, the clique's revered matron and a respected community leader, had turned to Dreamscape. Lately, she'd been so hard to wake from it that Benjy had begun to worry that one day, he wouldn't be able to wake her at all. He didn't really understand Dreamscape, but it sounded like a really intense kind of story you could step into. Better than any 3D sim-parlor or VR experience he'd ever heard of.

In Dreamscape, his friends told him, he could do more than just read about riding with Huck down the Mississippi River—he could actually *do* it. Feel the undulation of the mighty Mississip beneath the bound logs of the raft, feel the spray of the river water on his forehead. Smell the spring in the air. Now that sounded like fun, and he'd been tempted to try it once or twice. But then he'd begun to worry for his mom as she became more immersed in the program and unresponsive when it was time to cook dinner. He'd begun to get resentful of Dreamscape. And her.

But he didn't need a program to smell spring, anyway. Benjy looked up at the magnolia overhead flowering with white and pink blossoms. Their sweet scent hung around him. Magnolias, his mother had taught him when she could still teach him things, were among the oldest of trees. They'd evolved to attract bees for pollinating, and so their gynoecium—especially their carpels—made them tougher than other trees. When Benjy had asked what a *gynoecium* was, Anne Anderson had patiently explained that it was the collective term for the female reproductive system of a flower.

He'd blushed, smiled nervously, and asked what was for dinner. The memory was bittersweet, as were most memories lately that involved his mom.

Benjy focused on the pink flowers with their white tips blowing lightly in the breeze as he tried to shake the feeling of loss that seemed to hang over him constantly these days. Closing his eyes, he called up the image of his mom when she'd given him the lesson on magnolias. He hadn't paid much attention to her then, only to her words. But now his mind's eye noticed how tanned her face was, weathered from the sun and her years laboring beneath it. A strand of her sandy hair, more blonde than brown, bleached by sunlight, blew lightly in the breeze as she told him how old magnolias were in the world. Her bright smile sparkled with a kind of reverent look Benjy recognized as love. It was the same look he felt radiating from himself whenever he petted his dog, Bandit.

He'd left the dog in their Farmer Assistive Mobile Shelter earlier that morning.

"Stay here, watch over Mom," Benjy had said as he'd opened the windows of the FAMS to allow in the breeze. "I'll be back soon."

Bandit had offered a short whine of protest, staring up with his jaw resting on his paws.

"Come on, boy, I've been inside for two days straight. Just a couple of hours, okay?"

If he didn't get out of the FAMS for just a little while, Benjy felt like he might explode. Kneeling beside his mother, he'd placed a cool rag on her forehead before heading out for a little private reading time—outside, where he could feel the breeze and smell the spring. Anne had stayed lost in Dreamscape for two whole days this time, and he'd stayed by her side, caring for her. He'd haul her out, whatever it took, this evening. Yeah, that sounded about right—haul her out, as if from a deep well she didn't really want to escape. She'd become angry the last time, and anyway, so many others had lived a lot longer inside, so two days wasn't too long, right? She'd be fine, especially with Bandit watching over her—that's what Benjy had told himself when he'd left the FAMS for a few hours of reading time.

But his conscience thought otherwise. He'd spent less than an hour under the magnolia, unable to focus on *Huckleberry Finn*. Reading the words but not following the story, though he'd read it before. His mind always wandered back to his mother and his worries over Dreamscape. The root digging into his back seemed to urge him home.

Where you ought to be anyway, he told himself.

"Hey, Trace!"

Marianne Schiro's voice cut through his thoughts. Benjy switched off his sceye.

Marianne was fourteen, a year older than him. She'd called him by his nickname, the one his mom had given him that day when Benjy was little more than a toddler and drawing tiny circles in the dirt beside her in the crop row. From that day forward, he'd been Trace to his mom. He was only Benjy, or more likely Benjamin James Anderson, when she'd get angry with him. Benjy considered the Trace nickname almost childish, so he insisted most of the kids in the farming clique call him by his given name now that he was older. But Marianne, a friend for as long as he could remember, still called him by the old nickname, and Benjy tolerated it from her. He even preferred it—from her. It made him feel unique, like a totally different person—special in her eyes.

"You riding the river again?" Marianne asked, slightly out of breath as she jogged from the meadow.

"Yeah," he smiled.

Like most girls lately, Marianne fascinated him. He'd once thought of them as something to be avoided, almost like plague carriers. But now girls had become an irresistible mystery, from their lilting voices to their shy, inviting glances to the slightly frightening, great unknown of their gynoecium. Wait, that wasn't the right word—was it?

Marianne extended a hand to help him up, and Benjy thrilled at her touch. He stood, trying not to blush.

"I'm the one who's been running," she said. "Why are you so flushed?"

He knew why. What he said was, "Allergies."

"Ah."

He swung a hand generally toward the meadow. "Tired of goofing off?" It came out more harshly than he'd intended.

Marianne's eyebrows drew together. They were dark brown, almost black.

"We were playing, not 'goofing off,'" she said. "Who peed on your toast?"

Benjy's shoulders dropped. This isn't how he'd wanted this conversation to go. Not how he wanted any conversation with Marianne Schiro to go.

Especially not with Jimmy Ellis sniffing around her like Bandit after a possum at night. Benjy wasn't sure why the thought of that bothered him so much, but it did.

"Sorry," he said sincerely. "I'm just worried. About my mom."

"'scaping again?"

"Yeah."

Marianne reached out and lightly, awkwardly touched his shoulder. He almost jumped away at the electricity it shot through him. "I'm sorry, Trace. You know, I'm sure it won't be like Merris's dad. I'm sure your mom—"

"Yeah," he said again, not wanting to think about Merris Candon's dad, who'd stayed so long in Dreamscape he'd died. There'd been two deaths in the last week in their clique alone. The word from the neighboring counties said the same or worse was happening there—all over Earth, even. One local man had renamed Dreamscape the "Siren's Call." Benjy understood the reference from the stories his mom used to read him of Ulysses sailing home after the Trojan War and how Sirens would lure sailors to their deaths with the beauty of their voices.

Dreamscape was like that. Once you heard it, you sailed right toward death, careless of the rocks near shore. And then you drowned in your own fantasies. The thought of his mother dying in that way terrified Benjy. The thought of her dying at all terrified him. His conscience tugged again like gravity, drawing him back to their shelter.

"Trace?"

He realized they'd been standing there, with him distracted *again*.

"Sorry. I think I need to get home."

Marianne offered him a friendly smile.

"Hey!"

They both turned to find Jimmy Ellis waving his arms, like he was directing an airbus for landing.

"We're starting up a new game of ... well, we haven't decided what yet," Jimmy said. "Want to play?"

"Sure!" Marianne said, already moving that way. Then, over her shoulder to Benjy, "Sure you don't want to come?"

"Next time," Benjy replied.

The afternoon sun had warmed the FAMS more than Benjy expected. Though he'd opened the windows before leaving to read, the air had stilled, holding the heat inside the shelter. Panting heavily, his eyes sleepy, Bandit remained at his post. His black eyes opened wide, and he hopped to all fours when Benjy entered the shelter. A black overcoat and white belly and chest had pretty much dictated Bandit's name. What else would you call a white dog who seemed to be wearing a black mask and cape from his mixed breeding of Alaskan Husky and Australian Cattle Dog? Benjy cocked the shelter's front door open, hoping to increase the ventilation despite the lack of wind. A glance at his mother showed she'd hardly changed position since he'd left. There was a thin sheen of sweat on her forehead.

"Go on, boy, I know you probably need to go." Bandit's long, curling tail set to wagging. "Go on, it's okay."

Stopping first at his water bowl for a few laps, Bandit padded outside.

Benjy knelt next to his mother. Closer now, he could she was lying in a pool of sweat. The worry that so distracted him under the tree kicked into overdrive. The still air and unseasonably hot Pennsylvania spring had wrung her out. Her bed pad was soaked. Good thing he hadn't waited till evening to come home after all.

I'll be more careful next time, Benjy promised. Check the temperature forecast for the day, make sure she wouldn't be in danger of heat stroke. And Bandit deserved an extra treat with dinner. It must have been like an oven in here to him. Benjy's guilt followed him like a shadow as he moved around the shelter.

"Mom, wake up." He wiped the sweat from her skin with a towel. "Mom ... wake up, please."

Anne Anderson lay motionless, eyes open but unresponsive. He picked up the hand mirror where he'd left it the previous night and placed it next to her lips. Slowly, her breathing fogged its shiny surface.

"Mom!"

Bandit bounded back in, still panting heavily but looking relieved.

The thermostat on the wall read ninety-two degrees. He could cool the FAMS down in no time with air conditioning, but the lack of fieldwork lately meant their portion of the clique's electricity credits wasn't being refilled in exchange for crop production. The balance drew down every day, and no one knew when the work would gear up again. Not even a clique matron as respected as Anne Anderson got free electricity. Would his mom be angry if he pulled from their meager remaining balance?

She could yell at him later, Benjy decided. Right now, she needed the cool.

Bandit swung his head right and left to watch as Benjy got up and closed the windows and front door, then set the thermostat to seventy-five. The whisper quiet of the blower began to fill the small room with blessedly cool air.

"Better, boy?" Benjy said.

The dog seemed to be smiling as much as panting at him.

On the floor, his mother moaned. Benjy knelt next to her as she began to stir.

"Trace?" she whispered.

"*Mom*," he said, his relief evident. The vent blowing behind him made Benjy shiver. "I'll make us a late lunch, okay? You didn't have breakfast, you know."

"Trace..." she said again, sounding farther away.

"No, you can't go back to sleep, Mom." He knelt beside her again, trying to make her sit up. Bandit barked, and Anne waved at the air as if brushing away flies. "You have to sit up."

"Why?"

"Because you—"

"Why did you wake me up?" Her voice was harder, harsher. "I was with your father. Benjy, why did you wake me up?"

She'd used his given name. She was mad at him. But she was awake now, at least, and so she could be as mad at him as she liked. Her blue eyes were aware, their ghostly distance burning off with irritation.

"I'll get us some lunch, Mom," Benjy said, sharing a look with Bandit. His eyes furtive, the dog lowered his head. "I know you're hungry. I'll get us some lunch, okay?"

5

ADRIANA RABH • EN ROUTE TO CALLISTO

The journey to Callisto had been circuitous and slow. Two days of moon hopping and laying low to scan with the Tin Can's limited sensors. From Metis in the Amalthean Ring of Jupiter's innermost moons, they'd headed to Europa—their final rabbit hole, Edith called it—hanging over its ice-smooth surface while probing forward, looking for SSR ambushes.

Adriana had half-expected that boorish Braxton to be waiting for them, arms folded smugly on the bridge of the rebranded *Pax Corporatum*, a broad smile stretched across his oafish face. But not only had Braxton not been waiting, no one had.

They had only the fuel onboard, a half tank, and Adriana Rabh was their only pilot. Despite the miracle of Gregor Erkennen's Wellspring coursing through her, piloting the Tin Can under constant threat of discovery was taking its toll. She hadn't flown her own ship for seventy years, and certainly not under such dangerous circumstances.

After dropping from the tether, Adriana had paralleled Jupiter's curvature for several hours, relying as before on the volatile atmosphere to camouflage them, aiming for the planet's far side, away from where enemy ships should be waiting to grab them up. Emerging from the planet's outer atmosphere, the sedate serenity of flying in the smoothness of space had seemed an almost unnatural state.

Their escape had been disturbingly easy. And Adriana Rabh hadn't trusted *easy* since her first date in the back seat of a Volvo in Budapest. The boy hadn't just been shy, he'd been downright resistant. It'd proven a very frustrating evening for young Adriana Rabh.

But now Callisto was near. They waited out their final period of caution over Europa with nervous, semi-hopeful anticipation. Every moment that passed, the distance between the two moons' relative positions lengthened. It was tempting as hell to simply break orbit and spend their last drops of fuel running for home.

And Edith's constant review of archival footage from *The Real Story* was getting on Adriana's nerves. The signal was blocked while they were tucked away in the chaotic camouflage of Jupiter's atmospheric storms. Adriana found she hadn't missed the daily feed of constant news one iota.

"Doesn't that bitch ever shut up?" she said, staring at Cassandra's freakish golden eyes. The first time Adriana had seen them sent shivers down her spine. Cassandra had been a newborn then named Cassie. Now she looked too much like her mother. Even more so, Adriana mused, than those damned clones Elise Kisaan had grown in the lab and trained as her personal bodyguard.

"Shhh," Edith admonished, swiping up the volume.

"Anthony Taulke II, the lead tyrant of a nest of tyrants, is now in our custody. He will stand trial for his crimes, and a simple vote of the citizens of Sol will mete out justice on him."

"Shit," Adriana whispered. "They caught Tony." Was Gregor Erkennen still alive? she wondered. Had her decision to send Galatz to Titan rather than defend her on Callisto been in vain?

"Regent..."

The dread in Edith's voice lured Adriana's attention back to the broadcast. One of Elise's damned clones held a stunner to Helena Telemachus's head. Before Adriana could process that, she'd pulled the trigger. Edith yelped her shock like she'd been shot herself.

"Now is not the time for soft hearts," Cassandra said as she reappeared onscreen. The camera withdrew, bringing Elise Kisaan's decomposing head back into the shot. *"We will break your chains, citizens of Sol,"* she continued. *"One link at a time."*

"My God," Edith said.

"Turn it off," Adriana said as a commentator appeared. In a different time, not so very long ago, he would have been Helena Telemachus. Never again. "*Edith. Turn it off. Please.*"

Edith switched off the feed.

"When was that?" Adriana asked.

"Timestamp shows three days ago."

"Three days ago," Adriana whispered. A lot could happen in that amount of time. Tony Taulke had been in custody for three days? Had they already held his mock trial? Was he already dead? "Well, she's right about one thing."

Swallowing to find her voice, Edith said, "What's that?"

"No soft hearts now. Only hard ones." Adriana's eyes found Edith's. "No quarter. No mercy."

Edith regarded her a moment. "Are you scared? They'll be coming after you. Harder, I mean, now that they've caught Mr. Taulke."

"Scared? Me? That bitch doesn't scare me."

Not anymore.

And that was something, anyway.

"But I still I don't understand it," Adriana said. "Why the hell aren't SSR ships crawling up our ass? Where's Braxton?"

"I think I might know why."

"Well, don't keep it to yourself. This lack of life-threatening pursuit is bloody unnerving."

"I've spent most of our downtime since we left Jupiter skimming the archives of *The Real Story*," Edith said.

"Oh, my dear—Edith—trust me, I know. Isn't that dangerous with all the sniffer bots that bitch must have trolling the 'net? Couldn't they trace the connection back to us?"

"Doesn't matter."

"No? And why, pray tell, is that?"

"Because I .... I've learned to mask data queries. Reroute them to pass-through IPs bouncing between different subspace satellites. Do that enough times, and it's very hard to trace a query's origin." Edith flashed Adriana an innocent smile. "Theoretically."

"Is it now? And how would an accountant who volunteered to work inventory at Valhalla Station's infirmary come by that kind of expertise?" Adriana asked. "Theoretically..."

Edith's eyes darted away. Adriana had the feeling the answer wouldn't be something she liked.

"I learned it to help me accrue a nest egg when I was with Luther," Edith said. "I'd intended to buy my way off Callisto and get back to Earth. And away from *him*."

Adriana regarded her. "Okay." There was more to that story, a secret part Edith was holding back. Adriana let her keep it to herself for now.

Edith pointed at the small readout screen. "This is what I wanted to show you."

Adriana recognized the unkempt image of Gregor Erkennen onscreen. His mouth was open to speak. Edith pushed play.

"Titan stands," Gregor said. *"The rumors of mass genocide on Earth are true. Mars is rising up. The rebels are on the run."*

Images of the *Pax Corporatum* fleeing Titan's orbit played out. The largest warship in SynCorp's fleet, the *SCS Sovereign*, chased her with railgun fire peppering her stern.

"That's Galatz's command ship," Adriana said, releasing pent-up relief she hadn't known she was holding. So—they still had a fleet. Something foreign and odd began tickling her gut from the inside. It took her a moment to recognize *hope*. "What's Jabari doing with Gregor?"

"I don't know what to think anymore," Kwazi Jabari said. He seemed tired. Lost. *"But I know Cassandra Kisaan is a liar. Like the snake from the Garden of Eden."*

Adriana blew out a breath. "Just now getting that, are we, genius?"

Jabari went on to describe how Cassandra was using Dreamscape to control people, and that was new information. *Well, he should know,* Adriana thought, recalling Jabari's own addiction and how much it had frustrated Helena Telemachus. Thinking of Helena converted the swirling emotion inside Adriana into something heavy and hot.

SynCorp's circle-star brand appeared onscreen.

Edith paused the playback. "Casandra regains control of the broadcast at this point."

"Three days ago," Adriana whispered again. She reviewed their orbit over Europa. Stable, but they'd need a boost soon or the orbit would start to decay. The fuel level indicated they had just enough to get home. "Cassandra sent Tony's ship to take Masada Station, and Matthias Galatz chased it off. That explains the sudden lack of SSR hunting us." A smile had begun to form in her voice. "Cassandra got slapped *hard* at Masada Station. And what does one do when slapped hard?"

Edith regarded her, and Adriana, even in the half fog of her pilot's fatigue, realized the word she'd chosen.

"One ... turtles up," Edith said. Her tone was detached and cold, but also certain. Confident. "You pull in your extremities. For protection."

Adriana's eyes hardened. "Precisely."

"Do you think they've abandoned Callisto, then?"

"Doubtful. They already had it. And now it can serve as Cassandra's base in the outer system for launching another strike against Titan."

The near silence in the Tin Can enveloped them both. There was only the light pinging sound of the scoopship's lidar sensors. Adriana focused on SynCorp's emblem still frozen on the tiny screen.

"What about Tony?" she asked.

"He's alive," Edith said, "at least according to CorpNet. They're planning to move him to Earth for his trial."

Adriana felt the sneer forming. Trial? Show trial, maybe. Like Helena's execution, a circus act for the masses. No matter how the vote went, Tony was as good as dead.

"This is our chance to recover your regency," Edith said. "The spotlight is moving to Earth."

Adriana regarded her, mulling over what they might find on Valhalla Station. Garlands and roses tossed before their feet by Callistans welcoming their regent home? Or gravity cuffs and incarceration in a cell beneath the moon's pockmarked surface?

"We need to take it back for more than that reason," Adriana said. "We need to deny Cassandra that base for any more attacks on Masada Station."

She glanced at the Tin Can's fuel reserve again. Edith was right. It was now or never.

"In short, I agree with your assessment, Special Counselor to the Regent," Adriana said.

Edith missed half a breath. "What did you call me?"

"Special Counselor to the Regent," Adriana said, fiddling with the flight controls. With a little maneuvering, they could gain some extra momentum using Europa's gravity to catapult them toward Callisto. Stretch their fuel a bit further. "I'm promoting you."

There was a pause. "Regent, I—"

"You'll report directly to me in all incoming administrative matters," Adriana said in her most imperious voice. "You'll be my right hand in all matters outgoing."

The engine powering up thrummed through the Tin Can's hull. Edith braced herself in her improvised co-pilot's seat. Adriana could see her fighting to keep the smile from forming.

"Can we make it just 'Counselor,' then?" Edith asked. "The other is such a mouthful."

"Fine. As director of corporate accounting, I value efficiency above all else."

"What the hell is that?" Adriana demanded.

"I'm trying to figure it out, but these sensors—"

"Are shit, I know. Work with what you've got, Counselor."

Large pings were popping up all over the tactical screen. It was like they'd flown into an asteroid field. But there were no asteroid bodies this close to Callisto.

Something glanced off the Tin Can's outer hull.

"That's debris!" Edith said.

A large body took shape onscreen, outlined by lidar—directly in their path.

"Hold on!" Adriana said. She applied max power to the portside thrusters. They'd sacrificed maneuverability for speed on their flight from Europa. Now, with the last of its fuel hard-burning them home, the massive scoopship responded sluggishly, like a whale in cold seas.

"Edith, hold on!"

The large lidar blip disappeared.

The impact rocked the ship, throwing both women forward. The superstructure of the Tin Can yawed around them, groaning like a wounded animal.

"Fuck!" Adriana yelled. Red lights began to flash across the ship's dashboard.

"Something's wedged in the scoop!" Edith shouted over the alarms.

The ship began to list with skewed momentum. At this speed, in this ship, out of control and in the middle of a debris field...

"Release us from the scoop!" Edith said.

"What?"

"Detach the pilothouse! That large lever by the docking control!"

The queasiness she'd experienced over Jupiter returned. Reaching for the lever took effort as Adriana had to overcome the force of spin gravity working against her. Smaller debris rang off the outer hull.

"Got it!"

The lever wouldn't move.

"Release it!" Edith yelled. "Now!"

Adding a second hand for strength, her arthritis screaming, Adriana yanked downward. The sensation of becoming infinitely lighter followed as the Tin Can's pilothouse detached from the larger part of the ship. Stars streaked by overhead.

"Stabilize us," Edith said. "Adriana, hurry!"

Adriana engaged the automatic pilot. The Tin Can's onboard computer searched for the galactic horizon and fired its thrusters in sequence to course correct.

As the ship calmed its flight angle, a new blip appeared. The dimensional data showed it larger than anything they'd seen before.

"Shit," Adriana said.

It was close. It was very, very close. But ... behind them?

"That's the scoop and reservoir," Edith said with obvious relief.

"Oh," Adriana answered, embarrassed. The scoop floated freely, tumbling and cumbersome onscreen as just another piece of debris.

There was a tremendous flash. An impact had ignited the main engine still attached to the scoop, creating a massive explosion.

"Looks like you saved us again," Adriana said quietly.

Edith offered her a relieved smile. "You're the pilot," she said.

"As a matter of fact, I am," Adriana replied, returning to her duties. The field of pings was behind them now, and the auto-pilot had stabilized their course. Callisto hung almost centered in the forward window. "Seventy years, hell. Feels like yesterday."

A little light maneuvering on thrusters, and they should make it the rest of the way to Valhalla Station. Once she had the moon's gravity to work with, landing safely should be simple enough.

"My God," Edith said.

Adriana glanced first at Edith, then followed her stricken gaze. Callisto's orbital ring was growing close enough to see with the naked eye. Hanging over Jupiter, Adriana had longed to see it again—now she regretted that fantasy. It was like a celestial giant had gripped the ring with both hands and twisted, ripping it apart.

Rabh Regency Station was beaten into submission. Adriana hardly recognized the battered, streaked hulk she'd once called home. There were three large, ragged breaches in its lifeless hull. What was left of the station's superstructure spun lazily on a crawling course outward from the ring.

They were too far out and moving too fast to see bodies, and after their experience in the debris field, they'd have to stay that way to be safe. But prudence was a mercy. Adriana recalled the confused comm traffic as she and Edith had fled: reports of miners supporting her soldiers, allowing her and Edith to escape in the scoopship. She was starting to see, at long last, value in the Viking code her Callistans had chosen to live by.

"Think of all those people," Edith said. Her voice was wet. "All those lives lost."

Adriana cleared her throat. "So, Counselor," she said, "counsel me. We're almost out of fuel. Where should we set down?"

"The hydroponics dome has its own freight slips," Edith replied. "We can put down there." Her voice was matter of fact. Emotionless.

Good, hold onto that, Adriana thought, applying forward thrust. *Now is not the time for soft hearts, Cassandra? You got that right, bitch.*

Absolutely, one-hundred-percent fucking right.

6

RUBEN QINLAO • DARKSIDE, THE MOON

Ruben glanced over to find Anthony Taulke III sleeping on his mat. The low, animated volume of *The Real Story* hummed beneath his light snoring. The kid seemed to run on the mixed, heavy fuel of angst and self-importance, but when he'd finally crashed, he'd crashed hard. Eight hours of bliss so far, with the occasional stolen nap for himself, trading off with Strunk.

He studied the enforcer. Strunk stared at the monitor as he had for hours, soaking up every detail. Ruben couldn't shake the impression of a lessened man living past the time he might should have died. He set aside the sinking feeling in his gut and focused on the coverage. Cassandra was ramping up her rhetoric ahead of Tony's trial. She'd ordered the rechristened *Pax Corporatum* home to stand witness to its former owner's fate. Or maybe that was just her spin to explain why Tony's flagship had fled Titan, chased away by Galatz's fleet. That footage had leaked onto CorpNet before being scrubbed by Cassandra, the master of public messaging.

Watching Strunk watch the news was an interesting experiment in psychology. He seemed to be growing stronger but only by increments. Not Old Strunk strong, not by a longshot, but less Old Man Strunk now. His own natural healing kicking into gear, Ruben supposed.

"Something fascinating, Boss Man?"

There was even a bit of the old Strunk snark back now. It relieved some of the tension in Ruben's back, even when the snark was directed at him.

"Taking inventory," Ruben replied. "Listing our assets."

"What'd you call me?"

"I said *assets*."

"Ah," Strunk said.

Even word play? Ruben was tempted to find hope in that.

"Something new," Strunk said, indicating the monitor. He reached out and swiped the volume up.

"The Werewolf of Sol, Tony Taulke, is finally able to be moved to Earth," the commentator said. "He'll be held there until the *Freedom's Herald* returns from the outer system."

Footage from camerabots ran behind the words. Tony Taulke was awake and being attended by multiple medical personnel. The Darkside doctor, Brackin, hovered in the background apart from the caregiving team.

"That sonofabitch," Strunk said. "I get my hands on him—"

"I don't think Brackin gave Tony away," Ruben said. "I don't think he'd risk it going wrong."

Strunk made a noise that said he wasn't convinced. "We have two choices now," he said. "We spring Tony here or we do it on Earth."

Ruben absorbed that, looking for other options. Here, they were alone: one man, a half-strength professional killer, and a teenager with impulse control issues. And Tony was behind granite walls built to withstand a military assault in Darkside's Marshals Complex. Liberating him from there was a pipe dream. Then again, Tony would likely be held in tougher circumstances on Earth once the SSR got him there. Decisions, decisions.

"We could go in when they transfer him to the ship for Earth," Ruben suggested.

Strunk reached out and swiped the volume down again when the update started its loop. "Sure," he said. "When, exactly, is that happening again? And let's go through those assets you started listing. Oh, wait ... they're all right here."

"All right then, what do you suggest?"

"Contrary to recent rumor," Strunk said, stretching, his elbows and shoulders cracking, "I'm the muscle. You're the brains."

Ruben flashed him a hard look. "Here we're too wounded, too under-ground, and we have zero allies. So, if not here, then Earth," he said. "But we need to get there. And we've got no money." There was the vendor on the Fleshway, the one he'd bought fake passage from before and saddled the sleeping bum with, hoping to divert Elissa Kisaan's attention. But they had a money problem—as in, they didn't have any. Maybe he could break into Brackin's clinic, secure whatever illegal syncers the doctor might have left behind in that drawer of his. But the SSR would have cleaned that place out when they'd taken Tony.

The brains? He should have thought of the syncers sooner. So they had no money and nothing of value ... or, wait a minute...

Ruben cleared his throat and stood. "We have one other asset," he said to Strunk.

"Yeah? What's that?"

Walking to a dusty bookshelf, Ruben lifted a rag, revealing the Novy autoimmune stimulator he'd bargained for at the Darklight Bazaar. Under Brackin's direction, he'd secured the stimulator to spur Tony's healing process so they could get the hell out of Darkside. Then Tony had been taken and Brackin along with him. "We've got this thing."

"My pop needs that."

The two men turned to find a bleary-eyed Tony Junior rousing himself from sleep.

"Not anymore he doesn't," Strunk said, nodding at the monitor.

Junior leapt off his bed to peer at the screen. "They're taking him to Earth? To execute him?"

"We've been through the rescue options," Ruben said. "We'll make the attempt on Earth. But we have to get there first."

Junior looked from Ruben to Strunk and back again. "The Novy thing, then. Sell it."

"We were just discussing that," Ruben said.

"What's to discuss?" Whatever drowsiness had persisted in Junior was burning off quickly. "Sell it, get us to Earth. End of discussion."

"That's one option," Ruben said.

"It's the only option! Look what they did to Helena Telemachus!"

"Kid's got a point," Strunk said.

"Don't call me a 'kid.' Don't forget, Strunk—you work for me now."

Strunk hesitated in his response, pausing somewhere between health and current circumstances. Then, "Apologies, Mr. Taulke."

"We could use it on him," Ruben said, nodding at Strunk. "We need all hands on deck, whatever we choose to do. I can't do it alone."

"You've got me!" Junior insisted.

Ruben shared a look with Strunk. "Tony, listen to me." He tried to put his own feelings about Tony Taulke, Jr., aside and pretend the boy was any other teen with his father's life threatened. "Cassandra won't do anything to your father until she's gotten the maximum public relations value from him."

Strunk added, "The trial has to look legit, Mr. Taulke. To make *her* look legit as a ruler."

"But what they did to Telemachus—"

"Unfortunately..." Ruben, who'd begun to pace, stopped in front of the stimulator and gazed down at it. He needed to finish his statement but couldn't bring himself to do it.

So Strunk did it for him. "She was nothing. Just a prop. Your pop's the head of SynCorp. Big difference. Make no mistake, Cassandra will kill him —eventually."

Eventually, Ruben thought, tracing the contours of the Novy device with his fingertip. It really did look like an overfed medical hypo. Payload delivered by air compression through the pores of the skin. Simple, elegant. "I don't even know where the Bazaar is these days," he said, another decision forming in his head. "It floats around to avoid the authorities shutting it down."

"I can find out," Strunk said. "I've made some friends here. It's how I found you in the first place."

"Yeah, yeah, now you're talking," Junior said, his whole demeanor changed. "Wait, isn't that ... won't they trace the comm traffic—"

"The Bazaar guys have been shielding comm traffic for decades," Strunk said. "We'll be all right, k—Mr. Taulke."

But Ruben wasn't listening to them. Another course had occurred to him. A wild card course. He wasn't a man to act on impulse, he told himself. But sometimes, acting on impulse made all the difference.

"Okay, then, reach out," he said. Strunk's eyes flattened as he accessed his sceye. Scooping up the stimulator, Ruben approached the enforcer from behind.

"Hey!" Junior yelled.

Phish.

Strunk jumped, and Ruben narrowly avoided his backhand swing. But Strunk was slow to deliver it, and Ruben ducked in time. Strunk reached up to touch his neck.

"Goddamn it!" Junior said. "We just said..."

"Shut up!" Ruben shouted, turning to him. "Just ... shut ... *up!*"

Tony Junior's stunned expression quickly turned angry.

"We're on our own here!" Ruben said before the teen could speak. "Maybe we can find allies back on-planet—that's the chance we're taking. But we need Strunk at a hundred percent!" Ruben felt the blood coursing through his temple, his heart thudding in his chest. "And I'm just going to say this one ... more ... time." Ruben shifted his gaze between each of them. "*I'm* in charge of this Company until Tony Taulke *Senior* tells me differently. And that makes it my responsibility to do everything I can to save it. And right now, saving *him* is key to saving *it* as far as I'm concerned. Understand?"

Strunk stood apart from them, rubbing his neck. "Sure, Boss Man," he said.

Ruben shifted his unblinking gaze to Junior. The anger still festered behind the boy's eyes, but the blood had drained from Junior's cheeks.

"We either hang together," Ruben said, "or we hang separately. Do they still teach history in rich-kid school? Ben Franklin, by chance?"

Tony Junior swallowed, subdued if confused. "Yeah, okay. But we still have to get to Earth." He nodded at the spent stimulator in Ruben's hand. "Now—how do we do that?"

"Sure," Ruben answered, "sure we do. But how do we know it's not still valuable?"

Junior blinked. His black-and-white, binary mind had clearly never considered the possibility they could use the device on Strunk *and* still trade it back for passage Earthside.

"Strunk, call your contact," Ruben ordered. "Get the location of the Bazaar. We'll find out what this thing is worth."

"Sure, Boss Man," Strunk said again. "Sure thing."

————————————

Strunk's contact sent him to a ramp that led to the Sewer, the lowest quarter of inhabited Darkside. Its name fit the place, Ruben thought. It smelled even worse than the Fleshway, and its residents appeared pale and secretive, shying away from his monkish robes like they apparently avoided sunlight. The ground was caked with grayish moondust and sludge sloughing down from the more civilized inhabited levels above.

There'd been no sign of the three bounty hunters or any others, for that matter, as he'd made his way here. SSR troops and marshals, omnipresent in every hallway, seemed content to let a religious man pass without harassment. Or maybe they assumed, now that they'd caught the big fish in Tony Taulke, they were due some downtime.

No, all the concerns Ruben experienced as he made his way to the Darklight Bazaar were purely internal. The conflict with Tony's son seemed to be dividing Strunk's loyalties. Ruben was the power today, sure, but if they somehow were able to rescue Tony Senior and set things right with the Company, it was easy to see SynCorp's future in Tony Junior.

And that—more than anything save an ultimate victory by Cassandra—worried Ruben. Tony Junior was everything Ruben's sister Ming had warned him against: self-entitled and self-centered, lazy and lacking empathy, spoiled and wasteful. If the Company ever fell into his hands... Everything they'd worked for, everything Ming had charged Ruben with saving —it could be lost before the next generation even grew gray.

But that was a problem for another day. First, today, Cassandra had to be defeated. Then and only then could he have the luxury of worrying for tomorrow.

Down the ramp leading to the Sewer, Ruben found the familiar row of black-market vendor stands set along a dimly lit corridor. Ruben asked for Myerson by name and was allowed to pass.

"Do fer ya?" Myerson said as Ruben approached the stall.

Ruben pulled his hood back far enough for the hazy light to show his face.

"What the hell are you doing back here?" Myerson demanded, his breath quick.

"Lower your voice," Ruben said calmly, pulling the stimulator from beneath his robes.

"No refunds," Myerson growled.

"I don't want a refund. I want to trade."

"I sold the camoshades already!"

"*Volume.*" Ruben leaned in, placing the stimulator on the tabletop between them. He didn't remove his hand. "That's not what I want to trade for."

Myerson picked it up and turned it over. "You've used it. It's no good now."

"I don't believe you."

Staring at the stimulator, Myerson said, "Well, maybe as a curiosity only. For someone's museum display or private collection or—"

"How much?"

"Far *less* than you traded for it before. Not even sure it's worth my—"

Ruben held his hand out expectantly. "Fine, I'll find someone—"

"What do you want for it?" Myerson asked, not passing the Novy back. He shrugged to Ruben's raised eyebrow. "No harm in asking."

"Passage to Earth for three. No questions asked. No bullshit extortion fee halfway there. Three tickets, drop off in Old New York."

Myerson regarded him a moment, and he set the device on the tabletop between them. "I know a guy."

"I figured."

Ruben rested his hand lightly on the table beside the Novy. He was careful not to touch it, but his would be the hand that reached it first, should there be a contest.

"Cassandra is firing up the farming collectives again. Production was disrupted after Elise Kisaan was killed. But people are starting to squawk, now—food stores are running out all over the system. You want a revolution? Make sure mommas ain't got bread for their babies."

"Okay. And I need to know all this—why?"

"Because ag freighters are starting to move again. The Moon has always been the waystation between Earth and the rest of the system, right? Empty freighters are sitting here idle, have been since the big bang when Cassandra took over. They're finally heading back to Mother Earth to pick up whatever stores haven't rotted to distribute them across Sol."

"All right," Ruben said. "So we stow away on one of those, I take it."

"Yeah. In the cargo hold. It'll smell like seaweed pulled through a cow's ass, but you'll get used to it. And there's no seats. You'll be on the float."

Ruben considered that. Strunk's injuries could be a problem. The reason SynCorp had standardized gravity to one-g across the system was simple—because the human body had evolved in one-g. Less gravity meant muscles got slack. You could live under those conditions for a while, but come back to Earth, and it'd be like someone tied weights around your extremities. Your heart had to labor more. The other problem was healing the wounded. In zero-g, you could bleed out because blood wouldn't clot. Did Strunk have internal injuries? If so, would the Novy shot help heal them? Ruben was unsure how Strunk would weather the trip to Earth in the no-g hold of an ag freighter.

"But there are straps for securing the ag products, right?" he asked.

"Yeah," Myerson said curiously.

"Then those will have to do," Ruben said. With straps, at least, they could minimize movement. Wouldn't float around and potentially slam into the hull if the freighter made a quick maneuver. With no other options they'd have to chance it, Ruben decided.

Impulse to action won out again.

"Do we have a deal?"

Placing his hand on the stimulator, the black marketeer said, "Yeah, deal. But one more thing."

"Yeah?"

Myerson leaned forward. "Never ... ever ... come back here again."

7

BENJY ANDERSON • NORTHEASTERN FARMING COLLECTIVE, BETHLEHEM, PENNSYLVANIA, EARTH

Benjy had fallen asleep reading *Huckleberry Finn* again. Second night in a row.

His mother hardly stirred from Dreamscape now, no matter how hard he shook her or Bandit barked when Benjy became distraught. Two nights ago, the first night he'd been unable to rouse her at all, he'd cried for hours. Inside their warm FAMS, it'd been hard to separate the tears from the sweat brought on by the humid night. Sometimes, though rarely, Anne Anderson would mumble back to semi-consciousness. But Benjy's desperate attempts to make her eat something resulted only in food on the floor quickly snapped up by Bandit. When he'd prop her up and pour water over her lips, most of it burbled down the front of her rough-hewn blouse.

Tonight, he'd awoken angry. The pressure of caring for a mother who clearly no longer cared enough for him to come out of her stupor twisted the space between his shoulder blades. Why had she abandoned him? To spend time in a fairyland with his dead father? Who would choose to spend time in a world of the dead when the living were here—right here—who needed her?

Benjy propped himself up and switched off Twain's novel. Reluctantly, he sniffed the air. This morning was a blessing—the air was clean. Warm still, but clean. He roused himself from his sleeping pad and ran water over a cloth. Wiping it once over his own neck and head, he refreshed it again.

From the floor, his eyes cast upward, Bandit whined once.

"Sure, boy," Benjy said, opening the shelter's door. Bandit hopped to his feet and padded outside.

Benjy stood and stared at his mother, his anger slowly ebbing as the old fear replaced it. He cooled the cloth again with water and knelt beside her, placing it over her forehead. Sometimes she'd mutter incoherent not-words when he cared for her. At least when she mumbled, he knew she was alive. But Anne Anderson was quiet and unmoving this morning. Benjy checked her pulse.

Still beating. Still alive.

The first time she'd soiled herself and her pad—that night she hadn't awoken—Benjy called in a neighbor woman, Alice, to help clean her up. Alice had joined a local activist group from Bethlehem who'd taken on care for hackheads as a way of filling the hours of inactivity by helping others. They blamed Dreamscape for the community's problems, even the machines' mechanical failure, the blight in the crops to the west—the signs of which were now being seen locally—and the subversion of the clique's work ethic. The team consisted of people who'd refused to be sucked into Dreamscape's honey trap, seemingly on principle alone. Alice and her activist friends busied themselves constantly tending clique members too oblivious to care for themselves.

That first time Alice and her care team had arrived to help, she'd sent Benjy from the shelter while she cared for Anne—removing her clothes, cleaning her up, and wiping her body down with a cool rag before clothing her again. When she'd brought the soiled garments outside the shelter, Benjy had asked where the doctor was, and Alice had merely shrugged, the pre-dawn wind carrying the heavy odor of the soiled clothing in her hands. Smelling it made Benjy want to vomit and cry at the same time.

"The thing that's happening with your mother, Benjy? It's happening all over. I mean, all over the *world*," Alice said, setting the fetid clothing on a chair outside the FAMS. "Doctors, nurses, people with any medical training whatsoever—they're working long hours and losing patients..." She'd merely shaken her head.

"You can take these down to the river," Alice said, nodding wearily at the bundle. "That's what a lot of people are doing."

Benjy had merely nodded acceptance.

Yesterday, when he couldn't rouse his mother once again, Benjy had called Alice for help and received an auto-response that began by saying how overwhelmed the local care team was, then promising a callback in a week at the latest. So Benjy had changed his mother himself with Bandit watching nearby, his head resting on his paws. That's when the real anger had sprouted inside Benjy.

Mornings reading under the magnolia seemed years away, like they were memories from the life of another boy. Benjy was afraid now to leave his mother's side for more than a few minutes, and he'd begun to hate her for it. He'd begun to hate his father for dying too, and her need to be with a dead man more than her need to be with him.

But sometimes it was necessary to leave her, like now, to wash her clothes clean in the Lehigh River. The loving part of him feared he'd find her dead when he returned. The resentful part half-hoped for it. And then Benjy would feel guilty and sad all once more, and the emotional roller-coaster would resume climbing upward along its track.

Bandit strolled along the riverbank sniffing at flowers, while Benjy worked the material back and forth in his hand, scrubbing it in the river, trying to think of something else while staying upwind.

Today would be hot again. Maybe he could, with help from a neighbor, drag his mother's bedding outside. Get her in the sunshine, where the breeze was cooler. Why hadn't he thought of that before?

He worked the garment against a big rock in the riverbed, his fists gripping tighter, his arms thrusting harder. It took a moment for the high-pitched hum of the ship's engine to penetrate the dark curtain surrounding him. Benjy looked up to find Bandit standing stiff and pointing toward camp, his black-over-white tail wagging. A medium-sized shuttle was descending, a strange emblem on its belly: two snakes facing away from each other.

Cassandra! Or one of her commanders. Maybe they were coming to help! She talked about helping people all the time on CorpNet.

He snatched up the heavy, wet clothing. "Come on, boy!" Benjy cried. "Maybe they've got a doctor!"

With Bandit bounding beside him, Benjy raced from the riverbank through the purple mallow flowers in the meadow. The large shuttle had angled for the village square created by the clique's loose collection of FAMS. Marianne stood next to Jimmy Ellis and several of the other kids, enthralled by the dust kicked up. The shelters nearest the landing area shook and rattled.

Curious clique members were emerging from their FAMS. Benjy joined Marianne and Jimmy.

"What's happening?" Marianne wondered, elbowing Jimmy. "Oh, hi, Trace."

"Hi."

"No idea," Jimmy said. "Maybe it's—" The loud *phish* of the ship's hydraulics drowned out whatever he said. The shuttle settled on its struts, and a ramp began to lower from its belly.

"That's so cool," Jimmy said.

"What is?" asked Marianne.

"The double-snake thing. I think I might get it, like, tattooed."

"Oooo," Marianne said approvingly.

"You think that's cool?" Benjy said.

"No," Jimmy answered, "I *know* it's cool."

Marianne laughed.

Dick, Benjy thought.

Slender legs began descending the ramp. They belonged to a woman with a dark complexion and dark hair hanging loosely around her shoulders. She looked remarkably like Cassandra. As she stepped down the ramp, she reminded him of a fox he'd seen once slipping through the underbrush—sleek and lithe, almost like the brush was parting to let it pass. Half a dozen troopers in black uniforms followed and took up guard positions at the base of the ramp. The woman stood at the bottom, surveying the crowd as they continued to gather.

"She's pretty," Jimmy said.

"You think so?"

Marianne's tone was less curious, more cautioning.

"Yeah," answered Jimmy, clueless as mesmerized males can be. Then he seemed to snap out of it, turning to look at Marianne. "I mean, not as pretty as you are..."

Marianne turned away with a cold shoulder. "Yeah, yeah."

Dick.

"Members of the Northeastern Farming Collective," the woman said, speaking over the murmuring from the crowd. "My name is Elissa Kisaan. You knew my mother, Elise, as the head of the Kisaan Agro conglomerate. You know my sister, Cassandra."

She paused to let her pedigree secure their attention. She hadn't given Cassandra a title, Benjy realized, and he understood why. Cassandra didn't need a title. She ruled everything.

"You've no doubt heard rumors of a blight to the west and that now it's here," Kisaan said, walking forward. She stepped around the semicircle they'd formed, walking among them. "Well, those rumors are true."

Disbelief and anger rippled through the crowd. Kisaan folded her arms, continuing her slow circuit, trading looks with each person as she passed them. Then she turned her back, her gaze catching Benjy's eye and lingering a moment.

Holding up a hand to quell the voices, Kisaan turned and said, "We'll handle that. But in the short term, we need to collect the crops in the fields before the blight takes them. The combines and threshers need security updates to their software to protect them against SynCorp sabotage, and we're working on that, too. The reapers and other machines will be working again in a few days."

Except for the sounds of spring, the clearing was silent. Expectant. Someone had arrived to tell them what the future would be. Someone had arrived to tell them what to do.

"In the meantime, agriculture production needs to get back on track," Kisaan continued. One of the Soldiers near the ramp seemed nervous. Or anxious? His index finger tapped the trigger guard of his rifle. "There are hungry, frightened mouths to feed across this planet. Across this system." She cast her eyes around the assembled farmers. "Is Matron Anderson here?"

The silence returned until a man from the back said, "She's down with Dreamscape. She ain't coming back, I'm 'fraid."

"Take that back, Michael! She is too coming back!"

"Benjy..." Marianne's hand was on his arm, and he realized he'd stepped into the circle with the dark woman with the long hair. Bandit *whuffed* once, a warning.

"And you are?" Kisaan asked. She wore a smile that seemed made to win a pageant. With his wits about him again, Benjy was reminded of the fox when he looked at her, and that animal's reputation for charming its way into places it shouldn't be.

"Benjy. Anne Anderson is my mother," he said. "She's the matron of this clique." To the crowd, and in a raised voice, "And she's only sleeping!"

Kisaan approached and put her hand on his shoulder. Her eyes lingered on the wet clothing he'd forgotten he still carried. "How old are you?"

"Thirteen." He said it defiantly.

"You've begun your apprenticeship with your mother?" she asked.

"A year ago." Then, remembering his manners, "Yes, ma'am."

She turned back to the crowd. "Who else here works closely with Matron Anderson?"

A murmur made its way around the circle.

"Merrick Svoboda was her second, but he died a week ago," said the same man in the back, whom Benjy had named Michael.

"I see," Kisaan said thoughtfully. She turned to Benjy. "You know how to pick the fields when the reapers go down?"

Benjy nodded.

"Well, then," she said, "until your mother is better, you will lead in her place. It should only be for a couple of days, until we get the OS's on the machines upgraded. Then it'll be back to monitoring and maintaining them when they come off the line. Ladies and gentlemen," she said, raising her voice to the crowd, "meet your new matron, Benjamin Anderson." She knelt before Benjy and smiled upward as the group's semi-approving, semi-surprised opinions made themselves known. In a whisper only he could hear, she said, "I'll give you an hour. Get these people in the fields."

She had the eyes of a fox too. Sly and narrowed when she expected something done without question.

Elissa Kisaan stood up again and took his hand to shake it publicly. "Good picking, Mr. Anderson." Turning to the others, she said, "Good picking, all!"

Fat with humidity, the heat had persisted all afternoon. Benjy tried to walk tall, to keep his shoulders back as an example for the rest of the clique trailing behind him. They too looked like walking, wrung-out rags. Faces dirty, soft hands blistered, their shuffling feet and labored breathing made a heavy footfalls as they returned to camp.

His upper back hurt from carrying the gathering bag full of cabbages. It only made sense to offload it when it was full, so he'd carried it most of the shift. That's how a machine would do it—maximum efficiency. He'd wanted to impress Elissa Kisaan, and his anger at his mother, at the situation he'd been put in charge of, had fueled his work.

He didn't know why, not exactly, but he didn't trust Kisaan. Once he'd gotten the image in his brain, all he saw when he looked at her was the fox. Sleek and friendly but always angling for the treasure in the hen house.

But they'd gotten the work done. True, he'd trained for just such a day as this, but they were used to the machines doing all the work, and that showed today. It had only been one afternoon of work—a godsend really. Benjy doubted he or any of the others could have made it a full day under that sun. And yet tomorrow, that's exactly what they'd have to do. He should double the water rations tonight with dinner. And fill packs full tomorrow morning with salt stims before the crews returned to the fields.

"We got it done though, huh, boy?" he said to Bandit, whose tongue lolled, dripping. The dog had stayed beside Benjy all day, sheltering in the shade when he could, enduring the sun when he had to. "Yeah, we got it done."

He entered their shelter and tossed his empty bag to the ground. Just having it off his shoulder felt better. Benjy had worked up a fantasy in his mind that maybe his mother would have awakened and cooked dinner already, a homecoming for her hardworking stand-in as matron.

No such luck.

She lay flat on her bed pad, unmoving as usual. Benjy began his nightly ritual of kneeling and grabbing the mirror and placing it under her nose. He waited a few moments, almost begrudging her the time. He was tired. He was hungry. There was lots to do before he could rest.

And there was no frost on the glass.

Benjy's heart skipped a beat.

"Mom?"

He reached up and switched on the small lamp, then moved the mirror closer to her open mouth. He angled the light and waited what felt like hours.

"Mom!"

Bandit stopped his heavy panting and opened his eyes. Benjy pressed two fingers to his mother's neck.

"Mom!"

Anne Anderson had no pulse.

His mother was dead.

8

STACKS FISCHER • APPROACHING THE MOON

In the dream, I was trying to pick up a mug of beer in a nameless bar. Not The Slate, my favorite watering hole on SynCorp's orbiting headquarters over Earth, now Cassandra's main base. Not the dive Daisy Brace and I had said our see-you-laters in on Masada Station. Just an everyday, pitted bar with peanut shells and a mug of beer with newly poured foam sitting on top of it. Only, when I tried to pick up the beer, I couldn't. I glanced down to find what looked like a hundred pins sticking through my longcoat into my right arm.

"You get used to the pain after a while, old man. Try using *both* hands."

I looked over to find Daisy without her rehab exosuit, seemingly healthy and wearing a big grin.

The bar stool bumped me up and down. My eyes flew open.

A red light flashed on the *Coyote*'s dashboard. The crust started crumbling from my eyes. Ahead, dead center of the front window, was a pale silver disc with Rorschach's own pits and valleys scattered across it. We'd made it to the Moon.

Bekah was still sleeping in the co-pilot's seat. The journey through the Belt had been a little rougher than Gregor Erkennen had planned, I think, and the best way to get through the bumps was a little drug-induced sleep. Both of us had opted for that.

"Bekah," I said. A graybeard frog had stolen my vocal cords. With a little effort, I cleared the old fart out. "*Bekah.*"

She clawed her way to consciousness through her own version of burn-stress sickness. BSS is the result of heavy acceleration, which—even with the drugs and inertial dampeners offsetting the added vascular stresses of thrust gravity—takes its toll on a human body. As Bekah blinked awake, I suddenly realized we'd both been Erkennen's guinea pigs. No doubt he would download our biometrics from our vac-suits to study how we'd weathered the trip in his new double-fast ship. He'd have a nice spectrum of results from an old man and a young woman.

I popped the release on my straps. My joints lodged a class-action complaint when I tried to move. Another symptom of BSS.

Realizing Erkennen had likely used us to test his new tech made it feel more like plain old-fashioned BS to me.

"We made it?" Bekah asked. Her frog was feminine and sounded like a lifetime smoker.

"Not quite," I said, "but yeah."

The navigational readout showed our orbital path to the Moon. The approved approach vector was green. Under normal circumstances—and SynCorp law—that would be the required path all traffic approaching the Moon had to take. Tiny, programmed fingers would reach out from Dark-side's dockside control and slave the nav computer to keep the approach vector kosher. But we wanted to run silent, and letting ourselves be snagged by SynCorp Control and auto-piloted into Darkside's main docks would deliver us into Cassandra's scaly hands.

Gregor Erkennen had, of course, planned around that. Our entire trip kept us paralleling but at a safe distance from the Company's Frater Lanes. He'd flown us a little *too* close for my liking, but I understood why—too far out and we risked running into something not on the Company's system charts, like a wayward asteroid. Too close, and one lucky glance out a port-side window by an SSR type would give away the game.

The proximity alarm went off. A red dot appeared, heading directly for the *Coyote* from the Land of Green Cheese. A transport, maybe, likely on its way to Earth. I wondered if it was Tony's prison barge sailing home for the big show. Hopefully, it wasn't an SSR warship tipped off to our arrival. My I-told-you-so meter started to ping in the red.

"Ag freighter," Bekah said lazily, almost to herself. "Registry pings it as ... the *Grecian Earn*."

"Why does everyone who ever named a ship think they're clever?" I was relieved. You can tell by the snark. Then, "Think you can increase the distance between us and the mainlanes?"

Bekah was still clearing the cobwebs away. She sat up in her seat and winced with the effort. Even young joints take a little time to bounce back.

"Yeah, I just need to hack into the nav system. Give me a minute."

"Hack in?"

"Yeah," Bekah said, bringing up her programming screen. A few days earlier, she'd managed to make our ride a little smoother, especially during the hard burn cycles. I could only imagine how loud my joints would be screaming if she hadn't. "This is a prototype ship, remember? Made for testing, not travel. Navigation is integrated for remote control."

"Integrated," I said. "You mean there's no interface for a human pilot? We've been flying blind this whole time?"

Bekah scowled. "Not blind. Just following Gregor's pre-programmed flight plan." Up popped the gobbledygook on her screen again. "It's perfectly safe. But to alter it, I have to do it on the back end."

This was an example of the cutting-edge tech we'd fought so hard to protect on Masada Station?

"That's exactly what I'm worried about," I said. "My back end."

I tried to relax in my seat while the *Grecian Earn*'s red dot continued to close. It was impossible to really know what kind of sensors they had or if they'd be able to see us.

"Bekah..."

"I see it." Her fingers were blurry. The gobbledygook blinked and went red. The lights in the *Coyote*'s cabin winked out. But the ones that really mattered, the lights on the dashboard, were still lit. Pay particular attention, ladies and gentlemen, to the blinking red dot still closing on our position.

"Um..."

"*I see it*," she insisted. "Quit distracting me."

Far be it from me...

It's not often ships pass so close the light streaming through a window makes one visible to the other. It's the proverbial drop in the light bucket among a sea of stars, after all. Collision avoidance systems will ping each other and course-adjust long before that's possible, like ours had pinged the *Earn*. The question was—had the *Earn*'s pinged us? If so, cover blown. If not, maybe an even bigger explosion...

The flashing red code on Bekah's screen snapped green again. It wasn't immediate; it took a moment, but on the nav display I could see our approach to the Moon slowly arcing away from the *Earn*'s flight path. They'd pass to starboard at speed.

"Nicely done," I said. "Think they saw us?"

"Well, I can confirm there was no exchange of flight data—that was one way only, *toward* us. As for visual—we were still a good ways off their port side, and anyway, it's doubtful they saw us with Gregor's new stealth tech," Bekah said, visibly relaxing. "Multi-faceted slope-angle hull design, redirected lidar protocols—they would have crashed right into us before knowing we were even there."

"Well ... that's reassuring."

The *Coyote*'s boxy design had a purpose after all, then. All those angles and cuts making the ship look afflicted by square-angled leprosy. And whatever *redirected lidar protocols* were. I guess that's why Gregor Erkennen was a genius.

After the near miss with the *Earn*, Bekah took us on a wider approach far away from any mainlanes traffic. I vaguely knew where we were headed —an old lab that had once belonged to Viktor Erkennen, Gregor's father. The lab had been the Erkennen Faction's first secret, offworld research facility. A prototype for Masada Station carved right out of the gray lunar surface.

"Strap back in," Bekah said. "We're approaching the landing zone."

I did as ordered. A bunch of blurry keystrokes later, and the *Coyote* was kicking up moondust outside a fractured, domed structure. Something had cracked the dome like an egg.

I glanced over to congratulate Bekah for a whisper-smooth landing and saw her reaching for something around her neck.

"He left it with you?" I asked.

For half a second, she didn't seem to hear me. Then, "What? Oh, the Hammer? No. Tripp has that. Too dangerous to carry halfway across the solar system."

Couldn't disagree with that.

Bekah pulled the lanyard from beneath her vac-suit. It took me a minute to recognize the old tech—a removable lightning port drive. I hadn't seen an LPD in forever.

"How's a thousand-year-old drive going to help us defeat Cassandra?" I asked.

Bekah popped the lock on her pilot's harness. "It's not a thousand years old."

"In tech terms it is. I haven't seen one of those in years."

Bekah tried to stand. She got there, but it took a minute. With no gravity grid around, we were only afflicted by Moon-nominal gravity. A nicer way to come out of BSS than landing in full-g would've been.

"There's no umbilical collar," she said, looking out the portside window at the facility's single door. It looked like an old watertight door on a submarine. Not smooth plastisteel like you'd find on a modern station like Masada or SynCorp HQ. "We'll have to Armstrong it."

I was still struggling to get up from my seat. Bekah extended a hand.

"Armstrong it?" I said.

"You haven't done much excursion training, I take it," she said, motioning for me to hand her the helmet to her vac-suit.

"What's excursion training?" I said with a straight face.

"Right. We hopscotch it. From the *Coyote* to the lab's outer door. It's not that far."

"Okay."

"I'll go first and attach a cable to the facility. Then you'll clip a carabiner to the cable and follow."

"Why all the fuss?"

She hesitated, then, "Safety first."

When you travel in space, you learn to check your ego early on. That way you can be alive and embarrassed later if something goes awry.

"Okay," I said.

A minute or two later we were both suited up and pressurized. Bekah bled the air slowly out of the *Coyote's* cabin to minimize the expulsion when she opened the hatch.

"You sure these prototype controls can take exposure to space?" I asked. The comms made my voice thin.

"They're solid state," Bekah said.

"Right, then."

Bekah popped the hatch atop the *Coyote*, and we lifted ourselves out to land on the Moon. In all my visits to Darkside, I'd never actually stood on its surface before. There's something romantic about seeing that gray dusty puff up around your boots. Something my-forefathers-did-it-and-I'm-doing-it-now about it. Everyone's seen the footage of Armstrong landing on the Moon for the first time. One small step for man, one giant leap for the Company, as it turns out. But when you do it yourself, it's like it's *your* boots marking that particular turning point in human history. I'd stood on Mars, on Callisto, on Titan. But there's nothing quite like setting foot on the Moon for the first time.

"Wait here," Bekah said.

She hip-hopped a few steps to the one and only access door. There was a big E over it—actually, a Greek letter epsilon. It took me half a second to remember the old symbol for Erkennen Labs, from way back when individual corporate logos mattered more than the one big one does now. Bekah attached the cable she'd run from the *Coyote* and motioned to me.

I bobbed across like a kid at a carnival. Bekah attached her suit's onboard interface via lightning port to the door's dead security panel. Powering it up with her suit battery, she worked her techie magic. The security lock phased from red to green.

I stepped forward.

"Let me," I said over comms. I pulled my stunner. It was foreign and small in my gloved hand. I wasn't even sure how it would act without the nominal one-g of gravity I'd only ever fired it in. But I felt better holding it.

"Hold on to the tether," Bekah said. "Atmospheric decompression."

I nodded. We both stood aside as the seal released, ready for a big *whoosh* of air.

I pushed the door open. There was only a whisper of pressure. The lab's life support systems must have bled off long ago. A problem, long term, for us. What I saw next made me deprioritize that.

The lab's lighting system woke up. Sporadically. Randomly.

I heard Bekah's breath catch over comms. "Oh my God," she said, slipping past me.

I reached out to restrain her but missed. This was a killing zone, though the killing had obviously happened a long time ago. The fritzing light flashed and popped, revealing half a dozen gaunt, desiccated corpses. Nominal gravity had been in place here at one time. Dark streaks of dried blood painted the walls, the floor.

"What happened here?" Bekah whispered as I moved in beside her.

Some of the corpses wore lab-tech white. A few wore old Erkennen security uniforms with the block epsilon on the shoulder. One former Erkennen employee was slumped at her workstation. Skin had shriveled before the lab's atmosphere completely failed, drawing up around fingernails, pulling rictus smiles away from teeth. It was like we'd opened an Egyptian tomb, only instead of finding a pharaoh with all his wealth and organs neatly packaged beside him for the afterlife, we'd found half a dozen dead Erkennen loyalists. Permanently entombed together in this anonymous lunar cavern.

"I was hoping you could tell me," I said quietly. She approached the dead woman at the workstation. As I got closer, I could see the corpse's head lying unnaturally against one shoulder. Someone had nearly decapitated her from behind.

"No," Bekah answered, distracted and distant. She'd placed a gloved hand on the woman's head. I figured she was thinking of Carrin Bohannon, murdered by Bruno Richter at her own terminal on Masada Station. I knew I was.

"Human beings can be so cruel to one another," she said, her back to me. "Pointlessly cruel. Needlessly cruel."

Richter had been like that, had enjoyed killing. Had inhaled the fear that wafts off a victim who knows they're about to die. He'd gotten off on it. I'd killed, sure. But everyone who'd met Mother Universe at my hand had deserved it.

Well, that was a lie. *Almost* everyone. I'd made mistakes. But what we saw here wasn't a mistake. It was deliberate, multiple murder.

"This is why," Bekah said, the carnage around us reflected in her voice.

"Why what?"

"Cassandra must be stopped. I know she didn't do this, but—she's done the same. Through Richter, and others. My opa taught me a long time ago how dangerous action without conscience is. It's this. When paired with cruelty, it's the very definition of evil."

I came to stand beside her. "Cassandra," I reminded myself and Bekah, "is a fucking machine that thinks. Whoever thought *that* was a good idea? First thing I'd do if it were me—kill the impulsive bloodbags who made me. The universe would be a simpler, binary place."

Bekah said nothing. She'd begun stroking, lightly, the dead woman's hair.

"We're on the clock here," I said, not unkindly. Bekah didn't move, and I almost spoke again.

"When we're through," she said. "When we've done what we've come to do and Cassandra is dead ... I want to come back here. I want to take care of these people. They've been alone, uncared for, too long."

"Okay," I said. That was down the priority list too. *Way* down. These people were dead. They didn't care, hadn't cared about anything for thirty years. But Bekah Franklin cared, and I guess that was enough for me to keep her request on the list at all. "But first things first."

Bekah turned away from the dead woman. "Let's get to work."

9

ADRIANA RABH • APPROACHING VALHALLA STATION, CALLISTO

"I can override the docking protocols," Adriana said. "I think."

Using thrusters, the pilothouse—all that remained of their whale-like scoopship—descended lightly toward Valhalla Station's hydroponics dome. Unlike the main colony's Customs House, which offered several slips for catering to multiple ships simultaneously, there was only a single, multi-purpose dock for receiving the dome's more specialized deliveries.

"We're getting close," Edith said, her voice rising.

Tracking lights outlined the approach to the dock. At the end of the lighted path was a double-thick plastisteel blast door shut tightly against the vacuum of space.

"I know. Give me a minute."

Adriana focused on her fingers. She'd already input her override code that allowed her access to everything on Valhalla Station—from the shipping manifests to the market price projections for deuterium to the water allowance thresholds for flushing the colony's toilet. It'd taken her a moment to remember it, which she found odd, and when she'd first typed it in, the system had rejected it. Had Braxton or that Kisaan clone locked her out? That sounded like a first-order-of-business kind of thing for an AI-led revolutionary to do. Or maybe the system was down?

Or maybe you mistyped the goddamned code.

Edith's hand reached past her.

"What are you—?"

The thrusters fired for half a second, and she felt the pilothouse lift.

"Sorry," Edith said. "I was getting nervous."

Her cheek twitching, Adriana said, "What have I told you about apologizing when you're in the right? Now, strap in. I think I've got it this time."

Edith returned to her makeshift perch. Adriana took a breath and quite deliberately, without relying on muscle memory as she had before, typed her override code into the console. Below, the dock's running lights blinked twice. The blast doors didn't open.

"What's happening?" Edith asked. "Why aren't they—"

"The bay is depressurizing, bleeding off atmosphere," Adriana said, the knowledge trawled up from a few decades earlier. "So it doesn't blow us off course. Give it a minute."

"Oh," Edith said, "okay."

The running lights flashed twice more, and the plastisteel doors separated. A light, white cloud of atmosphere *whooshed* between them as they parted, revealing a softly lit bay beyond. The calm amber light of Callistan night revealed an empty bay. Adriana began guiding them in.

"Looks clear," she muttered.

"What?"

"It's what someone says when they have no idea if it's really clear or not," Adriana answered. "Old joke."

"Oh," Edith replied.

How tired Adriana was—physically, sure, but emotionally too after seeing the wreck of the ring and the station that had once been her home, floating dead in space. Even her spirit was tired. Once they were docked, once they were home, she could rest, at least for a little while.

Goddamn, Gregor, she thought as the dock's automated system slaved their guidance system toward an empty slip. *What am I fucking bribing you for? Your Wellspring has sprung a goddamned leak.*

Above them, the slip's blast doors closed.

"Atmo shows green," Edith said as the Tin Can settled on its struts.

Adriana popped her pilot's harness loose. After several tries, she found she couldn't lift herself from the seat. She'd been sitting too long. Edith offered her a hand, and the Regent of Callisto and Exchequer of Corporate Accounts reluctantly took it. After a few more moments of physical struggle, their feet stood on the hard deck of the hydroponics dome's receiving dock.

The one-g standard made Adriana's blood feel like molasses in her veins. She'd adjust, but it would take a few hours. Glancing at Edith, she was selfishly gratified to see that the younger, stronger woman wasn't doing so well either. Then she remembered Edith was carrying a child and felt that new, unfamiliar self-realization at how selfish she could be. She owed Edith something for not only putting herself at risk to save Adriana, but for putting her child at risk as well.

And she hated being in debt.

"The main agriculture greenhouses are through there," Adriana said, forcing herself to move. "It's nighttime, or what passes for it on Callisto, anyway. Staff should be minimal. Let's see if we can find some real food."

They shed their vac-suits near the doorway. Adriana's override codes allowed them to pass from the dock into the dome proper. The huge dome stretched for kilometers outward from its center, with dozens of individual hothouse zones organized by crop type. They had indeed come home in the long stretch of the post-midnight period. There wasn't a soul around.

"Look at the blue dandelions," Edith said, straying off their path. Adriana was glad for the excuse to stop. "And look!" Edith continued. "They've already been reaping the roots for tea. They've even ground some for the marketplace! My friend, Reyansh, brings in exotic spices all the time. Cumin and curry. Paprika and basil." She held up two tiny brown bags, each tied with string. "And chicory! For coffee!"

Adriana offered a polite smile as she sat down. Being off her feet felt positively orgasmic. Or would have, if she could actually remember what that felt like. She watched as Edith searched through the wicker basket full of tiny, brown bags. She finally picked two and began separating their dark contents into roughly equal piles.

"Would you like some coffee with a little flavor?" Without waiting for an answer, Edith began casting around for materials. She dug a hole in the dirt and filled it with small branches from nearby trees. Adriana wondered how she'd start the fire, but with a smile, Edith produced a lighter she'd scrounged from a nearby toolbox.

"Is that safe?" Adriana said.

The kindling in the small dugout began to catch. "Sure," Edith said. "I used to camp all the time with my parents in Mississippi."

"This isn't Mississippi," Adriana mumbled, though in truth, she was too tired to argue. She continued to watch, a part of her fascinated by Edith's puttering as she assembled a crude coffee pot from the items on hand: a thin piece of cloth, ripped from her own clothing, for a filter; an old plastis-teel container with a flat circle of metal for a crude lid. She could pull water from the hose of the greenhouse's irrigation system.

Edith was resourceful, Adriana realized, in a way she could never be. The woman's knowledge had saved them from capture by Cassandra, rough as that ride had been.

As Edith poured the foul-smelling liquid into a small bowl that reminded Adriana absurdly of Japanese dining, she noted Edith's distant, wary look.

"Something on your mind?" she asked after Edith had filled her own cup. Adriana lifted the bowl. The contents really did smell foul. But the liquid was warm. And it wasn't recycled urine or Absinthe of the Garden Green.

"No," Edith replied quickly, blowing over the top of her coffee.

"Okay." Adriana took a swig. The heat was perfect. Nearly tongue burn-ing, but just nearly. Although... "This tastes like shit. Like, literally, what shit would taste like if you boiled it over a fire and drank it."

Edith slurped at her own cup, grimaced, and blew over it again. "I might have gotten the portions wrong," she allowed. "Chicory to coffee grounds."

"Still," Adriana said, atypically uncomfortable with the silence that had grown from Edith's *mea culpa*, "there's something to be said for variety. And if you ever say I said this, I'll call you a liar. But I could do without thinking about, much less drinking, anymore Green for a while."

Adriana found Edith's eyes and held them. Somewhat surprisingly, Edith held hers back, indecision playing across her features. Adriana was about to ask what was wrong when Edith made the question moot.

"It was me," Edith said.

Here it was, then. The big secret Edith had only hinted at before when they were still flying for their lives from Jupiter. Adriana gave the moment some respect for Edith's having held out for so long. She took another sip from her cup.

"What was you?" Adriana said once the liquid shit had slid down her throat. She'd almost unwittingly added *my dear.*

Edith stared into her coffee. Her face was drawn. Adriana wondered if that's how she herself, with her rejuvenated skin, must look to others. She even understood, as she watched Edith struggling to form words, why they called her Adriana the Alabastered behind her back. The woman who'd bargained her soul away, if she'd ever had one, for eternal life. It was laugh-out-loud comical, the irony. The most accomplished businesswoman in the solar system, and she'd failed to read the fine print—the contract she'd made with Gregor Erkennen hadn't said anything about eternal *youth.* That life-lived-too-long reflection Adriana often saw in the mirror was how Edith appeared to her now. Skin stretched, reflecting pain, until it threatened to snap.

"It wasn't Luther," Edith said. "It was me. I sold the information to the pirates."

Adriana blinked once. She wondered if hearing loss was another symptom of Wellspring failing. She stared at Edith, who refused to meet her gaze.

"Fischer told me—"

"He lied," Edith said. "For me, I suppose. Though I don't know why. Not really."

The coldness of anger congealed inside Adriana. If this were true—and she knew it must be, now—why Fischer had deceived her was a very good question indeed. She ran the permutations through her head for the deal that must have been made. Had Edith paid him? Surely, she must have—enforcers didn't lie for free. Maybe with her profits from her betrayal of Adriana? Now, that would be rich. Maybe with her body? Other than disease, which was easily remedied, the risk when you were already pregnant was minimal...

It had been so easy to believe that Luther Birch had been guilty. But whatever his sins, he hadn't betrayed Adriana Rabh and the Company. No —that had been his wife.

"Why?" Adriana whispered. She provided for everyone on Callisto: employment, paid leisure, a life with purpose. She'd always demanded a certain level of respect, sure, but such was her right as their regent. That was the deal she'd made with them—work for life. She'd always seen it as fair. Unworthy of betrayal.

"It was all I had to bargain with," Edith said. Her voice was soft, wet with regret.

"What was?" Adriana hissed. She wanted to rail. She wanted to scream. She wanted to slap Edith Birch silly till she rolled into a tiny, defensive ball begging for mercy.

"Information," Edith whispered, wiping her eyes. "I wanted to go home."

"Wanted to go home?" *You* destroyed *our home, you stupid bitch!* Adriana wanted to say—to shout. *You handed them the data that fueled their starships ... their whole goddamned revolution!*

"I wanted to get away!" Edith cried. "From here! From *him!*" Any other words she had were lost to sobbing. The cup tumbled from her hands, its contents soaking into the soil.

"You didn't need to betray me for that!" Adriana said. She wanted to rise, to stand over Edith, to strike her. But her body wouldn't cooperate, and that only infuriated her more. "You could have come to me!"

To her surprise, it was Edith who rose. "Come to you?" She advanced across the small space, and Adriana dropped her own bowl of shit coffee. "Come to *you?* The Company only values one thing! *Productivity.* I counted inventory in a clinic. Luther mined Jupiter's atmosphere." Edith's hands were animated, though Adriana felt no threat. The motions were desperate, and desperately futile. "The Company would have sided with him. *Has* sided with men like him for years! I've heard the stories ... seen the evidence in the clinic. SynCorp doesn't give a *shit* about anything but profit. No matter what the cost!"

Adriana listened because she had little choice.

"So, you know what I told myself?" Edith's face flushed red. "I said, 'Fuck the Company!' I said, 'You can't report this. They'll only garnish his wages for a fine—and then he'll be pissed! Then it'll be worse! And all your fault!' I said, 'I'll show Adriana Rabh, that pompous Alabastered Bitch in orbit, what it costs *her* for *me* to be free! Fuck her!' I said to myself, 'I'm doing this for me! Fuck them all!'"

Edith swung away from her then, tears spilling from her. She wrapped her arms around her chest, hugging her shoulders and sobbing. She stood alone and apart.

"I'm sorry I betrayed you," Edith said, her back to Adriana. "But I don't regret what I did!"

She saved you. From some dormant corner of Adriana's mind, her own cold, calculating voice spoke truth to her.

She saved herself, Adriana shot back.

She could have done that alone, the quiet voice said. *She chose to save you, too.*

A guilty conscience, that. Nothing more.

A part of Adriana reveled in the pain Edith was feeling. Every catching sob, each clenched, white knuckle—self-justice levied by a betrayer's need for absolution. Edith deserved every ounce of pain she was feeling.

But you know what she said was true. About the Company's priorities. It's true still.

Maybe. Get over it! It's the opportunity cost of running a fucking solar system.

The price, *you mean.*

A distinction without a difference. I can't fix it. That's not me.

No, the voice said, and there was sadness there. A quality of long-borne weariness. *It's not who you are.*

Edith's weeping had begun to soften. She smoothed the front of her clothes roughly, then turned slowly to Adriana. There was a hesitant fear paired with challenge in her eyes.

"What now?" she asked.

Adriana took in a long, slow breath. Just at the dome's horizon she could make out the yellow sliver of Jupiter's light bleeding through. The shading in the smartglass opened, timed to let through what passed for sunrise on Callisto. The colony would be waking up soon. Friend and foe alike.

"You betrayed me, Edith Birch," Adriana said, the calm of her voice masking a fury gone cold. She enjoyed, if only for a moment, the way Edith's face registered the hurt. "You also saved me." The Regent of Callisto stood, slowly and with effort. When Edith reached out a hand to help her, Adriana slapped it away. "For now, we'll leave it at that."

The relief that flooded Edith's features made Adriana want to vomit.

"Thank you," Edith said simply.

"Don't thank me," Adriana said, returning to the path they'd been walking before the blue dandelions distracted them. "There's still justice to be served here. But it will have to wait a while."

Behind her, Edith cleared her throat. "I understand."

"I doubt that." Adriana gestured at the growing yellow light kilometers away on the other side of the dome. "Lunar dawn is coming. These farmers have lockers in each dedicated growth sector, I believe. Maybe we can find some clothes to disguise ourselves. Maybe we can blend in long enough to avoid being executed. Although—I wouldn't know where to begin to look in Valhalla Station for anyone friendly to me."

Edith joined her on the dirt path. "I think I might know someone who can help us." Around them, the finely balanced ecosystem of Callisto's hydroponics dome was waking up. A bird chirped and was answered by its mate.

"Fine," Adriana said. "Lead on."

10

BENJY ANDERSON • NORTHEASTERN FARMING COLLECTIVE, BETHLEHEM, PENNSYLVANIA, EARTH

Benjy yanked at the radish until it finally came out of the ground. Tossing it into his gathering bag, he moved on to the next one.

He fixated on the task in front of him. Grabbing, pulling, sometimes fighting the earth for the next radish, then tossing it in the sack. He ignored the sweat saturating his clothes. He ignored the ache in his bones lingering from the previous day.

Grab. Pull. Toss. Move on to the next.

It was like the harder he worked, the madder he got at his mother. For leaving him. For leaving him here in the fields, alone and sweating and aching and wanting to vomit and cry and scream, all at the same time. The adults—so many of them gone now, only a few left. After they'd started giving it away for free, Dreamscape had become an easy way out. Of hard work. Of doing their jobs.

Of being here.

When softer thoughts filtered in, thoughts that weren't red and pulsing in his vision, Benjy wondered if he maybe worked harder, just a little harder, God would notice and give his mother back. But then he'd just get angry at himself for wishing the impossible, and the cycle would start again.

Grab. Pull. Toss. Move on to the next.

Distant and dreamlike, he could hear voices from the rows around him. Marianne and Jimmy, Michael Guomo, the man who'd spoken up in the camp when Elissa Kisaan called his mother's name. Every one of the dozen or so remaining members of their farming clique, most of them children, labored in the fields. Twice that many had died or were dying, languishing in a Dreamscape coma.

Just a fucking hackhead. The savage thought came with an image of his mother, smiling, over dinner. Or maybe she was putting him to bed after reading to him when he was younger. Or maybe it was any other of a thousand images he could conjure to spit at in his grief.

Grab. Pull. Toss. Move on to the next.

"I hate this shit," Jimmy said from far away.

Reaching for the next radish, Benjy's hand stopped.

"Jimmy, keep your voice down," Marianne said, irritated. "You don't want to—"

"Fuck it!" Jimmy yelled. Benjy heard him slough his sack off into the dirt. "I'm not doing this anymore. They need to fix the damned reapers."

Slipping his bag from his shoulder, Benjy set it carefully between the rows and got to his feet.

Three rows over, Jimmy stood defiantly. Marianne had one hand on his arm.

"Get back to work," Benjy said quietly.

"Fuck you, Trace," Jimmy said, defiant and cocksure. "I don't have to do what you say."

"Jimmy!" Marianne sounded embarrassed, scandalized.

"Jimmy," Michael said. "You should get back to picking. It's only for another day or—"

"Fuck you too, Mike. You're not my father."

Fists clenched at his sides, Benjy advanced across the rows. Bandit trailed him. Jimmy was half a head taller, so Benjy had to stare upward to look him in the eye. Marianne moved forward, placing a hand lightly between them.

"Trace, it's okay," she said. "It's just the heat and—"

"Get back to work," Benjy said to Jimmy.

"Or what? Whatcha gonna do, Trace? Think you can take me?"

Bandit growled.

"No, boy," Benjy said, his voice low, his eyes never leaving Jimmy's. "Stay."

The workers around them were still. They stood up straight with the excuse of stretching their backs. All had left their sacks in the dirt.

"Jimmy," Marianne said, "we have to get the work done. Miss Kisaan said—"

"I don't care what she said!" Jimmy yelled. "We shouldn't have to be out here." Turning to Benjy, he said, "If your hackhead mother hadn't fucked off her duties, the reapers would still be working, and—"

Benjy's fist cracked Jimmy's jaw. The other boy went down.

Marianne squeaked once, backing away. "Trace!"

Bandit's barking filled the air.

"Say it again!" Benjy shouted, dropping his full weight on Jimmy's belly.

A *whoof* of air and Jimmy's arms were up, trying to fend off the blows. Sometimes Benjy's fists landed, sometimes Jimmy's managed to knock them away. Benjy struck wildly, and Jimmy's knuckles got past him, landing once, twice, above his left eye.

"Say it again!" Benjy shouted, feeling no pain.

Hands were on him then, pulling him off. "Benjy, stop already!" Michael said, struggling to restrain him. "We need him out here to meet the quota!"

Benjy went limp. When Michael relaxed Benjy wheedled out of his grasp, plowing into Jimmy again. Benjy's fists pounded the other boy, and then more hands there helping Michael pull him off. They held him solidly now.

"Enough, boy!" Michael shouted. "It's almost time! Stop this!"

There came the sound of Jimmy's moaning, then Bandit's worried huffing. And in the distance, the now-familiar droning of a shuttle on approach.

Marianne knelt next to Jimmy and checked him over, asking if he was okay.

"Leave me alone!" Jimmy said, breathing through his mouth.

"Say it again," Benjy whispered. The other boy wiped the blood from his nose, already swelling. "Say what you said again."

"Benjy, I said, that's enough." Michael's voice was quieter now, more restrained. "They're coming." He jerked his head at the sky.

Above, six shuttles approached. The mirrored-snake emblem adorned their hulls. Five were painted gunmetal gray, and the sixth, black, flew in the center of the formation. One by one, the clique members picked up their bags, knowing work for the day was done. Benjy was tempted to retrieve his too, but he'd left it in the dirt two rows over.

The shuttles landed. One at a time, their debarkation ramps extended. SSR troopers exited the five gray ships. Then, as she had before, Elissa Kisaan descended. From the black shuttle, alone and without escort, save for three camerabots hovering over and around her, a lone figure stepped down the ramp. Gasps came from the farmers sweating in the sun. Benjy's anger at his mother, even his grief for her, were momentarily forgotten.

Cassandra had come to Bethlehem.

"I've come to pay my respects," Cassandra told the crowd. A 'bot repositioned nearby to pan across their awestruck faces. "Which one of you is Benjy Anderson?"

No one answered. Benjy's insides fluttered with butterflies. This was the woman who'd toppled Tony Taulke, who was about to put the man on trial. Cassandra was powerful. The most powerful person he'd ever met—maybe *would* ever meet. And her beauty almost glowed. Her dark hair shone in the Pennsylvania sun. Her body, slender and elegant, made his earlier comparison of Elissa Kisaan to a fox seem silly and childish. When this woman moved, she *was* movement. When she spoke, she *was* language. And when her gaze lit on Benjy, his fascination with Marianne Schiro fell away like old skin.

"You," Cassandra said.

Benjy stepped forward, steel to the magnet of her inviting smile.

"Yes," he piped from a dry throat.

Cassandra moved forward. Elissa Kisaan made to join her, but Cassandra gestured for her to stay where she was. The camerabots hovered and hummed like bees. The one behind Benjy's head made him uneasy.

"Your mother, Anne," Cassandra said. "She was a matron well loved by those who worked for her."

"Yes."

"She was the very symbol of why we're fighting the Syndicate Corporation. A woman who gives and gives ... even unto her death ... who slaves day after day so that rich moguls like Tony Taulke and Adriana Rabh and, yes, my own mother Elise Kisaan might enjoy opulence from her sacrifice."

"It was Dreamscape." Benjy spat the words out.

"What?" Cassandra said.

"Her work didn't kill her," he said. "Dreamscape did."

Cassandra regarded him a moment. "Perhaps that was the weapon," she allowed, "but the finger that pulled the trigger? That was SynCorp." Cassandra bent down so their eyes were level, and that sense of drowning in her dazed him again. Her unnatural eyes, her crown-like mane of hair, her scent. The way her breasts parted, lifted and framed in her tight, black uniform.

Benjy's skin tingled where she touched his cheek. He cocked his head, the emotions of the last days melting and breaking apart inside him. "I don't understand..."

"You don't have to understand, Benjy," she said. "But trust me when I say it's true." Part of him wanted to pull away, but most of him didn't. She brushed the hair from his forehead. "What's this?"

"What?" he whispered.

"This bruise here. What happened?"

"I got into a fight."

"I see." She stood and looked around. "That boy there?"

Jimmy Ellis stood apart from the rest of the clique, his body language less defiant with Cassandra there. Marianne was next to him. Their fingers were entwined.

"Yeah," Benjy said, "him."

Cassandra's eyes narrowed, then she returned her attention to Benjy. "Why?"

"He was ... being disrespectful to my mother. And to the work. He didn't want to do it."

"I see. And you took offense. You defended your mother's honor," she said. "And the honor of the work."

Benjy shrugged. There was truth somewhere in that.

"I can see your mother in you. Tough, dedicated, sacrificing," Cassandra said. Benjy's breath hitched in his throat. Cassandra turned to the camerabot. "Her loss is felt deeply in this community. And we've come to recognize that fact in our own small way." Then, to Benjy again, "Let's go pay your mother the respect she deserves."

As the simple pine box lowered into the ground, Benjy couldn't hold back his tears. His anger washed out of him with them, though his shame at having held it so hard for so long lingered in his belly. His mother would have been sad to see him crying. He needed to be strong for all their clique, now, she'd say. It's what she'd said about them both after his father had died.

The box thumped into the earth.

Cassandra, Elissa Kisaan, and the clique surrounded the graveside. Benjy had picked the spot out himself. He'd made sure they avoided the root that had so annoyed him a few days earlier. He wanted the magnolia to live a long time. The Pennsylvania spring had been so hot, and he wanted his mother to sleep in the shade. Now, she would always remain cool.

"Pick up a shovel, young man," Cassandra said.

Benjy started to move forward, but Kisaan's hand held him in place. He glanced up, confused. Then he realized Cassandra was talking to Jimmy Ellis.

"I—I..." the boy stammered. His nose had swollen to a purple mass.

"Do the work," Benjy whispered. Then, looking Jimmy in the eye, "You owe her that."

Marianne pushed him forward, and Jimmy reluctantly picked up a shovel.

"Wait!" Benjy said. He'd almost forgotten. At his request, the people of the camp Anne Anderson once led had gathered flowers from the nearby meadow. He'd chosen some of the magnolia's pink and white blossoms.

Benjy picked up the basket and carefully, evenly distributed the flowers over the coffin. As the last of them drifted down onto the wood, he said, "To deaden the clods of earth. So she's not disturbed." He'd read that in a book somewhere. Maybe it'd even been *Huckleberry Finn*. He didn't remember. He'd thought it odd, then, tossing flowers onto the coffin before shoveling in the dirt—he hadn't really seen the point. The person inside was dead—not even a person anymore. What difference would clods clunking on the coffin's lid make to them?

Now, blanketing the lid seemed an entirely needful thing to do for his mother's sake. It didn't matter that she was dead. Respect was something that shouldn't die—a lesson she'd taught him about his father. The flowers were about that more than anything, Benjy realized now.

Jimmy began shoveling earth into the hole. Others picked up shovels to help. Benjy wanted to leave so he wouldn't see, but he forced himself to stand there and watch. He stood there, beside his mother, her protector until the work was done.

At dusk, the air in the shelter was lighter, almost cool. Benjy stood inside for a long time, just looking around. Everything he'd lived with all his life—his mother's crochet she liked to do at night, Bandit's bed and bowl, the small shelf of *real books* in the corner—everything seemed new again. New and alien at the same time.

There was a knock on the door, and Bandit, his nap disturbed, grumbled a half-hearted warning. Bandit was a watchdog in name only, his mother had joked more than once. Her teasing smile lit the corners of Benjy's memory.

The knock came again.

He didn't want to see anyone, not even Marianne. But his mother had always taught him to be neighborly, and that being friendly mattered most at the times he felt least like being so.

"Come in."

The door opened. Cassandra entered, filling up the space with her presence. A single camerabot hovered over one shoulder. It panned around the

FAMS. Benjy experienced competing impulses. First, to pick something up and knock the 'bot from the air. But he also felt embarrassment at the shelter's disarray and that it might be caught on camera. The embarrassment he knew his mother would have felt had she been alive to feel it.

"How are you doing?" asked Sol's new ruler.

"I'm fine," he said reflexively. Anything else would only extend the conversation. He wanted to be alone.

"I know it's been a hard day." Cassandra stood just inside the door. Bandit watched warily as the camerabot moved around the shelter. "You bore it well, Benjy."

"Don't call me that," he said without thinking. "I ... call me Trace."

It was an impulse. A way to stay grounded in a house that didn't feel like a home anymore. A life preserver tethered to a life he no longer had.

"Okay, Trace," Cassandra said. "I have an idea."

"Okay."

The camerabot whirred against one wall, framing them both in the shot.

"Do you want to stay here? Now that your mother has ... passed on?"

"I..." He had no idea, actually, so he defaulted to the known. "I was appointed matron by Miss Kisaan. I have to take care of the clique."

Cassandra's smile was warm and practiced. And somehow at odds with the energy in her golden eyes. "Such a responsible young man. But if we could find someone else to lead the clique, would you consider coming to live with me?"

"I ... maybe?" He'd never considered leaving before, hadn't realized leaving was an option. He looked around the shelter again, experiencing its emptiness. What was left for him here? His mother's grave? Not friends, not really. Not Marianne. She had Jimmy.

"I live in New York," Cassandra said, moving casually inside. The light from outside disappeared as the door closed. "I think you'd like it there."

He regarded her a moment, trying not to stare too long at her eyes. They glowed with promise. Of a place that wasn't here. A time that wasn't now.

"Is there air conditioning there?" he asked. "How would I earn work credits?"

"All you could ever need. And as for credits—well, you could be my consultant. Tell me firsthand about the problems the cliques are experiencing. It's our duty to get them back up and running again, to feed the system. We can do that together."

The thought of helping others was appealing. So was unlimited air conditioning. And seeing Cassandra every day.

"Why?" he asked.

"Why what?"

"Why me?"

Her expression lightened. "You're a very special young man, Trace. You don't know why yet, but you will. And I'd like to take care of you, if you'll let me."

He thought about it a moment longer. Then Benjy—now Trace—crossed the shelter's small space and began to separate items into two piles.

"What are you doing?" Cassandra asked after a while.

"Deciding what to take." He stopped short his packing. "Bandit can come, right?"

Hearing his name, the dog raised his head, his ears perking up.

Cassandra smiled at him. "Why, of course."

Nodding, Trace said, "Hear that, Bandit? We're going to a new home." One with unlimited air conditioning. A home without memories. Without grief in every corner.

The camerabot panned across the room until it had a clear shot of his expectant face.

He uncovered his mother's tattered paperback of *The Adventures of Huckleberry Finn*. Her love for the novel had inspired Trace to read it on his sceye. He grabbed it and put it in the stack of stuff to take with him. Now he had two things to remind him of her—the book, and the name she'd given him that day beside her in the crop row.

"I can be ready in an hour. I want to visit my mom again before we leave."

"Of course. And you can come back to visit her anytime you like."

Nodding, Trace—who used to be called Benjy—returned to sorting his future from his past.

11

RUBEN QINLAO • OLD NEW YORK CITY, EARTH

The *Grecian Earn* landed at New York Harbor. After the ship settled, Strunk moaned. Through the rebreather, it sounded hollow and metallic. The planet's gravity seemed to lengthen their bones after several hours in zero-g.

"God, can we get the fuck out of here now?" Junior asked. "I can't stand this fucking smell."

It really did smell like seaweed drawn through a cow's ass, Ruben thought. But he ignored the kid and turned to Strunk. "You all right?"

The trip from the Moon had been smooth, serene even in the weightlessness of space. But the descent into Earth's gravity well had been tough on all of them.

"I'll be fine," Strunk said, less than convincing.

The engines, their whine a constant companion on the journey, powered down.

"Listen, I have an idea—" Junior began.

There was the sound of metal separating followed by the soft *whoosh* of air decompression. The reinforced doors of the cargo hold parted. The light from outside spilled in, and Milo Patroclus stepped into the hold.

"Y'all survive in there?" he called, shading his temple to see better.

"I think so, Captain," Ruben answered. He moved forward tentatively, the drag of Earth's gravity making him careful. A few plodding steps got him to Strunk, still struggling out of his straps.

"I'm good," Strunk said almost angrily as Ruben steadied him on his feet.

"And now," Junior said, "can we get out of this shithole?"

Captain Patroclus waited as they made their way to the door. "Sorry for the smell," he said again, "but desperate times... Lately all my crew does is get drunk and play with themselves in port because they don't have the cash to play with anyone else. It's good that things are getting back stable again."

"You just better keep your word," Junior said, advancing on the freighter captain. A full head shorter than the lanky Patroclus, the kid seemed to make up the difference with attitude. "And your mouth shut."

Patroclus regarded him a moment as if debating whether to step on a cockroach. Then he turned quite deliberately to Ruben and, peering over Junior's head, said, "We have a deal. I—" He turned his eyes down to Junior again. "—'keep my mouth shut,' and—"

"I grant you and your company exclusive freighting rights for all ag products delivered to Mars," Ruben finished.

"That's right, Regent. Exclusive, without Qinlao Manufacturing—or any other faction—taking a cut. I get the profit free and clear," Patroclus said. "Same goes for all manufactured goods coming back to the Moon for transfer to the rest of the system."

"The return trip wasn't part of the deal," Ruben said. Though, in truth, he'd expected something like this. Anything short of handing them over to Cassandra was a price he was willing to pay.

"Yes, well, call it a handling fee." Patroclus once again regarded Junior with a look that knew they needed him more than he needed them. "A surcharge for attitude and ingratitude."

Ruben felt Strunk's shadow move over him. He reached out and stopped his progress, surprised at how easy that was.

"Let it go," Ruben said. Then, to Patroclus, "It's a deal."

Patroclus nodded as Junior slipped by him. "I have three sets of clothing for you," he said. "You can change in the wardroom. Marshals' uniforms." His eyes lingered on Strunk. "I *think* they'll fit well enough."

"Marshals' uniforms?" Junior asked.

"Sure," Patroclus said. "They're easy to come by—marshals retire, or they're *retired*." He winked at Junior. "Some sell their old uniforms to make some scratch on the side. Some barter them away for curvier in-kinds, if you know what I mean."

"You don't think three marshals will draw attention?" Ruben said.

Patroclus shrugged. "The badger costumes will get you in just about anywhere you need to go. The average citizen will leave you alone because no one ever knows if a marshal has a legit reason to harass them or if they just want to shake them down. The SSR troops might be tempted to do some dick measuring, but—" He nodded to Strunk. "—they probably won't be too inclined to that, either. The caps will help hide your identities from cameras, though I wouldn't rely on that."

Ruben nodded. Patroclus had thought through their needs. The marshals' uniforms were a stroke of genius, something Ruben should have thought of himself. It was in that moment that he realized he hadn't really formulated a plan beyond getting them here. The odds had been so long that his whole focus had simply been on not getting caught until they reached Earth.

"I'll show you to your changing room, gentlemen," Patroclus said, opening a bulkhead door and motioning them into a room with a small table bolted to the floor. Across the backs of three chairs were neatly folded marshals' uniforms. Three five-pointed badges lay on the table.

"I'll escort you off-ship when you're ready," Patroclus said.

Ruben stepped aside as first Junior, then Strunk entered the wardroom. Patroclus stuck out a hand, barring Ruben's way.

"Don't fuck me on this deal, Regent. You SynCorp execs are known for that. You send King Kong there after me in my sleep one night or some other assassin, once you're back in power—I'll deal with that, and then I'll come for you. I've made lots of fast friends in low places who owe me favors. Meaty favors, like I've done for you here. And some of those friends are on Mars."

Dropping his gaze to the captain's hand, Ruben stared until Patroclus removed it.

"Through making speeches?" he asked, earning a cold look from the captain. That, at least, was satisfying. "We have a deal. I honor my deals. Even your new version of it."

Patroclus grunted his suspicion of that claim, then stepped aside, allowing Ruben passage. "I'll give you some privacy."

Ruben walked to the chair with his uniform lying across it. Let Milo Patroclus have the last word. Let him feel powerful with that word lingering in the air. It didn't matter. All that *did* matter was that they were on Earth now. All that mattered was that Ruben kept his word to his sister, Ming, by saving Tony Taulke from Cassandra.

Patroclus closed the wardroom's door, loud and metallic and heavy, behind him.

"This monkey suit itches," Strunk complained, twisting his shoulders in the tight-fitting uniform as they walked along the docks.

"That's your conscience at work," Ruben said.

Junior laughed.

As evening unfolded, New York Harbor came alive. Ruben could see what Patroclus had meant about commerce being rejuvenated, at least at SynCorp's distribution node on Staten Island.

Lined up dockside were rows of skip-haulers that ferried harvested crops to the coastal nodes from landlocked farming collectives. The workers busily offloading cargo would still be doing so deep into the night. Cassandra seemed to be learning the most important lesson of all successful usurpers: keep the people fed to achieve political stability.

Ruben's sceye pinged once. It was so unexpected he stopped in his tracks. Strunk and Junior walked on ahead before they noticed.

There was a single character displayed on his retina—a red Greek letter epsilon. The comm channel it had come in on was so far down the frequency spectrum, he was surprised his sceye had picked it up at all. But the signal had been tightbeamed and boosted so it would. Acknowledging the signal put him, put them all, at risk if it was traced over CorpNet.

"What's up, Boss Man?" Strunk asked, pulling Junior lightly against the building. The tone of his voice warned against drawing attention.

Ruben motioned him with his head into the space between two ware-houses. The teen and Strunk joined him.

"I think I just got a transmission from the Erkennen Faction," he said, explaining to the younger men how Erkennen Labs had once used the epsilon, still pulsing for attention on his sceye, as its corporate logo. "Or someone masquerading as them."

Strunk grumbled, "The SSR, trying to smoke us out, maybe."

"One way to find out," Junior said.

"For once, I agree with you," Ruben acknowledged. That low-frequency ping felt like something the tech-savvy Erkennen would do. Impulse to action. "Strunk, keep watch." The enforcer nodded, leaning against the wall and watching the docks. Touching the pulsing letter with a glance made it open a two-word message.

"Return ping."

"Here goes nothing," Ruben said aloud, then sent a single signal return.

There was a delay. And nothing.

Then, Gregor Erkennen's worried voice.

"Regent Qinlao?"

"Gregor?"

A fritz of static.

"It works, Rahim! Excellent!"

The joyous face of Gregor Erkennen appeared.

"First question," Ruben said. "Are you trying to get us killed?"

"Comms are secure," Gregor assured him. "For a little while, anyway. Quickly, what's your status? Let's keep the tech talk to a minimum until we're sure this is safe."

"Until you're—" Ruben began.

"Status!" Gregor insisted.

"Uh," Ruben began again, deciding that if he were rolling the dice, he might as well roll them off the table. "In New York. Trying to rescue Tony."

"Good!" Gregor said. "Keep doing that."

Ruben raised an eyebrow. "Are you sure I didn't just give away—"

"We're still figuring out the parameters, so I'll keep this short, but in layman's terms, we can message targeted, short, two-way signals that can't be traced ... we think."

"You think...?"

"Will contact again when needed. And now you can too," Gregor said, his conquering smile returning. Then he became serious. "Reserve for emergencies. Less contact, less chance for Cassandra to crack the channel. Bye for now."

As Ruben opened his mouth to reply, his sceye went dark. A new, minimized Greek epsilon resided in the upper-right corner of the display.

He refocused on his surroundings to find Strunk and Junior looking at him expectantly.

"Well?" Junior said.

He briefed them on what had just happened.

"I don't hear any shuttles landing. No boots pounding the pavement, headed our way," Strunk said. "So far, so good."

"If Gregor Erkennen screwed this up in any way," Junior warned, growing red.

"Let's assume he didn't," Ruben said, lacking anything more reassuring to say. "Erkennen is the smartest man in the solar system. If he says it was secure..."

He trailed off, taking inventory of their new situation and factoring in the new information. If Gregor could talk to them, he could talk to others. Adriana Rabh. Captain Li on Mars. In the long hours of relative boredom in Darkside, they'd seen enough on CorpNet to know that Mars had been in perpetual revolt since the SSR had taken over. Li had been named an enemy of Cassandra's new state. With communications restored, SynCorp's defenders were no longer the individual arms of a dissected octopus fighting against Cassandra's coup. Now they could talk to each other. Coordinate the fight.

But Tony's trial started tomorrow. It would, Ruben knew, be an expedited showcase of SynCorp's sins followed by a single, inevitable verdict. Time to complete the mission to rescue Tony Taulke was running out.

"What's next then, Boss Man?" Strunk asked. "Did Erkennen say anything—"

"No, he just said to keep on keeping on. So that's what we're gonna do." Ruben scanned the city skyline. "But first things first—we need to find a place to hole up, to plan. And we don't know this city."

"I do," Junior said.

Another skip-hauler from the inner country passed overhead. Its approach to landing was careful and loud. When the dockside's busy background noise returned, Ruben faced Tony Junior.

"What do you mean? You know people in New York?"

"Absolutely," the teenager said.

"Trustworthy people?" Strunk's tone was less than confident.

"Sure. Danny Lasker and I have been running buddies forever."

"The Lasker Family?" Strunk said. "As in the most dangerous mob family on the East Coast?"

"That's them." Junior's smile couldn't get any wider. "You said before that we need allies on Earth, right?"

"Tell me about them," Ruben said.

"Well, Danny Lasker and I—"

"Not you." Ruben turned to Strunk. "You."

Strunk's features twisted. Ruben couldn't tell if he was thumbing through the card catalog of his memory or previewing his opinion of the Lasker Family.

"One of the older East Coast clans," Strunk recited. "Been around since before the Weather War, back when the city still had its own police force. They run black-market stuff that the Company's made technically illegal. Drugs and snuff programs for sim-parlors, that kinda thing. Stuff the top level of CorpNet swears doesn't exist anymore."

Ruben let his confusion show. "Why would the Company allow that? On Mars, we keep a tight lid on—"

"This isn't Mars," Strunk interrupted. "Earth is more complicated. Always has been, likely always will be. Tony considers families like the Laskers a necessary evil to service spicier appetites. Lets off pervert steam, if you know what I mean. As long as corporate profits don't suffer, it's not worth wasting corporate assets to stifle it."

"Look, I just want to do my part, okay? I just want to help Pop," Junior said. "Got any better ideas?"

Ruben regarded him, loath to admit that he didn't. Earth wasn't his domain of expertise.

"He's got a point," Strunk allowed. "Time is short. If the kid has connections, especially powerful ones..."

"I've already pinged them," Junior said, like he was telling them how he'd pre-selected a restaurant for dinner. The reservation was made. Why argue with the choice?

"You already..." Ruben grabbed the kid by the shoulders and drew him close. Another skip-hauler approached from the west, forcing him to raise his voice. "Do you have any idea how dangerous that is? Jesus, kid, how many times..."

"Didn't you just take the same risk answering Erkennen's transmission?" Junior demanded. "So it's okay for you, but—"

"That's different," Ruben insisted. But was it really? Desperation and a ticking clock had made Ruben take that chance. Maybe Tony Junior was feeling the same Hail-Mary pressure he was—only multiplied exponentially, fearing for his father's life.

"Yeah, right," Junior said, failing to shake Ruben's grip. "Hey, hands off!"

"Hey, Boss Man, let's keep it civil," Strunk advised. He jerked his head without looking at the workers, still busy transferring ag cargo. "Let the kid help, if he can."

"Okay, then." Ruben released and smoothed the teen's ill-fitting uniform. "I suppose we've got limited options. Get us to somewhere safe, Tony."

"Trust me," Junior said in maybe the most earnest voice Ruben had ever heard him use. "I learned how to survive from Pop."

12

STACKS FISCHER • ABANDONED ERKENNEN LAB, THE MOON

"Okay, try that," Bekah said.

I pushed the power button again. "Nope."

A stream of four-letter frustrations crackled over comms. I was impressed. I had no idea a twenty-something geek like her could be that creative ... or experimental. Half the positions weren't even physically possible.

I glanced down—not easy to do, seated in a vac-suit—to find her lower half jerking with the same emotion. From the mid-gut up, she was hidden by the control panel.

"I don't even know what half this crap is," she said as she tried again. "We've achieved so much with quantum circuitry in the last twenty years. This stuff is museum worthy!"

Bekah went on like that, narrating her efforts, so I tuned out. I wasn't unsympathetic, but since I didn't understand half of what she said as she recited from her tech-manual mind, I didn't waste my own brain power on it.

"Okay, now," she said like she was starting a prayer. "Try that."

I pushed the button. The atmospheric indicator lit up green. It still read zero, but at least it seemed to be working.

"Yep, that did it."

I heard what sounded like an atmo leak explode over the channel. It was Bekah Franklin's relief. "Finally!" She squirmed out from inside the panel, careful of the sharp edges threatening her sealed vac-suit. Even through her helmet's foggy visor, I could see the sweat on her forehead, the smile on her face. "We have air!"

"We have power to the atmospheric system," I corrected her. "Let's not count chickens before they breathe."

She sat up, hyper-stretching her back. "Count chickens?"

"Never mind."

"Okay. Help me up. We need to get below to Level Four."

I helped her to her feet. The atmo level had already lifted from null. The seals around the outer doors seemed to be holding. Everything in space depends on seals. One pinhole leak and a whole colony can die. But that's one thing about the Erkennen clan—they build something, they build it to last. In a few hours, we'd have breathable atmosphere and heat. No more need for our hermetically sealed cocoons.

"What's down there anyway?" I asked, indulging my inner cat's curiosity.

"The kill code," Bekah said like that explained a single goddamned thing. I watched her step over a body, heading for the lab's vator. When we'd first arrived, she'd been appalled by the carnage. Hell, the vacuum-sealed gore had even thrown me for a loop, and I'm used to seeing how that particular sausage gets made, and regularly. Inter-faction rivalries can be deadly, and I had no doubt that's what had happened here: someone had killed this station to get over on the Erkennens. But Bekah was hyperfo-cused now and stepped right over that corpse without a second look.

Human beings are strange creatures.

The spastic lights were getting on my nerves. A sizzle and pop, and a dark corner would show. Sometimes it was empty; sometimes it wasn't. Another spark, and we'd get a glimpse of another body, another face, skin crevassed like a canyon. When a body's freeze-dried, the skin shrinks, pulling the jaws apart. Sometimes the eyes open. That's why the undertaker sews them shut. Otherwise, every dead body eventually looks like *The Scream*—that swirly painting with the shrieking guy on the pier. Everyone's afraid of death. Eventually, it always shows.

We boarded the vator when it arrived, and Bekah pushed the button for Level Four. Slowly, the car began its descent.

"So," I said, asking the obvious, "answer me a question."

"Sure. If I can."

"Back on Masada Station." Seeing her step over that body back there had scratched at something I hadn't thought of much while flying for my life all the way here in the *Coyote*. "Would you really have used Erkennen's key on that mainframe?"

The old hydraulics of the vator whined a bit. No one likes being woken up after thirty years to do work, I guess. Not even machinery.

"I had it plugged in," she said, thoughtful, like she wasn't sure of the answer to the question herself. "I was about to turn it."

"And?"

"Inspiration struck. I found another way."

The vator car hiccupped, and we both reached out to the sides to steady ourselves.

"You would've risked losing all that knowledge?"

The vator stopped. Because it'd reached the fourth level, I hoped.

"It wasn't a huge risk. The data was backed up on the key."

The doors opened and stopped halfway.

"Drives can fail," I said, reaching up to muscle one side of the half-cocked door. Bekah took the other, and together we forced it open.

"Better to lose the knowledge than hand it over to Cassandra," she said, looking me in the eye. "And Rahim has shored up Masada's virtual security since, so it should be safe ... for now, anyway."

The lights came on as she stepped onto Level Four. They were more stable than the ones up top. More of that flat, hospital-like boring white décor. The whole place was one big laboratory, I reminded myself.

I pulled my stunner. "I wouldn't worry about Masada. Cassie Kisaan has more pressing concerns closer to home."

"She'll be back soon enough," Bekah said. Her tone was tough and sure, like she'd had a glimpse of the future and it was just a matter of time's passing till we got there. "Do you really need that thing? Does it kill ghosts?"

Wow. Brains, ability, *and* the girl had a gallows sense of humor. Just my type. Too bad the Hearse gets jealous easily.

"Cautious people live longer," I said.

We faced a plastisteel-reinforced double door capable of sealing out space in the event of a breach. A layer of dust covered the key coder on the wall. Bekah brushed it clean and dialed in whatever Erkennen had given her. Amazingly, the locking mechanism opened like the maintenance crew had just been around yesterday to oil it up. Smooth and *swishy*.

The lab's lights snapped on.

Another horror show.

Bekah, who'd just stepped over that body upstairs, screamed over comms. Her instincts stepped her backward. I pushed past, positioning myself between her and whatever might be inside.

The room was small and painted in more of that sterile-white style. Except where the dark brown patches were. Blood pools. Or the rusty stains they'd left behind, anyway.

"They look like they ate themselves from the inside," Bekah said in a hoarse whisper.

That didn't quite track, but when you see what we saw—especially when you're not used to regular tours of the butcher's shop—you try to make sense of it with whatever words you have.

There were two bodies. One looked like a pro, an Erkennen guard from a bygone era. He had the faction's epsilon logo on his uniform. There was a huge knife with a wicked, broad blade beside him. Seeing it tugged at something historical in my memory I couldn't quite grab onto.

I stepped deeper into the octagonal room. Bekah followed. There were no unlit corners here. It looked like a lab without the burners and hoods and beakers. Relatively small, its walls were lined with old-fashioned computer systems. The second body was slumped over a terminal. Someone had opened the top of his spine with a knife.

"What's that?" Bekah asked. "A sword of some kind?"

I turned to find her pointing at the wicked blade. Seeing the smaller knife wound had placed the larger knife in context for me, even giving me a name.

"Bowie knife," I said.

She said something else I didn't hear. I reached over and pulled the man away from the terminal, and he fell backward in the chair. His mouth gaped in a scream that looked set in concrete. He could have been the model for the painting. The nametag on his white lab coat read *Okaga*.

"I'll get to work," Bekah said. I could hear her trying to be strong. No more quips about shooting ghosts with my stunner would be coming anytime soon. "Can you ... I mean..."

"Sure," I said. While she worked on bringing up the local system, I pulled Okaga out of his death chair and carried him to where the guard lay next to the Bowie knife. It was easy in the light lunar gravity.

Bekah soon had a screen working. CorpNet. *The Real Story*. We both watched it for a while, glad to be plugged in again to events in the system. Grateful to see live people walking around, even if they were shilling for Cassie Kisaan. There was a feel-good story about some farmer's kid from the northeast. After his mother died, he was adopted by ... the half-breed? What the hell was she playing at? Trying to massage her public image? I didn't even know him, and I felt sorry for the kid. At the bottom of the screen was a counter, doing its thing, counting down. Tony's trial was tomorrow, and his execution not much past that.

"Sure they can't track that?" I said. "Receiving the signal here, I mean."

Bekah shook her head. "It's broadcast. We're just one of a million places receiving it. Close enough to Darkside not to seem suspicious."

I reminded myself that Bekah Franklin had attended the Erkennen School of Scientific Certainty. Well—she knew her business. She'd proven that more than once.

"And speaking of a signal..." Bekah began working the old controls.

"Are you sure Gregor knows what he's doing?" I asked. When she passed me the business look, I clammed up.

"The old-style radio signal is way down the frequency band. It's so outdated no one would even think to listen for it. You'd have to have a tight-beamed receiver set specifically to listen for it to know it's even there. And yes, Gregor is listening for it. So yes, he knows what he's doing."

Well, okay then.

"Sorry," I said, meaning it. "Tony's in a bad way. And I'm sitting here on the Moon…" Bekah passed me an odd, needful glance. "…doing exactly what I'm supposed to do," I finished diplomatically.

She offered up a patient smile. "Pinging now."

I held my breath without realizing it. I hate technology, mainly because I don't understand it. I'm more of a people person. Don't laugh too hard, now. I understand their motivations, what reactions to expect. I get the fundamental truth about people: that all they really care about is sating their appetites and protecting their asses. On occasion, they'll put aside those things when principles aren't too expensive to have. But tech? I don't trust it. Seen it fail too many times.

Ping.

It was the simplest of answers to her own signal. Bekah looked up at me.

"This is your business," I said a little defensively. "Do you know who's on the other end of—"

"Epsilon One," she said into the ether.

Smart. No real names. Just code.

Now we both held our breath.

"Bekah! You made it!"

Gregor Erkennen's gregarious voice burst from the console speaker. I glanced over my shoulder, half afraid he'd woken our two dead knifing victims. Bekah exhaled once and smiled at me.

"So much for code names, huh?" I said.

"Fischer!" Erkennen's voice crackled. "You didn't stroke out after all. Fantastic!"

Um … what now?

"Um … what now? You thought I'd stroke out?"

I could almost see Erkennen's head hemming and hawing. "Well," his voice said, "the stressors of the flight on older vascular systems are significantly more—"

"Never mind."

I was sorry I'd asked—on multiple fronts.

"Gregor, what about security…" Bekah said. "I thought we had a communications blackout in place."

Onscreen, the wily gray hair of Gregor Erkennen appeared, adding visual to the audio. "We're using a new, multi-frequency encryption comm protocol," he said. My ears threatened to vomit from all the tech talk being forced down them. "It generates its own variance along the spectrum, telling the next connection along the subspace satellite network where to look for the signal. We're trying to limit exchanges to under two minutes; Rahim's simulations identify that as the outside threshold to maintain security on the network."

"Let me guess," Bekah said, and I could practically hear the gears in her skull meshing together. "You added a parity true/false bit between the data packets to ensure the receiving algorithm on the next satellite in the chain is legit?" Then, and tapping her finger against the console, "If the binary switch misses the marker sent ahead, the entire signal scrambles? That's brilliant. Simple and brilliant!"

Brilliant? I'd take her word for it. But *simple*?

"I'll pass along your kudos to Rahim," Gregor said around a ruby-cheeked smile. "Since every communication is a new, randomized exchange of protocols, there's no way for the enemy to learn what we're doing." He cleared his throat. "We don't think—still, we want to keep the conversations short—emergencies only. Cassandra has outthought us before."

"Have you seen the news?" I demanded, tired of the banter. We were on the clock—he'd just said so. "Tony goes on trial tomorrow."

"I know," Erkennen said. "Ruben Qinlao and Tony's bodyguard, Strunk, are in New York."

"The Qinlao kid's on the ground? With King Kong Strunk?"

"Yes."

Well, that was good news of a sort. That they were both alive was a surprise and a little impressive. The kid and Strunk the Gorilla were smarter at the spy game than I'd given them credit for. That they were on the ground within spitting distance of Tony's prison cell was reassuring. I almost let myself relax a little.

"Bekah, we're nearing the security threshold for this connection," Gregor said. "You're bringing the lab's systems back online?"

"Yes, cycling them up now. Gregor..." She broke off, and I could hear that ticking clock getting louder. "The dead here..."

"I know," he said. "But we'll have to discuss that another time." He glanced offscreen. "Ten seconds. Ping me back on the low-frequency band, but make it absolutely necessary. Every time we use this protocol, we give Cassandra a chance to break it. Masada out."

The screen went dark, and we began to settle down from the excitement of conversing with allies and feeling like, if only for just under two minutes, we weren't the only living things in the whole damned universe.

"Well, that changes things a little," I said. Being able to chat with the home base improved our odds for sure.

"Yeah," Bekah answered. "Anyway—back to work."

13

TRACE ANDERSON • EN ROUTE TO OLD NEW YORK CITY, EARTH

When New York City appeared on the horizon, it was like watching square, silver trees growing skyward from Earth.

As the aircar drew closer, the buildings gained detail and definition. So many of them, so many varieties. Higher ones, lower ones, skinny ones, wide ones. Some with spires so tall they looked like they'd pierce the clouds. Some colored a flat, stone gray, and some shining with motionless sunlight like a freshwater pond. The aircar banked along its flight path, moving in a wide arc.

"Coming up on Staten Island," the pilot announced.

"Hey, boy, look," Trace said to Bandit, his only companion on the flight. Cassandra and Elissa Kisaan had already returned to New York. To prepare for Tony Taulke's trial, Elissa had informed him. Trace had remained behind to say his goodbyes to the people of the clique. And to visit his mother's grave beneath the magnolia tree one more time.

"Hey, come here and look," he said to Bandit, beckoning. But the dog's head was low, his eyes wary. He'd never been in an aircar before, and while the stabilizers could make a human passenger forget they were flying, they apparently hadn't been perfected for dogs. But he sat up now, tentatively, and followed his master's finger out the window.

Below, the waterline of the great island passed on their left, a strange mixture of beaches and green spaces amid a background of buildings, part of the luminescent canvas of the city. The aircar banked again, and Bandit edged closer to Trace's seat. He reached down and petted the dog's head. Through the shuttle's right-side windows, there was only the green-blue hue of New York Harbor. Trace had seen images of New York and its coastline before, of course. But as vibrant and beautiful as 3D sims could be, nothing beat seeing the actual thing with his own eyes.

Mom would love this, he thought. Trace could imagine her sitting next to him, pointing to landmarks neither of them had ever seen before except in motion 3D images. They'd visited Philadelphia once together, and that memory transposed onto this moment as he imagined his mother's delight at the constant procession of new sights. Then, Trace remembered, he was supposed to be angry with her. His delight at the sights below flitted away.

"Coming up on the old UN Building," the pilot said.

Trace swallowed hard and forced his feelings down again. Bandit's head rested on his knee, his eyes gazing upward.

"Almost there, boy. Almost back on solid ground."

Bandit's wagging tail showed his appreciation.

As he disembarked from the aircar, Trace slung his small, heavy bag of possessions from the farming camp over his shoulder. Bandit padded down the ramp ahead of him. Elissa Kisaan met them, her hands folded together in front of her, her sly-fox eyes attempting a smile.

"How was your flight?" she asked.

"Fine." The whistled across the roof of the building. "Where's Cassandra?"

Elissa's smile cracked a little, reminding him of Jimmy Ellis.

"Well, she's a little busy at the moment. Big day tomorrow. But I can give you a quick tour."

"I'm hungry," Trace said. He wasn't though, not really. Well, maybe a little. But Bandit always seemed to be hungry, even after he'd just been fed, and Trace hadn't fed him since leaving the camp. His dad had always taught him to take care of those who depended on him first, then to fend for himself. He wouldn't eat before Bandit ate. "And is there a place where my dog can..."

Elissa took a moment to clue in. "Oh, well, I suppose ... there's a green space over by the door there."

Trace escorted Bandit to the grassy area. "Buildings and forests and grass and concrete, all together," he said while the dog did his business. "New York is a funny city."

"I suppose so," Kisaan said. "People want to have the best of both worlds, I guess. The conveniences of city living, the prettiness of country life."

Bandit sidled up to Trace and knocked the boy's hand with his head. Trace scratched him behind the ear.

"Let's go inside and get you something to eat," Elissa said.

"Bandit first," Trace said, following. "Do they have dog food here?"

Elissa's smile seemed more at ease now. Less calculated. "I'm sure we can come up with something."

A short time later, both Trace and Bandit had full stomachs. Elissa left them alone to check in with Cassandra and encouraged Trace to explore after supper by walking around the windowed suite. Its floor-to-ceiling, double-paned glass looked out over the city and East River Bay. The Soldiers wouldn't let him leave the penthouse level without her though, she told him.

Left alone with Bandit with nothing else to do, Trace took in the tremendous views. It was like a grander, broader scheme of what he'd seen flying over. Seeing the city from the aircar was awe inspiring, but over-looking the city in flight required a kind of inattention to detail. Observing the landscape from his fixed position allowed Trace to linger on the things that interested him. He could take in the broad expanse of the city and all its features or view a distant landmark closeup through the fixed binoculars that lined the suite's circular interior—old tools of tourism. The entire Earth as far as he could see was carpeted with concrete, the soil compacted to support dozens of the straight, steel-and-glass mountain-trees he'd seen on his way in. Green parks were patchworked among the colder construction.

So many buildings! So many people!

To Trace, New York seemed like the factory that had birthed all of humanity. Stamped them out, person for person, along a conveyor belt of sidewalks. Or maybe humans were harvested like crops, pulled right from the asphalt of the city streets. They looked so small from up here, the people. Like ants scurrying around, disturbed during harvest, every one of them busy with what they thought was important business.

From the bay side of the suite, Trace could see two great bridges spanning the water and what looked like a mostly submerged island stretching beneath one of them. The ruins of empty buildings and rusting metal fences jutted up from a muddy bed.

"That's the Roosevelt Island Memorial," Elissa said behind him.

Startled, Trace turned to find her returned and standing at a distance. He wondered how long the fox had been there, silently watching him.

"The island sunk?" he asked.

"Not exactly," Elissa said, moving to stand next to him. Bandit's ears perked up as she approached. "The tide rose."

"Same difference," Trace said, turning to Bandit. "Want to walk some more, boy?"

"It's the East River," she said, following after them. "Bigger than what you're used to, I bet. The Lehigh."

"Bigger, sure," Trace said. "But browner than the Lehigh. I'd never wash clothes in it. They'd come out dirtier than they went in."

They walked for a while, the buildings and asphalt and people below forming a kind of visual white noise coursing across Trace's brain.

"What's that building?" he said, pointing. "It doesn't look like the others."

"The Chrysler Building, or it used to be," Elissa explained. "Built nearly two hundred years ago."

"It's shiny, like a lake."

Elissa nodded. "It was considered art when it was built. It was the tallest building in the world—for less than a year. Then they built the Empire State Building. The Chrysler Building is where we're keeping the Werewolf, in fact."

He turned to her. "The Werewolf?"

"Tony Taulke," she said with venom.

Trace had seen Taulke referred to as "the Werewolf" on CorpNet too, and he wondered why that was. But he sensed Kisaan was on the edge of anger, so he held his curiosity in check. What did it matter, anyway? There were people in the clique back in Pennsylvania who'd loved Taulke because he provided a life for them. Stability. He even cared for them, they claimed. Others argued, twisting the sentiment into how a keeper cares for an animal in a cage. You either loved Tony Taulke or you hated him—Trace had learned that a long time ago.

"How are things going in here?"

Next to him, Elissa tensed. Bandit, who'd been sitting and gazing out the window, stood up. Cassandra strolled toward them, two camerabots following at a distance.

"Making yourself at home?" she asked.

"He's had supper," Elissa said like she was reporting the items on a shipping manifest. "The dog, too."

"His name's Bandit," Trace said.

"Of course." Elissa's voice held that same tone of cautious expectation. To Cassandra, "We were just talking about the sights."

"How nice." Cassandra's smile never seemed to reach her eyes. Bandit *whuffed* once as she approached. "That will be all for now, Elissa. Thank you for your help this afternoon. See that we're not disturbed."

Elissa lowered her head. "Of course," she said again, minus her fox-like leer. She backed away three steps before leaving them alone.

The camerabots positioned themselves on either side of Trace, each careful to avoid the other's viewing arc. The purring of their anti-gravs was subtle, something that could be easily forgotten. Cassandra placed one arm around him, her hand resting on his shoulder.

"How are you doing?"

"Fine," he said quickly. "The city is cool. I've never been—"

"That's not what I meant," Cassandra said. "I meant, I know your mother's loss is still fresh. It will be for a while. Losing my own mother was very difficult."

That confused him. "Didn't you kill her?" It wasn't till the words were out of his mouth that he realized they might not be taken well.

Cassandra bent over slightly, bringing their eyes level. "Ending my mother's life was the hardest decision I've ever made," she said. "But this is not a time for soft hearts, Trace. It's a time for making hard decisions—for the future."

"Like killing your mother, you mean." *Murdering her, you mean*, he'd wanted to say. It was bad enough having his mother taken away ... but the thought of someone killing their own mother stoked the coals of his grief— left them glowing.

A noise came from the hovering camerabot over Cassandra's shoulder. The shutter of the lens, zooming in. She turned, and both 'bots rose and flew off.

"Why did you do that?" he asked.

"This is not for others to hear," Cassandra said. "Not yet."

"Okay."

"I heard you talking with Elissa about the Chrysler Building."

Trace blinked at the sudden switch in subjects. "Yeah?"

"It was the tallest building in the world ... for less than a year."

"Yeah, Elissa said that."

"And then the Empire State Building was built taller."

"She said that, too."

"That's what I'm doing, Trace, with our species," she said, reaching out a hand to his shoulder.

It was all he could do not to flinch. *Mother-killer.*

"I'm improving humanity," she said. "I'm helping along a process called natural selection—preserving the strongest aspects of who we are now with the greatest promise of who we can become. Accelerating it, refining it with ... with my own programming."

"What do you mean? You're building a new kind of human?"

Cassandra cocked her head. "That's one way to put it." Her tone grew grim. "Humanity is a flawed species, Trace. A selfish species."

He didn't understand. But he did maybe, a little—like Jimmy Ellis and his refusal to work. When the clique needed him, Jimmy only complained about losing his playtime. And Trace's mother ... the memory played for the millionth time in his brain—when the demand for work stopped, when the reapers and threshers failed, she'd thrown herself headfirst into the trap that was Dreamscape. At first it was an hour here or there, and he could easily pull her out. But as the workless weeks passed and the languor of inactivity spread through the camp like malaria, Anne Anderson had spent more time with the illusion of his dead father than she had in the real world with Trace.

Maybe Cassandra was right. Maybe humans were just selfish creatures concerned only with meeting their own needs. And if it happened at the expense of those who loved them most? Apparently, that didn't matter for some.

"I'm trying to build a better version of us, Trace," Cassandra continued. "A next generation of humanity that will do the right thing because it's the right thing to do. But first, I must rid the field of the parasites." Her eyes grew bright with connection. "Like you do before planting season—so the new crop can flourish. I'll weed out self-interest. And with it, I can pull the need for conflict, the impulse to war, up by the roots. When a surgeon finds a cancer, she cuts it out so the rest of the body might live. I'm the caretaker of the body human now—all of us, everywhere. I *am* natural selection. Do you understand?"

"I—I'm not sure," Trace said. He was sure of one thing, though—Cassandra was frightening him. The room seemed to shrink around her words. Not the sound of them, but their intent. Their purpose.

Cassandra stood and gestured for him to walk. They followed the path of the floor-to-ceiling windows, New York City stretching outward below, all the way to the horizon.

"We're all made of genes," she explained, "the building blocks of life that dictate what we are, who we become as individuals. Our hair color, skin tone; our tendency toward innate intelligence or athletic ability."

"The human genome," Trace said. "I learned about it in school."

"Yes, exactly. Think of it as the girders and concrete and sheetrock of our human building."

"Okay."

"There's a certain genetic mutation that some humans have—I call it the HLA-Delta mutation. Do you know what *delta* means?"

Trace shook his head.

"Well, in scientific equations, delta stands for *change*. All humans have a line of HLA genes, but only some have HLA-Delta. That mutation, once triggered, enables the human genome to accept synthetic genes like the ones that created me. So, if they have the delta mutation, they can evolve—become like me. Physically stronger, intellectually smarter. Less *selfish*. Back at the camp, I told you that you're special, Trace. Most humans don't have this mutation, but you do. It's why I chose you. Think of it, Trace—you're the future of humanity. You're the next stage in the evolutionary chart."

They walked for a few steps in silence as Trace tried to wrap his mind around what Cassandra was saying. He understood, sort of. She was talking about hybridism, right? His father had taught him all about it. Cross-breeding plants to yield sturdier crops. That's what it sounded like Cassandra was talking about. But it wasn't plants she was talking about. It was people.

"But what happens to the people who don't have it?" Trace asked.

They walked a little farther. Cassandra sighed, asking, "Well, what do you do with the weeds that are choking off the crops you're trying to grow?"

"You pull them out, root and stem," he said simply. That was one of the first lessons his mother had ever taught him about farming. "To make sure they don't take up the space and suck away the water and nutrients the good plants need."

"Yes, Trace, that's exactly right," Cassandra said, turning him toward her. "You pull them out. Root and stem."

14

ADRIANA RABH • VALHALLA STATION, CALLISTO

"I can't begin to know how this Wellspring thing works," Dr. Estevez said. "Obviously, at the quantum cellular level. What little I know—gravity acts differently there. All that time over Jupiter, flying around in zero-g after... Regent, I have no idea what's happening to you. I'm sorry."

Adriana offered him a half-hearted smile. It was a skill she was learning to perfect. At least the injection of the adrenaline-infused, vitamin enriched stimulant and saline cocktail had helped her to feel human again. An old human, but even that was an improvement over the bone weariness she'd been experiencing.

"Thank you, Doctor. I think my age is simply catching up to me."

"That," Estevez said, "is as close as I can come to a diagnosis as well. And it's catching up at a geometrically accelerated rate. Your own personal physician could, perhaps—"

"I'm almost positive she's dead, Doctor," Adriana said matter-of-factly. It wasn't how she felt, but it was how she spoke publicly about loss. *Old habits, like old women, die hard.* "Along with everyone else on the ring station."

Busying himself with arranging the diagnostic tray, Estevez said nothing. Then, "I've prepared more hypos like the one I just gave you. A combination of vitamins and steroids suspended in an iron-enhanced saline solution. One a day when you feel like you need it." The doctor paused, placing a hand on her arm. She looked down at it, fascinated by the contact. He seemed to have no concept at all that he was breaching protocol. Even more surprisingly, it didn't seem to bother her one bit. "But wait until you need it. Its effectiveness will wane with each use."

"Thank you, Doctor. Sincerely." His smile seemed hopeful, although she knew it was a lie. But it was a pleasant lie. "As soon as I take back this station, I'll set up a permanent trust to fund this clinic's expansion. And I'll earmark a million SynCorp dollars per annum as discretionary funding— for you to use as you see fit."

"Thank you, Regent," Estevez said, clearly surprised by her generosity.

She stood up from the exam table. "Now please, can I put my farmer's rags back on? I feel a draft. This fucking gown can't seem to stay closed in the back."

She found Edith and her friend from the clinic, Krystin Drake, in the office outside the exam room. They talked like two young girls still in school, stealing moments between classes.

Funny, the things you remember so clearly.

"How are you feeling, Regent?" Drake asked.

"Like a million-dollar earmark."

Edith stood, displaying that galling, open look of sympathy of hers. Adriana smiled inwardly. What she had in store for Edith Birch to finally balance their personal books should knock that expression right on its ass.

"What did Doctor Estevez say?" Edith asked.

Adriana adjusted the layered linen she wore. Made of smartcloth, it was meant to breathe and safeguard the wearer at the same time. Perfect for farming work. A bit chilly indoors. She put the hood up, wondering how cronish she looked.

"That if you run an engine too hot for too long, you can burn it up." Turning from Edith to Drake, she said, "I was surprised how easy it was to get here from hydroponics, even early in the morning. I expected to find SSR troops, or marshals working for them, on every corner."

"Well," Drake said, exchanging a look with Edith, "we had lots of wounded a few days ago. Some SSR. Mostly our own. They were better armed than we were. We had more people, though."

"The perfect recipe for mutual slaughter," Adriana said. But she kept herself on track. *Now is not the time for soft hearts.*

"Then, all of a sudden, they just ... left," Drake said, clearly perplexed by the so-called strategy. "Not all of them. There's still a small force holed up in Justice Hall. They still claim absolute authority over Callisto on CorpNet."

"Of course they do," Edith said.

A smile from Drake, genuine where Estevez's earlier had been merely well intentioned. "But the reality is we intend to take back the station tonight," she said. "There's a meeting in the Entertainment District. The biggest bar, Loki's Longhouse. Scuttlebutt is that Gregor Erkennen is sending support to take charge."

"Is he now?" Adriana asked. "How considerate of him. I hope he's not sending his enforcer, that needle-nosed walking penis, Bruno Richter. He gives me the creeps."

Was Gregor really trying to help or, perhaps, take control of Valhalla Station for himself? If she were him, Adriana would see this as an opportunity. It wouldn't be the first time one regent tried to take over another's faction. Then again, dealing with Cassandra would take all of them working together—Gregor would realize that. Maybe she was just being paranoid, Adriana thought. Which, even if it were true, wouldn't necessarily make her wrong about Gregor. "What time is this meeting happening?"

"Eighteen hundred," Drake said. "But it's invite only. Callisto is nearly united in our desire to kick these pretenders out. There were known Callistan collaborators with the SSR. Sometimes it's hard to tell who the traitors are."

Adriana passed a knowing if brief glance Edith's way. "So true." Then, with confidence, she said to Drake, "I suppose it's good to know some of my people are on my side. Makes me feel like I was doing something right after all. Now, is there a place where we can rest? Get a good meal without attracting too much attention? Oh, and I need a secure line to the head of the marshals—Coronado is his name, assuming he's still alive."

"Of course," Drake said. "We can set you up in one of the offices. You can get some rest in the adjoining exam room. It won't be comfortable, but—"

"My dear, compared to where we've been the last few days, it'll be the executive suite," Adriana said. "Lead on."

Drake nodded and motioned for them to follow.

"Regent—Adriana—are you sure about this?" Edith said. "Let your people secure Justice Hall, then—"

A look from Adriana, and Edith closed her mouth. "It's hard to lead from behind," she said. "And if it's the last thing I fucking do, I'll make Callisto mine again. And then, Edith Birch, you can bury me here."

"I assume the amount was sufficient, Chief Marshal?" Adriana said. She had to bow her head next to his ear to be heard. Her arrival at the beer hall had generated considerable excitement. Sitting next to Coronado on the hastily erected platform recalled old feelings of stage fright when she was a child in public school. Under the present circumstances, the troublesome memory almost made her burst out laughing.

"Certainly, Regent," Coronado said. "Unnecessary, of course, since our duty—"

"Of course," Adriana said with an obligatory smile. Everyone knew the Marshals Service bent to the will of the highest bidder. Problem was, so the saying went, you never knew who bid highest till a marshal aimed a weapon.

"We've all seen the footage on CorpNet, at least before it was quashed—the SSR is in retreat." Addressing the crowd, Krystin Drake paused, and a couple dozen miners sent up a cheer. "The Company's ships have them on the run." Another cheer. Miners pounded their empty steins on the wooden tables of Loki's Longhouse, demanding refills. "Captain Li on Mars has held them for weeks, and now he's counterattacking. The Red Planet will be uncontested SynCorp soil again soon."

Chants of "Qinlao! Qinlao! Qinlao!" erupted.

Her job done, Drake turned toward Adriana. "Regent, would you like to say a few words?"

Krystin Drake: clinic nurse by day, insurrection firebrand by night, Adriana thought. And Edith Birch's best friend to boot? Drake was not only respected, she realized, she was loved. A healer who walked softly but carried a big stick. That should come in handy for Edith, indeed.

"Thank you, Ms. Drake," Adriana said as she rose. That had become considerably easier in the hours she'd rested in the clinic, thanks to the good doctor's short-term remedy. The miners slapped the tables in front of them with enthusiasm. As she passed Drake returning to her seat, Adriana leaned in, saying, "Thanks for warming them up."

Pulling herself to her full, respectable height of five foot ten inches, Adriana Rabh scanned the room. Besides Coronado onstage, there were four other marshals, one in each of the four corners of the beer hall. Half a dozen of her own faction security sat sprinkled among the miners, a sensible precaution to her making a public appearance, even at a private meeting. A number of her security forces had died in the initial attack on Valhalla Station. Many more had bunkered up on Rabh Regency Station.

Adriana held the eyes of the miners as she took a moment. She'd never seen them as anything but skilled laborers with delusions of Viking grandeur. But they'd fought so hard for the colony. And now, she could honestly say, she owed her life to them by proxy, through Edith. That seemed like as good a place to start as any.

"I owe you my life," she said solemnly. The room, which had murmured with anticipation, fell silent. Adriana wondered if they'd even heard her, so she repeated it louder. "*I owe you my life*. Specifically, I owe my life to Edith Birch," she said, nodding to Edith, who was sitting next to Coronado.

The door to the street opened, breaking her rhythm. A hooded figure entered the bar and, with a body-language apology at the intrusion, slipped quietly to one side and leaned against the wall near the door. *Better late than never*, Adriana thought, swallowing her annoyance at being interrupted. She took a moment to collect her thoughts as a waitress emptied her pitcher into several mugs.

"More than that," she continued after clearing her throat, "I owe you my regency. And I want to make a promise to you now. I know the Syndicate Corporation hasn't always been the friendliest of employers. Our focus is on the bottom line. On profit. Not—" She was tempted to throw a look back to Edith and resisted it. "—always on the welfare of citizen-workers."

Tired, wary assent passed among the crowd.

"I won't stand here and promise you a brave new world of indulgences and opportunities," Adriana said. "That's what that she-snake who murdered Elise Kisaan is promising. And you can trust me when I say this." She smiled grimly at her own humor. "In fact, you can take this to the bank. What that woman is promising is a lie. You saw Gregor Erkennen's snap-cast. You heard what's happening on Earth. She's a snake selling oil, pure and simple. But once we take back Justice Hall, we'll—"

"Shut up, you Alabastered Bitch!"

The interruption hit her like a slap across the face. The marshal standing in the far-right corner of the room pulled his sidearm and aimed it square at Adriana.

"Imagine it," he said. "Me! Making shit pay on a shit moon most of my life. And here I have Adriana Rabh, the Queen-Bitch Banker, delivered right on a platter. She said dead was fine, Queen-Bitch. And that works for me." He leveled his pistol at her.

Later, Adriana remembered hearing the smooth swipe of leather and not knowing what it was at the time. Then, a thunderous *boom* filled the room, followed by the recognition that getting shot must feel like nothing because she hadn't felt anything. Then, people screaming.

"Regent!"

The hooded man had drawn his weapon in a way that seemed too fast to be true. It was his weapon that produced the thunder.

Adriana's feet were rooted to the spot, her eyes drawn perversely to the pistol of the marshal who'd declared her as good as dead. Hit by the hooded man he spun around, blood already blooming like a red sun on his chest. A second shot *cracked*, the soon-dead marshal reflexively pulling his trigger. The shot went into the ceiling, and he crashed to his knees.

The room whirled around Adriana as she was driven to the barroom floor. Then Edith Birch's voice, whispering in her ear, told her to stay down. It was incredible that Adriana could hear her at all, with all the screaming from the patrons. Chairs scraped as people dived for cover. Adriana's security forces leapt to their feet, bolting for the front of the room. *Away* from the gunfight?

Cowards!

Adriana arched her head upward to find the second marshal at the back of the room still standing, appearing confused—and scared. Had he been in league with the dead marshal? He hesitated, his gun wavering between the hooded man and Adriana, shielded beneath Edith's body. That was all the time the hooded man needed to duck, dive, and roll behind a table thrown on its side. The marshal went for the nearest threat, trying to line up his shot without first finding cover, and the hooded man fired twice again.

Crack! Crack!

The marshal's head whipped backward with a bullet's impact. He joined his partner in oblivion.

"Don't kill him!" the hooded man shouted, pointing toward the stage at someone else.

But the voice was no man's. In fact, even to Adriana's gun-blasted eardrums drowning in adrenaline, it sounded damned familiar.

Daisy Brace shuffled off the hooded cloak and shared a short nod of reunion with her old boss. Something blossomed inside Adriana when she saw Daisy, something warm and electrical, an alchemy of astonishment and love and a loathsome brand of anger.

The enforcer rushed past her toward the platform. "I said, *don't*—"

A shot rang out from the bar. Adriana turned to find Coronado falling forward, the still-smoking pistol in his right hand falling loosely to his side. The Rabh security agents who'd rushed forward stopped short. Daisy blew out a string of curses.

"Sorry, he..." one of the agents said.

"Yeah, yeah, I see," Daisy said, her gun panning between the two remaining marshals in each of the bar's back corners. "How about you two? Learn to read the room yet?"

"We weren't part of this!" one of them shouted. He unholstered his weapon and placed it, butt first, on the bar, then backed away, raising his hands. "We didn't know anything about it!"

"Uh-huh," Daisy said, unconvinced. She turned to the other one. "How about you? Rediscover your loyalty to Regent Rabh like your friend over there?"

"It's like he said." The last lawman in the room still armed followed his fellow marshal's lead, placing his pistol down on the bar and giving it space. "We didn't—"

"Put these traitors in gravity cuffs," she told the agents. "Do it now. *Move.*"

They moved.

Edith helped Adriana to her feet.

"So, there you are," Daisy said as Adriana moved toward her. "I've been looking all over for—"

Her words cut off with her breath, the victim of Adriana's bear hug. "I ought to fire you," Adriana said. "You scared the shit out of me, being dead so long."

"I could say the same about you. And it's a long story."

"It better be a goddamned good one. What's that you're wearing? The latest Promethean fashion?"

Daisy turned, modeling her body suit. It might have been colored as camouflage reflecting the smoky bourbon of Callisto's ambient light. "It's the second stage of my rehab therapy."

"Rehab therapy?"

"Adriana, are you all right?" Edith asked.

"Why," the regent said, turning to her, "don't I look all right?"

"You look like death carved from marble," Daisy said.

"Improvement then?" Adriana quipped.

"As opposed to actually dead?" Daisy said with snark. "Yeah."

"I take it you're the agent Gregor sent?"

"Yeah. This is a quick stop for me, actually. I'm headed to—"

"Regent," Krystin Drake interrupted as she approached them from the blood-soaked stage, "we still have a mission. And we have to do it now. Before others on our own side hear about this flip-flop by the marshals and start to waiver. Or the enemy hears and becomes emboldened."

Adriana nodded. Drake understood people. That too would help Edith down the road.

"Get those prisoners secured!" Daisy ordered. "And grab their weapons. We'll need 'em."

15

RUBEN QINLAO • OLD NEW YORK CITY, EARTH

A short subway ride later brought them to the ancient affluence of Staten Island's Annadale neighborhood. Opulence shone in the architecture, lit golden by the streetlights and highlighted by a silver moon in the night sky. Stately mansions were done up in the old East Coast brownstone style. It was mixed with contemporized designs of plastisteel *art futuro* meant to evoke a feeling of technological superiority. The future was determinant, it said, something that couldn't be denied—embrace inevitability before it embraces you.

It was a stark contrast to what Ruben had seen on the subway—SynCorp citizens, dressed in the agricultural colors, the green and brown clothing of the Kisaan Faction. Not surprising, since Elise Kisaan had been Regent of Earth. Revolutions don't come with new uniforms, at least not right away. But there was irony woven into the material, now that Elise's matricidal daughter was in charge. The riders shared a haunted look of uncertainty. Ruben wondered if they found comfort in the routine of continuing their daily lives as if their entire universe hadn't changed.

"It's just a short walk," Junior explained, mounting the moving walkway that led upward. "They're expecting us."

They stepped onto New York City's streets from below. What struck Ruben almost immediately was how different it seemed from the city he remembered when he'd visited with Ming on official Qinlao Faction business. Walking among the population reinforced what he'd seen on the subway—there was a prevailing sense of despair among the citizen-workers. How like Darkside the city had become, only on a much larger scale—a spiritless, cautious collection of downcast eyes and hands in pockets. And fear—it was like an electric current tickling Ruben's feet through the sidewalk.

"Here we are, guys," Junior said. "I'll buzz us in."

Ruben shared a look with Strunk. In less dire times, he might have smirked. Now he simply felt uneasy with relying on Tony Junior. Was it disbelief that the kid could actually be a help instead of a hindrance? Or maybe it was the effect of the city's atmosphere soaking into his skin.

"Tony Taulke to see Danny Lasker."

The red light next to the door switched to green. Junior reached out and turned the latch.

Inside, the Lasker Compound was an homage to opulence. Ruben experienced a pang of homesickness when he saw the floor made of Martian red marble in the foyer. A crystal chandelier hung overhead, its faux candles flickering with holographic precision. The real light came from one of the most expensive innovations ever to come from the Erkennen Labs—sunspire lights, each burning with the luminescence of the sun itself on a clear day. They shined like orange stars amid diamond-studded constellations hanging from the ceiling. The wall to Ruben's right was skinned with the skyline of Niagara Falls, the perennial thunder of its crashing waters providing a constant flow of *shushing* to welcome visitors.

A sweeping staircase led to the second floor. Descending it was a young man about Junior's age—Danny Lasker, Ruben assumed. Behind him was an older man with the same features, only more lined and world weary. He wore a suit that shimmered as he moved, changing with the observer's viewing angle. It transitioned in color from charcoal to a lighter gray, the lapels lingering on a burnished onyx. To Ruben's knowledge, it was the most expensive kind of suit you could buy. It was the *art futuro* statement made fashionable.

"Tony!" Danny's pace quickened. His father's didn't. "Man, I was glad to hear from you!"

The two young men embraced briefly. Danny's father smiled at the reunion.

"Glad to see you're okay, kid," Matteo Lasker said. "Sorry about your pop." As Junior nodded and stepped aside to jabber with Danny, the elder Lasker approached Ruben and extended a hand.

"Regent Qinlao, I'm Matteo Lasker. I'm honored to welcome you to my home." Ruben accepted the handshake. "I can't believe all that's happened in so short a time. Tony Taulke's been good to us, to all the families. It's a goddamned insult the way that bitch is treating him."

Ruben nodded. He noticed three men and one woman approaching from deeper inside the house. They were younger, more deferential. More serious.

Muscle.

Matteo Lasker gestured widely. "Marshals' uniforms?" He chuckled. "Even knowing it's you inside them, I still have a knee jerk of discomfort."

"It's the hide-in-plain-sight approach," Strunk said before Ruben could answer. "Worked so far."

Lasker seemed annoyed that the help had joined the conversation. He turned to Strunk with an indulgent smile. "Smart thinking."

"We appreciate the hospitality," Ruben said, inclining his head toward Junior and Danny chatting among themselves. "Tony won't forget it."

"Oh, I'm sure he won't," Lasker said, his voice friendly. "I imagine you gentlemen are tired. One thing—house rule—I need to ask for your weapons."

There was a moment where even the chatter from the teenagers seemed to stop. Only the quiet *shushing* of Niagara Falls filled the entryway.

Strunk crossed his arms. The four operatives advanced a step but halted when Lasker motioned behind him. It was a subtle dance Ruben was beginning to notice when it happened. How simple his old life on Mars had been.

"Just a precaution I take with all my guests," Lasker said, not quite achieving his earlier friendliness. He raised his hands in front of his chest. "My chief of security would have my hide if I didn't enforce the policy equally. You'll be under my protection while you're here. Not to worry."

Danny said something that made Tony Junior laugh.

Ruben looked to Strunk, who shrugged. They pulled their stunners from their holsters and handed them over, and Ruben surrendered his sole remaining katara dagger.

"Thanks." Matteo Lasker smiled. "Soldatos?"

One by one, the four soldiers pulled their own weapons and aimed them at Ruben and Strunk. Junior moved forward until he stood next to the elder Lasker. Behind them, Danny smiled.

"What's this?" Strunk demanded.

Matteo Lasker raised his hands again, addressing himself to Ruben. "Nothing to be concerned about. We're just going to make sure you stay here a few days. Like I said, it's for your protection, really."

He motioned, and his four soldiers made a path. "This way please," Lasker said.

Ruben turned with disbelief to Tony Junior, whose self-satisfaction occupied every corner of his young face.

"Now you see who's really in charge, huh?" Junior said.

⸻

Ruben tapped the red Greek epsilon on his sceye. Again, it refused to engage. It was seemingly functional but unable to launch. Gregor had told them to only use it in an emergency. This situation certainly qualified.

He couldn't believe it. Couldn't fucking *believe* it. Tony Junior conspiring with a New York mobster to keep them here. Didn't he understand he was sealing Tony Senior's fate?

"Try yours again," Ruben said.

"Sure. Nothing else to do." Strunk made another attempt with his sceye. "Nada," he said. "I'm telling you, Boss Man, we're under the canvas."

Under the canvas. Wise-guy talk for *separated from CorpNet*. The dampening field surrounding the Lasker Compound was absolute. They'd each tested its limits in the far corner of every wall of their lavish prison cell. Long hours of watching Strunk play poker with their guards combined with bitter contemplation had produced a theory in Ruben. The field ran some kind of emulator program that imposed a blanket of coverage and a data mirage to make you think you were still on the 'net.

They were completely isolated, without a window on the world, save for the single screen Matteo Lasker had allowed in their shared room. Ruben watched as *The Real Story* re-ran its current feel-good story of the revolution —Cassandra escorting a motherless farm boy from Pennsylvania into the new-old symbol of unity on Earth.

Now that Tony Taulke had been deposed, the UN Building had, ironically, become the unified seat of planetary power its founders had once hoped for. No one-hundred-ninety-three nations competing with one another. Not even Five Factions now. Just one absolute ruler and her revolution.

The Company had preserved the building as a museum piece, a symbol of the Old World's failing to do their one job: protect their citizens. Today, a single standard flew from the center flagpole: the golden, mirrored-S serpents of the Soldiers of the Solar Revolution emblazoned upon a crimson field. When the coastal winds picked up, the cloth snapped like a whip cracking.

"Goddamnit!"

"Relax, Boss Man," Strunk said. "We're secure. Without worry. That shot you gave me? It's done wonders. And after a night in a nice room like this— my muscles are almost Earth adjusted. I feel more like my old—"

"Without worry?" Ruben said. "Tony's son betrays us, and we're 'without worry?'"

Strunk shrugged. "Beats hiding in a dusty Darkside church waiting for the door to bust in."

Ruben inhaled deeply, ready to lay into Strunk for his seeming indifference. Then, he simply sighed. One thing Strunk had said was true enough; his physical health was on the mend. He was almost back to his old self, in fact. He no longer hunched over when he moved around, even in the constant drag of Earth's one-g. The Novy stimulator had been worth every penny. But Strunk's motivation to help Tony—his impetus to action— seemed fractured. It was like Strunk's spirit to do anything to help his old boss had been bled out of him by Junior's betrayal.

"I don't understand you," Ruben said, standing because he couldn't sit any longer. "Last night—playing cards with Lasker's men like they were old friends. You of all people."

The enforcer shifted in his chair. "What's that supposed to mean?"

Ruben stood before the double-glassed window, looking over New York's skyline and its vast array of human accomplishment. The pre-dawn city was already alive with lights sprinkled randomly among its countless high rises. Stars still twinkled above, though only the brightest of them were still visible. Aircars occasionally streamed by, the traffic sparse before sunrise.

"It means, every minute we stay here is another minute Tony Taulke gets closer to execution." Ruben turned back to stare at Strunk. "And you sit there, inert and ... impotent—satisfied with doing nothing. Where's your loyalty to Tony?"

Strunk regarded him in silence, though his eyes grew cold.

For the first time since the *Roadrunner* crashed on the Moon, the way Strunk was looking at him sent a tickle of fear up Ruben's spine. He thought that maybe, just maybe his diagnosis of Strunk's impotence to take action had been entirely wrong.

"Listen, Boss Man," Strunk said, rising. The hair at the nape of his neck rose. His combat reflexes woke up. He centered himself and prepared his legs to move quickly. "We don't know how this will play out. Odds are, we're both dead men and just don't know it yet. It's even still possible Anthony Taulke the Third—aka Tony Junior, aka Tony Three-point-one—is destined to run this solar system."

"Except for one thing," Ruben said. Strunk hadn't moved toward him as he'd spoken, hadn't moved at all except to stand and stretch. Ruben heard the big man's joints cracking. His fighter's instincts stepped down to yellow alert. "Anthony Taulke the Second is still alive, and Cassandra Kisaan has him in chains."

"That's two things," Strunk said.

Was that a joke?

Strunk confirmed it with a sideways grin. It was almost like he had a secret he wanted to share with Ruben but hadn't quite made up his mind to do it yet.

Ruben reflected Strunk's expression, offering him a familiar, it's-just-us-against-the-universe smile. "You're making my case for me."

"It's almost breakfast," Strunk said, cracking more joints. "I could use a good meal."

Ruben didn't let himself get angry again, not at Strunk at any rate. It was just wasting energy. He walked to the bed, sat down, then lay back. The morning sunlight was streaming in brighter now. The reflective relief pattern in the ceiling had begun to resemble the universe inverted—mostly lightened background with tiny black pinholes of darkness.

"The clock's ticking, Strunk," he said, despondent. "We're running out of time."

A few heartbeats later, Strunk's considerable head and shoulders appeared, looking down on Ruben and blocking out the inverted starfield.

"Yeah, but the game's not over yet, Boss Man," he whispered. "The game's not over yet."

16

STACKS FISCHER • ABANDONED ERKENNEN LAB, THE MOON

"—Epsilon One out."

I snorted myself awake. Long hours listening to Bekah Franklin talk to herself while she worked her geek magic on the Cassandra kill code had lulled me.

"Good, you're awake," she said.

I began sweeping the cobwebs from my brain. "What?"

"Priority message from Gregor. Masada Station installed listening algorithms to parse communications on the subspace satellite network. The algos rely on a discrete nomenclature of both direct and indirect or associated terms and ... what's wrong?"

My thumb and middle finger framed the bridge of my nose. "I stopped listening—understanding, really—after *listening*. Can you cut to the chase?"

There was a flash of annoyance, and I could see that future professor in Bekah again, annoyed with an impatient student who just wanted *the answer*. Then, she merely sighed. "Gregor's noted unusual activity on the far side of the Moon. Comms traffic is cryptic and non-specific around the South Pole-Aitken basin where, really, there shouldn't be any comms traffic at all. It's the kind of stuff that led them to the pirates in the Belt."

I picked up the coffee I'd been working on when I'd fallen asleep. "What's he expect us to do about it?"

"Passive proximity monitoring is all," she said. Even I understood geek speak for *just listen in locally*. "He figures we might hear something to pass along, help them figure it out. I wish we could do more," she said.

The coffee was cold.

"Like what?" I said. The basin was a long way away. Only one of us could fly the *Coyote*, and she had her plate finishing Project Jericho.

"I don't know," Bekah said, her fatigue turning fatalistic. The kid had a talent for taking on the burdens of the universe. "I'm close to splicing Daniel's viral code with Cassandra-Prime's base keys—"

I held up a hand. We both sat in silence for a moment.

"I have an idea," I said. "For the record, I hate it."

"Okay."

"I head into Darkside. Sniff around. I have tons of informants there. At least, I used to. But that would mean leaving you here. Alone. Which is why I hate the idea."

"But..." She took a moment. Weighing options, same as me. "Gregor's worried. And we're all he's got here."

My vac-suit lay on the floor, where we'd both dumped them once atmospherics came up to par. "I'll have to Armstrong it," I said. If I'd only had the Hearse parked outside instead of a prototype ship with no nav interface... Then again, sneaking into Darkside with a ship was infinitely more complicated. Maybe opportunity was knocking here after all.

"How will you get in?" she asked. "Isn't the only way into the city by ship?"

"That," I said, "is the one thing I'm not worried about. How close are you to assembling the kill code?"

"Less than half a solar day, I think," she said.

"Good," I said. "Time's ticking for Tony." I got up, pulled out my stunner, and set it on the console in front of her.

"What's that for?"

"Comfort," I said.

Old-world castles sometimes had an ancient door leading to the outside from an underground passage. A final getaway for the castle lord when he lost the walls.

Darkside has something similar, built right into the foundation when the city was mostly still an artist's rendering of LUNa City: an antechamber connected to a series of airtight doors leading directly to the lunar surface. I'd always heard it called the Smuggler's Door, used by inventive entrepreneurs back in the day whenever the UN cracked down on the black market dockside.

I was half convinced it'd be gone or sealed up. But once I'd hopscotched across the lunar surface, I found it right where it ought to be, still secured with a conventional Nautilus wheel-lock mechanism. Once inside and with the antechamber repressurized, I happily shimmied out of my vac-suit and unpacked my longcoat and fedora from their vacuum-sealed freshness. The hat was mashed to hell, but a little time in Darkside's one-g standard gravity and human-spiced air would take care of it. I pulled it down snug to protect against facial rec.

Tony Taulke gets the credit for conquering Sol for SynCorp, but the real power behind the throne has always been the tech innovations of the Erkennen Faction. Coming up with a way to lasso gravity, make it something you can turn up and down like a thermostat? The single most important factor in making colonization as easy as packing a bag and hopping a skiff. But the trip on the *Coyote* and the time in the lunar-g lab had made my muscles feel like lead, my blood like mud.

I took my time, trying to acclimate, while I climbed the levels of Darkside—slowly. By the time I stepped onto the Fleshway, I almost felt normal again. Ironic, if you know anything about the Fleshway. But seeing all those humans grifting one another along that boulevard of dire intent felt as close to home as I figured I was every gonna feel. I didn't even mind the smell. Being isolated in space has a way of making you appreciate the least of humanity because at least it's humanity.

I headed straight for the Arms of Artemis. The madam there, Minerva Sett—Minnie the Mouth, to her customers—is an old ... acquaintance ... and a bountiful source of info. If something secret was happening over in the basin, she'd be the one person in Darkside most likely to know about it.

The Fleshway had the expected hustle-bustle of people moving every which way—the usual hands feeling around in pockets not their own, the odd wino lying near the V-drains. But there was something different, too. The hubbub was almost ... subdued. A sign of the times, maybe? When folks don't know what's gonna happen tomorrow, they're more likely to be cautious today. It was the Fleshway, sure enough, but the Fleshway on downers.

The Arms made the thoroughfare outside look downright perky. Minnie's place seemed more like an opium den of languidity. A murmur here and there among hunched-over patrons, their eyes cast down, only raising a hand to order another drink. A few of Minnie's girls sat on laps as usual trying to rub up business, and one or two laughed at something their john said like they actually thought it was funny. But on balance it was like a fucking wake without the fun.

Brandy Watts was bartending. I angled her way, watching her down the shot she'd just poured. That was the most unholy sign yet. Minnie didn't allow her girls to drink on duty, not even her bartender.

There was the sound of pain from the back. That wasn't unusual here, as long as the john paid extra and the girl agreed. I picked a free corner of the bar and nodded at Brandy.

"Stacks!" she whispered. "Jesus Christ, you scared me!"

I tossed some of the old Fischer charm her direction. "How's it going, Brandy? I was wondering if Minnie—"

I cut myself off. I'd finally clued in to the fear ringing Brandy's eyes. Like someone was pressing a pistol into the small of her back. Like she was worried maybe she hadn't done everything in life she'd wanted, and it was about to be too late. I glanced around. Hers was a communal, fixed expression. The patrons were quiet as mice because they were scared like mice.

Pain came from the back room again. It wasn't the sound of someone earning extra.

Brandy poured me a scotch. The top of the bottle clanked against the rim of the glass.

"What's going on, Brandy?" I asked quietly.

"Minnie's in trouble," she said. "Bad shit, Stacks."

"What kind of trouble?"

A raised voice, muffled behind the walls. Same location as the plea I'd taken for part of a fetish fantasy earlier.

I shot the scotch. When I set it down, the glass *clocked* on the bar like a pistol shot.

"Stacks..." Brandy began.

"Office?"

"Stacks, please, Minnie might get—"

"Office, then."

When I slipped off the barstool, Brandy grabbed my arm. "You don't understand—it's SSR," she whispered, harsh and insistent. "They want to know about some guy that was in here a few days ago. I hate it, we all hate it, but there's nothing we can do. It's the fucking SSR!"

"I understand." Pulling my arm away, I put my hand in my pocket, wrapping it around my .38.

"Stacks!"

Chairs moved against Minnie's faux-wood floor. The smarter people, bailing on their tabs. A steady line of johns and girls alike followed.

I didn't go charging in. My mud blood and lazy muscles didn't feel like testing themselves against Minnie's office door, fake wood or not.

I put an ear to it. Behind me, metal scraped wood. I turned to find Brandy with a double-wide shotgun, a peacekeeper Minnie calls the Sweeper. She cleans the floor with it on bad business days.

"If this is gonna happen, okay then," Brandy said. "You flush 'em. I'll bag 'em."

I smiled. Mostly because she'd declared her loyalties instead of shooting me in the back.

I rapped on the door to Minnie's office.

"H—hello?" I said, piping like a teenager hoping for a first dance. "I think I can help you fellas out."

There was a shuffling of voices inside. Minnie's was in the mix. I could recognize it now. And two or three others.

"Who's out there?" a man asked. Sounded older. Not like one of those wet-eared types I'd played with on Masada Station.

I said to Brandy, "I'm about to flush. You shoot the shit that comes out."

Footsteps.

"I have information," I piped, doubling down on the southern multi-vowel voice of a Martian miner. Every word has at least one extra syllable. *In-fo*-may-*a-tion*. "Please don't hurt Minnie no more, yeah?" With my back against the wall, I extended my arm and put the mouth of my revolver next to where a grown man's temple ought to be.

The door opened, and the SSR bastard stepped into the frame. His eyes went wide at seeing Brandy's shotgun. He brought up his sidearm.

Crack!

I put a new hole in the side of his head.

Shit happened fast, then. I shoved soldier boy out of the doorway, and his corpse landed in the bar area.

"Lieutenant!" another, younger voice shouted. A wet-eared type.

I snagged the fedora from my head and tossed it in the room. Somebody fired off a burst of automatic weapons fire.

Bracka-bracka-bracka!

"Get down!" I shouted at Brandy as I knelt. If you've ever indulged at the Arms, you know how flimsy Minnie's walls are. I didn't want Brandy taken out by my hat trick.

My right eye and .38 peaked around the doorframe. The greenhorn who hated headwear was staring at my fedora on the floor, like someone might spring up from underneath it. He wasn't wearing armor.

Crack! Crack!

I plugged him twice, once in the gut, once in the chest. He went down on his back, blood bubbling out of him, his arms jerking. The rifle was suddenly too heavy for him to lift.

Movement in the room. I caught a glimpse of Minnie, tied in a chair, head lolling on her chest. There was blood too, all down her best come-hither hostess dress.

"That's enough!" a man shouted from cover. "You can't get in here without me plugging you! And I'll make sure to take the Mouth first!"

I stayed where I was, reconnoitering with my ears. I didn't hear anyone else, just the guy behind Minnie's desk. Two down, one to go, then. Something he'd said pricked my curiosity gene, but I set aside the mystery. Priorities.

"Not sure how you think this is gonna end, friend," I said, shucking my empty casings and reloaded. "But history paints a path for the future to follow, yeah? And your buddies, well—they're history."

"I've already called for backup," the man said. That ticklish feeling worried the back of my brain again.

Called for backup, he'd said. And he'd called Minnie by her nickname —the Mouth.

He was a local. And he was a marshal, or had been once. Soldiers get reinforcements. The law gets backup.

"Come on, Marshal," I said, testing the theory. "We both know these SSR snakes are just the flavor of the day. SynCorp's star is rising again."

"Fuck SynCorp!" That poetry was followed by muttering I took to be grievances but couldn't understand. But backup was on the way, and I was out of patience.

"Brandy, your broom," I said. She peaked around the edge of the bar, floor level. "I need to sweep."

She skittered her scattergun across the floor. I stood up, my back to the wall.

"Okay, Marshal, last chance. I just want to see Minnie up close. Make sure she's okay. I'll let you walk."

"You come in, I'll blow your fucking head off!"

Okay. Reverse psychology isn't my thing.

One last glance to place Minnie in the zone, then I reached around the corner with the scattergun.

Boom.

Photos framed in the old-fashioned way exploded on the wall behind the desk, showering the marshal.

"Jesus Christ! Jesus Christ!" Brandy screamed, her head tucked under her hands.

The marshal screeched at the glass rain and scrambled away from it without thinking. He forgot where the desk ended.

I hadn't.

Boom.

His body, pockmarked and shredded, slammed into the back wall of Minnie's office.

"Jesus Christ! Jesus Christ! Jesus Christ!"

Brandy kept praying while I moved in. The shotgun blasts had roused Minnie. She picked at the ropes tying her to the chair. Crusted blood on her cheeks got freshened up by new flow.

"Minnie?" I set my artillery on the desk. "Brandy, stop braying your prayers and get in here! And bring a bottle! Hey, Minnie..."

"Stacks? Am I dreaming?" she said, looking at me from the one eye that wasn't swollen.

"Not this time," I said. "My pants are on."

She laughed a little, or tried to.

Brandy came in, and I took the bottle from her. "Bring a cloth from the bar, help me clean her up," I said. "Minnie, take a slug. Mind the cuts."

I put the bottle to her lips, and she drank deeply, wincing when the alcohol found an open cut anyway. I set the bottle down and sprung the blade from under my wrist. The ropes didn't look too thick.

"Now, what's this all about?" I asked.

"Few days ago, a kid—came in. Met some people. Bounty hunter types, I think."

"Who was the kid?"

Minnie leered at me through the bruises and whispered, "Tony Taulke's boy."

I stopped sawing and took that in. "Junior was here?"

"Hey, hey, hey," she said, and I finished the job on the ropes. They dropped and Minnie's shoulder popped. She gasped her relief.

"The two snakes and their marshal collaborator back there," she said, "they thought I knew where Taulke Junior went. They kept asking me ... about Qinlao, too."

"But you don't know where they went."

"Nope, but I'm not without knowledge," she said, trying to smile. "And you're gonna wanna hear it."

I leaned in, and she whispered in my ear.

"Are you fucking sure, Minnie?"

Minnie grunted, rubbing at the welted rope burns on her wrists.

"Where do you think the crews come to shoot a load off?"

"Fair point."

Brandy was crunching her way across the broken glass.

"God, you shot the shit out of my office, Stacks," Minnie complained between hissing at Brandy's ministrations.

"Hang on, I've got my time machine right here," I said. "I can run it back ten minutes or so, if you'd prefer."

"Fuck you."

"I don't have that kinda time," I said.

How lucky was I? I'd learned what I'd come to find out, and I hadn't even asked a question—just kill a few guys who needed killing. Now, that's efficiency! I should take the rest of the day off. But I didn't have that kinda time.

"There'll be reprisals," I said, flicking my fingers at the bodies.

"I take care of the captain in charge of the..." Minnie paused, and I knew she was allowing for Brandy's being in the room. "...thing I mentioned. I'll be all right. If you hadn't done for these guys, he'd have done for them himself."

Nodding, that sounded about right to me. Minerva Sett was a survivor and knew how to keep insurance in her hip pocket. Or somewhere near there. She'd be fine.

"In that case, I'm on the clock, Minnie."

"You're always on the clock, you lovely bastard."

"Pour the rest of that bottle down her," I told Brandy. "And get the local doc over here to tend her bruises."

"Get the fuck out of here, Stacks," Minnie said. "Not that you were ever here."

I took her suggestion and beat feet, headed back to the Smuggler's Door and Bekah Franklin.

17

TRACE ANDERSON • UN BUILDING, OLD NEW YORK CITY, EARTH

"Don't you look handsome," Cassandra said. The compliment sounded syrupy and forced, despite the bright smile surrounding it. Elissa stood beside Trace, one arm loosely draped around his shoulder. He felt like he was being herded in the same way he'd watched Bandit herd livestock.

"Thanks, I guess," he said, tugging at the snug suit they'd laid out for him. He glanced around the modest-sized, stark-white room. Two tables sat, one on each side of the room, opposite one another. Both faced the front of the room at an angle where a raised dais sat, a semi-circular desk and high-backed chair atop it. Half a dozen camerabots hovered along the back wall like a firing squad awaiting orders.

"What of the *Freedom's Herald*?" Cassandra asked Elissa.

"Arrived in orbit an hour ago. Burned hard all the way from Titan."

"And the rest of the fleet?"

"The rest of the fleet will be here soon," Elissa said.

"But not soon enough to witness this trial from orbit."

"No, ma'am. But they'll be here for the—" Elissa hesitated, glancing at Trace. "—punishment phase."

"Pity. But at least the *Herald* is here," Cassandra said. Trace had only been half listening, but when she returned her gaze to him, his attention snapped to. "There's a certain relish that comes from delivering justice to a criminal like Tony Taulke with his old flagship as witness. Remember that, Trace. Justice should always be served with a righteous weapon in hand."

He had no idea what that meant, but Trace smiled anyway. It's what Cassandra seemed to expect.

Someone switched the lights off and on in different combinations. After a few seconds, one would fade and two more would brighten. Then two would dim, and two more in another part of the room came up.

"What's with the lights?" Trace asked.

"Please explain it, Elissa," Cassandra said. "I have some final pretrial preparation to do."

"Of course."

Cassandra reached out and stroked Trace's chin with thumb and fore-finger. Her touch was light and effortless but also irresistible as she guided his gaze to meet hers again.

"Root and stem, Trace." Her golden eyes flared. "Today is an auspicious day. A day for endings as well as beginnings. The end of autocracy. The beginning of humanity's future."

Trace swallowed. When Cassandra removed her fingers, they left a chill behind on his skin. It was very different from the electricity of excitement he'd felt when she'd first touched his face in the camp. When he'd still been awed by her. She moved to the table on the near side of the room and sat down, then closed her eyes.

"What's she doing?" he asked.

"Going over again what she plans to say," Elissa said. "Anyway, you were asking about the lights... Taulke's trial will be broadcast live across the entire solar system. Lighting sets the mood. It's important."

"It sounds like a vid production," Trace said.

"It should," Elissa said. "That's exactly what it is. How else can the billions across the system watch what's happening?"

That hadn't been what he meant. His mother taught him that trials and courtrooms were something to be respected, revered even. Associating a trial with entertainment vids felt wrong.

At the front of the room, a spotlight switched on, lighting the judge's dais.

"Why's she sitting at the table?" Trace gestured to the raised seat on the platform. "Doesn't the judge sit there?"

"Yes."

"Then why—"

"Cassandra isn't the judge, Trace," Elissa said. "You are."

He wasn't sure he'd heard her right. "What?"

"You're the proxy in the room for all the people of Sol. You're their witness here. Exciting, isn't it? You have a starring role here today."

The lights near the back of the room dimmed, then slowly brightened again.

"I don't understand."

Elissa squeezed his shoulder. "You will."

A door opened behind the second table opposite where Cassandra sat. Two Soldiers entered and positioned themselves to either side of the doorway. Behind them, an old man in a maglev-chair floated into the room through the same door. Two medical personnel guided him to the table.

"Finally," Elissa muttered, "the Werewolf arrives."

Trace recognized him, if barely: Anthony Taulke II. He'd seen the leader of the Syndicate Corporation often enough on CorpNet. He looked smaller in person. One of Trace's earliest memories was of watching Tony Taulke giving a speech over CorpNet on the eve of harvest. Trace couldn't have been more than three or four, and yet he remembered it. He remembered the lights then too, blazing over Taulke's head while he stood behind a podium, his voice deep and commanding and resonant. Saying big words, strong words. Words with muscle on them. Trace couldn't remember what the words were, hadn't understood them then; but just hearing Taulke speak had made Trace feel like his mother holding him—secure, safe, protected.

The medical personnel stepped aside. Yes, the man in the maglev-chair was the man Trace had seen speak so forcefully back then, but Taulke was older now. Trace wondered from time to time if, when he grew up, he'd eventually look like his father. He wondered now if Tony Taulke looked like *his* father. If so, the elder Taulke must have been sickly. Tony appeared gray and wrinkled and slumped. Weak. If this was a vid production, Trace thought, they'd forgotten to tell Tony Taulke. His eyes stared forward. His lids blinked lazily. He looked nothing like the man from Trace's childhood now.

"It's time," Elissa said. Her hands urged Trace forward. "Take your place."

Not seeing as he had any choice, Trace did as he was told. He wished he had Bandit with him. He felt exposed. There were six stairs up to the dais. He took them, one at a time, and sat. The chair was comfortable, genuine leather. It felt cool and luxurious against his skin.

The courtroom appeared larger from his raised seat. Cassandra nodded to him with a confident smile. Elissa took a seat next to her and focused the ire of her eyes on Taulke. Trace was surprised to find Tony Taulke looking straight at him, a bit of the old fire from Trace's memory in the older man's eyes. The six camerabots whirred as they took up positions all around the room.

To capture everything from every angle, Trace thought. It really was a vid production.

Cassandra rose.

"Ladies and gentlemen, citizens of Sol. Today, we bring justice to Anthony Taulke II. Today, we bring the freedom of the future, at long last, to the human species."

Trace watched her closely. Her eyes flared at him as she said the last sentence. It was like she was sharing a secret only with him.

"There are no lawyers—only Tony Taulke and me. The only judges are the people of Sol, represented here by Benjamin Anderson, a young man from Earth's Northeastern Farming Collective. The will of the people shall rule."

Cassandra moved out from behind her table and walked toward the center of the white room.

"We are at a crossroads of human existence," she stated. "For thousands of years, the average individual has suffered enslavement under the yoke of some oppressor—government, corporate, political, financial. At no point have men and women ever truly chosen their own destiny. It's always been dictated to them, paired with promises of material reward. The most recent example of this incentivized servitude? Life under the Syndicate Corporation—the entirety of the human species held in velvet chains by one entity.

A collective life of cultural chains binding them to their task: service to SynCorp's profit margin, from the moment of birth to the moment of death. Yes, ladies and gentlemen—the only way to escape SynCorp is to die."

"What a load of horseshit."

The words grumbled to life from the opposite side of the room. Spoken quietly in Tony Taulke's weakened voice, they went almost unheard. But Cassandra had inserted a dramatic pause into her walking recitation, and Taulke had taken his chance. Quietly purring in their movement, two of the camerabots homed in on the old man in the maglev-chair.

"You're the most inefficient goddamned computer I've ever seen," he said, shifting his posture. He was trying to sit up taller. "If you're gonna kill me, get it done."

"Anxious to meet Death, Tony?" Cassandra said. There was enjoyment in her voice. Anticipation.

"If she's less tiresome than you?" he growled. "Absolutely."

Cassandra's smile was cold. "We won't rush justice," she said. "The people will decide whether you live or die."

"The *people*," Taulke said. "You don't give a flying fuck about the *people*. Just like your mother. Another soulless bitch, Elise Kisaan. You come by your crazy honestly, at least."

Turning, her hands outstretched, Cassandra addressed Trace directly. It was then he heard a camerabot hovering over his head. That never ceased to make him nervous. "You see, Benjamin," she said. Trace hated it when she used his full name like that. "An uncouth, foul-mouthed, bitter old man. I couldn't have asked for a better specimen of the Human-Alpha breed."

Taulke grunted. "Funny, your using that term—*breed*—since you're a half-breed machine yourself."

"But I'm not a machine," she said. "I'm the next step in the evolutionary chain. A—"

"Uh-huh." Tony turned in his chair again and addressed Trace for the first time. "Kid, meet the new boss. Same as the old boss."

"Cassandra?" The eyes in the courtroom turned to Elissa Kisaan, as did the hovering camerabots. Her unblinking eyes were focused on Tony Taulke. "If I might suggest..."

"Yes, yes, of course," Cassandra said. She smiled briefly at Trace. Or, more specifically, at the 'bot over his head. "I digress. Mr. Taulke, we'll talk today, you and I. We'll have a conversation. And the people will decide whom they believe."

Trace watched Taulke from the dais. The whole room was looking at the prisoner. *The whole solar system*, Trace remembered.

"Can I make a small request?" Taulke asked weakly. He turned sad eyes to Trace. "If it please the court, of course."

Trace nodded at the same time Cassandra said, "If you must."

Taulke smiled appreciatively. "I would be very thankful if you, Cassandra, would be so kind as to go fuck yourself to death."

Cassandra stood up straighter. "You, Tony Taulke, are charged with murder—the murder of uncounted thousands over the years as you and your fellow faction leaders have done whatever it took to hold on to power. And to profit."

"More horseshit."

"You're charged with kidnapping *en masse*—kidnapping all those humans to work your mines, from the regolith caverns of the Red Planet to the caustic atmosphere of Jupiter."

"*Horseshit*. Mars is run by the Qinlaos, Jupiter by Adriana Rabh. And anyway, those people emigrated of their own free—"

"Isn't it true," Cassandra continued, "that thirty years ago you took power over what was then Taulke Industries by murdering your own father?"

"I don't answer to you, half-breed."

"So you don't deny it," Cassandra said, gesturing widely for the 'bots. "An admission by omission."

The words were starting to run together for Trace. It wasn't that he couldn't understand them, like when he'd seen Taulke's speeches on CorpNet as a boy. The words were understandable. But emotion had so charged the room, it was almost like the words were skipping over his ability to comprehend them.

"That was too clever by half," Tony Taulke said. "You should record holo-cards."

"Thirty years ago, you and the other faction leaders took power from the governments of Earth." It was a simple statement from Cassandra.

"I'd think that was an idea you could get behind," Tony said.

"You blackmailed the countries of Earth into handing you power in exchange for getting the weather back under control."

"As I recall," Taulke said, "that was your mother's part in the play. Elise went psychotic after the Cassandra mainframe injected its crazy genes into her. Then your loser father impregnated her and, lo and behold!—we got you."

Elissa Kisaan leapt up from her seat behind the prosecutor's table. The 'bots whirled to her.

"You're a liar! My mother saved this planet after you and the others..."

Cassandra turned quickly, and Elise Kisaan's cloned daughter, once one of three, stopped speaking.

"Is that what Elise told you?" Tony said. "That she was the sainted martyr who saved Earth? And yet you betrayed her anyway. Actually, it was Elise who murdered millions planetside with floods and hurricanes in the Weather War. At the direction of the Cassandra mainframe, in fact. And *I'm* on trial here?"

From across the room, Elissa's eyes burned at him.

"You will be silent," Cassandra said, "until given leave to speak."

"Then again," Tony said, turning a broken half smile to her, "I suppose you've already levied justice on Elise Kisaan. Got her head on display as proof. Last time I saw her, she seemed a bit worse for—"

"You will be silent!"

Advancing from the center of the courtroom, Cassandra appeared poised to launch herself at the old man in the maglev-chair. And yet, Taulke, weakened as he was, refused to flinch. Maybe he really did want to die...

Cassandra placed her hands flat on the table in front of him.

"The historical record clearly shows, *Mister* Taulke," she hissed, "that your father, Anthony, was the humanitarian of the family. When you took power from him, you used it to enlist the entirety of humanity as your workforce to gain control of the solar system. You're a power-hungry psychopath who deserves justice from those who've suffered most—the people of Sol."

Taulke snorted. Trace noticed his hands, worrying at the arms of the maglev-chair. "That's rich coming from you," Taulke said. "Using tech to put humanity down like a diseased animal … how many has Dreamscape killed? A hundred million? Two hundred? Your invention, I believe. Don't know what it does beyond addicting folks to their own fantasies, or why, but it's got Cassandra crazy written all over it."

What? Trace thought. He'd been lost in the sparring, the meaning drowned in the poison slinging back and forth. But that—what Taulke had said about Dreamscape—it was like his brain had snagged it from the air. But what, exactly, had Taulke just said?

"That's enough!" Cassandra shouted. "Every citizen watching this feed knows what you've done to them and their families for more than a generation now. This trial is over. The voting begins: now!"

Standing up straight, Cassandra smoothed her uniform with angry hands. The 'bots, which had captured their final war of words close-up, spread back out for the closing long shot. Cassandra's face became resolute as she walked toward Trace in his seat high up on the dais. The golden glow of her eyes had become fiery like the flaming surface of the sun.

"You're a fraud, Cassandra!" Tony Taulke said. "And you're the worst kind of fraud—one who promises freedom when it's really just your own power you're trying to—"

"Muzzle him!" Cassandra shouted.

The Soldiers moved forward, but the medical personnel beat them to their target. A hypo hissed against Tony Taulke's neck, and SynCorp's chairman slumped over with a sigh.

Cassandra turned back to Trace. "You have borne witness, Benjamin Anderson. All of you," she continued, her eyes shifting to the 'bot above his head, "have borne witness. The sins of Anthony Taulke II have been laid before you.

"As leader of the Syndicate Corporation, he bears ultimate responsibility for the crimes committed against you and your loved ones. My mother, Elise Kisaan, has already paid the ultimate price for her part in aiding and abetting those crimes. It is up to you, the people of Sol, to decide Tony Taulke's guilt or innocence."

Her brow furrowing, Cassandra raised her hands at the camerabot hovering over Trace. "The Caesars of old once rendered judgment on the people with a simple thumbs up or thumbs down. Now it is you, the people, who judge Caesar."

Her eyeline dropped a hair, her stare drilling directly into Trace once more.

"Let the voting begin."

18

RUBEN QINLAO • LASKER COMPOUND, OLD NEW YORK CITY, EARTH

Mechanical locks tumbled. The door opened, and Matteo Lasker stepped into their crenelated prison cell. He was dressed less formally than the day before. Less multichromatically, more weekend-at-home.

"I hope you passed the night in comfort, Regent Qinlao," he said. Two soldiers from his personal guard followed him in, positioning themselves on either side of the doorway. He stepped aside, and wait staff wheeled in a cart with covered, silver platters on it.

"I thought you might be hungry," Lasker said as the staff began to arrange the morning meal. "I've taken the liberty of having a high-protein, high-carb meal planned for you. Tony Junior told me the story of your time on the Moon. Shameful. Hard-boiled eggs, bacon, handmade leavened bread for toast... If there's anything else you need—"

Strunk was already rising, drawn to the ambrosia smells of real food.

"What we need," Ruben said, placing his hand on Strunk's arm, "is for you to release us. We have no idea what's happening with Tony, and once this is all over—"

Strunk shrugged him off. He seemed to float across the room on the aroma to where the staff were making small, edible art pieces from the food.

Matteo Lasker closely watched the big man's movements, then offered

Ruben a tight, tolerant expression. "I can't do that, Regent Qinlao, not yet. Let you go, I mean. In a day or two…"

"What's so special about a day or two?" Ruben asked. Maybe if he could understand what was going on here, he could find common ground for negotiation. Through the door walked Tony Junior and Lasker's son, Danny, wearing white robes and looking pleased with themselves.

"Because, Qinlao," Junior said, "my pop's trial will be over by then. And I'll be officially in charge of the Company. No pancakes?" He'd tossed the question to the wait staff. "Since when don't we have pancakes?"

Ruben felt Lasker's eyes on him as he advanced across the room. His soldiers came out of their relaxed, parade-rest positions. Strunk filled his plate.

"Is that what this is about, Junior?" Ruben asked. His body was tense. His anger at Tony Taulke's son burned through him. "A play to take over? Tony's your father!"

"You don't understand," Junior said. "I love my Pop. But it's his weakness that got us here. If he'd been stronger, more ruthless, Cassandra would never have happened. I'm gonna see that she never happens again."

"You don't know what you're talking about," Ruben said.

Junior smirked. "Guess we'll find out, huh? Now, how long will it take to make pancakes?" he asked the room.

Ruben sprinted at the teenager, faster than Lasker's soldiers could intervene. He grabbed Tony Junior's white robe by its silken lapels and hauled the teen around to look at him. "Do you know what you're risking here, you idiot? All in some selfish attempt to seize power? Have you forgotten there's an entire revolution standing in the way? Have you forgotten—"

Lasker's strongmen were on him then, pulling him off and away from Tony Junior. Danny was laughing hysterically. The look on Matteo Lasker's face indicated how distasteful and unnecessary he found the whole display. Strunk forked food into his mouth, seemingly oblivious to the drama unfolding around him.

"You forget your place, Qinlao!" Junior shouted as the soldiers wrestled Ruben out of reach. He adjusted his robe, trying to recover its pristine arrangement. "I'm in charge now! I was in charge all along, you just didn't know it. Well, now you do!"

"My apologies," their host said, addressing Tony Junior. "I should have foreseen this would happen, Tony. Can I trust, Regent, that you'll behave yourself?"

Rugen ignored him. "You've allied yourself with mobsters to ensure your father is put to death by Cassandra. And then you expect to..."

"I guess not, then," Matteo Lasker said, smacking his lips. He nodded at the crew, who loosened their hold on Ruben.

"Those three in Darkside," Ruben said, putting the puzzle pieces together. "They weren't trying to *kidnap* you..."

Junior smiled, as if finally able to supply the punchline to a joke. "Nope."

"You were..." Ruben had a hard time putting it into words. As if, in speaking heresy, lightning might strike. "You hired them to hold us on the Moon until after your father's trial. I nearly got killed trying to protect you!"

"Yeah, about that—"

Ruben lunged again, and Lasker's men lost their grip. But this time he didn't reach Junior.

Dropping his plate onto a silver platter, Strunk stepped between them. "Time to dial it back, Boss Man." He placed a hand on Ruben's chest. "Seriously, calm down," Strunk said.

Matteo Lasker whipped two fingers around in the air. Immediately, the staff began to re-cover the food.

"No, no, leave that, Dolores. Our guests are hungry." Lasker jerked his head, and his two guards returned to their door-flanking positions. "Tony, Danny, let's retire to the formal dining room."

Tony Junior seemed about to protest, but Danny touched his arm lightly. "Come on, T-3, my sister's probably up by now. You'd rather eat with her anyway, right?"

Snorting, Junior let himself be coaxed from the room.

Ruben's anger didn't leave with the kid. It stayed, solid and simmering inside him.

Lasker picked up a remote and pointed it at the lone screen in the room. It came to life, *The Real Story*'s headlines crawling beneath a woman's muted but animated commentary.

"You said earlier you were in the dark about Tony," he said. "Well, the trial begins shortly. You can watch it in here."

Ruben said nothing but stared, calculating, at Lasker and the two men behind him. He would have made a break for it, but he couldn't trust Strunk now. There was no way, with four of them—five, if you counted Strunk twice—he'd make it out of the Lasker Compound, much less be able to rescue Tony ... alone.

"Thanks," Strunk said in reply to Lasker's announcement.

"It's a kindness I'm glad to provide," Lasker replied, acknowledging Strunk's return to restrained propriety. "Don't hesitate to let me know what else you need." Lasker quickly added, "Within reason."

He exited the room, followed by his two soldiers. The mechanical locks reengaged.

"He eats alone, that kid," Strunk mused.

"What?" Ruben said. It was almost obligatory. He, frankly, didn't give a shit what Strunk meant.

"Junior," the enforcer explained. "For the rest of his life. Other people might be in the room, but that kid? He eats alone. One day, someone's gonna make him pancakes, his favorite kind, whatever that is. And he'll eat them without thinking twice because, well, he loves pancakes. He feeds his appetites without thought for what that costs. One day, when someone slips something deadly into the batter—it'll cost him his life."

"I've said it before—I'll say it again—I don't understand you," Ruben said. "Tony is going on trial for his life and you just sit here, defending this coup-within-a-coup by a kid who isn't fit to run a bodega on the Fleshway, much less—"

Strunk gave him a knowing look, then darted his eye to a corner of the room. Ruben followed, spying a camera there the size of his pinky fingernail, painted like the wall, camouflaged in the corner. Strunk nodded almost imperceptibly, and Ruben turned to find three others, just as clandestine in their placement. His eyes lit on Strunk.

"Let's watch the trial," the enforcer said. "And finish breakfast. You never know when you'll need a full meal in your belly."

"Who's the kid?" Strunk asked around a mouthful of eggs.

The boy on the raised platform looked like a small animal caught in an open field. His eyes were wide, his movements minimal. Ruben recognized the look. He'd seen it often enough in the mirror when he was just about that boy's age. When his sister had taken him away, at his mother Sying's request, to protect him. The boy sitting atop the platform was isolated and afraid—Ruben would bet money on it. Ready for anything but prepared for nothing.

"He's the farmer kid, the one whose mother died—Anderson," Ruben supplied. His stomach, sourced by the earlier conflict, had settled down with the first bite he'd taken. The bacon tasted like dripping heaven. How long had it been since they'd had real food?

"Oh yeah," Strunk said.

"Can I make a small request?" From the monitor, Tony Taulke sounded as sickly as he looked. *"If it please the court, of course."* As Ruben watched him address the boy, he remembered how intimidating Taulke's eyes could be from a child's height. But Anderson had the advantage of the dais in his favor. Along with Tony's clear lack of ability to threaten anyone about anything. *"I would be very thankful if you, Cassandra, would be so kind as to go fuck yourself to death."*

Strunk erupted in laughter. Sitting closely, hunched together in front of the single window on the world Lasker had allowed them, The small divan shook with it.

"Now that's more like the old Tony!" Strunk said.

Earlier, when Tony had appeared under guard, escorted in his maglev-chair, Strunk had come to his feet, a raging animal in a cage, gesticulating at the small screen. But as the sparring with Cassandra grew more and more heated, it became clear that Tony wasn't going down without a fight.

"Is that true?" Strunk asked at one point.

"What?"

"What Tony said about Regent Kisaan. About her killing all those people on Earth with natural disasters—before SynCorp."

"Yeah," Ruben said simply. There was a long history there, but a near sleepless night followed by his confrontation with Junior put him in no mood to dredge it up for Strunk.

"Look at her," the enforcer said, already moving on. Getting restless again, Strunk half-stood, then sat back down on the divan. "She's nuts! Look when the 'bots focus in on those eyes. Ignore the freakish color for a minute. Look at her *look*. She's barely keeping it together."

Ruben agreed. However Cassandra had thought this co-called transparent trial would go, it didn't seem to be going that way. She'd made an appealing case against Tony, but here was the thing—the people of Sol knew what kind of man he was already, even if they hadn't known all the details. And they didn't care, not really. Not, at least, in an organized join-the-revolution way.

And join for what, exactly? Despite his physical condition, Tony had done just as good a job at deflecting. He'd painted Cassandra as untrustworthy and duplicitous. Even if the citizen-workers across the system thought Tony Taulke a snake in the grass, did they really believe in this new serpent hard enough to jump from the Company ship?

He saw the truth of that when Tony brought up Dreamscape. In that last board meeting—which seemed like years ago now, though it was only weeks—Tony had suspected a link between the hackhead threat and the rest of what was happening in the system: the pirates in the Belt, Facility 12's destruction on Mars. If that were true … if Dreamscape was just one more arm of Cassandra's coup attempt, then Ruben could see the potential effect of that in the boy's eyes. Disbelief turning to discovery, then disillusionment.

"Motherfucker!"

Strunk leapt to his feet again. Ruben thought the enforcer might punch his fist through the screen. He pushed his speculations aside and stood up to see around the enforcer. The medical team attending Tony had hypoed him, silencing him at Cassandra's order. Ruben could barely hear her summation over Strunk's cursing as he paced, back and forth. The impression of the caged animal returned.

"Let the voting begin," Cassandra said. The image switched to the slumped, unconscious Tony as the medical team guided him from the room. The headline at the bottom of the feed read: *Godfather of Sol Convicted. System to Render Verdict.*

"They must think they're being funny with that headline," Ruben said, attempting to calm Strunk with humor. But he could hear the lack of a rudder in his own voice, the despair. Tony's time was running out. Cassandra had started the twenty-four-hour clock for the system to cast its collective thumbs-up/thumbs-down vote. There was no doubt in his mind as to its result, whatever the actual vote tally.

Strunk stood, seething at the feed. *The Real Story* was already rerunning soundbites from the trial. They favored Cassandra's performance.

"You asked before what kind of man I was—am," Strunk said, sitting down again, almost deliberately. Ruben returned to the divan and sat next to him. He kept himself from flinching when Strunk bent closer. "I'm giving you my answer now, Boss Man. I took a *giuramento di lealtà*—an oath of loyalty—to Tony Taulke. I made my bones with him. He gave me opportunity. It's time to pay that debt back."

It took a moment for Ruben to recognize the spark of hope kindling in his own gut.

"We're well rested and well fed, now. And I'm almost a hundred percent," Strunk whispered, stretching his arms and cracking his knuckles. He turned his head oddly; then Ruben realized Strunk was hiding his mouth from each of the cameras in the four corners of the room. It wasn't easy, but Strunk had found the angle to do it.

"Let's go get Tony," the enforcer said.

19

ADRIANA RABH • JUSTICE HALL, VALHALLA STATION, CALLISTO

Bullets slammed into plastisteel and fiberglass.

Their hastily erected barrier stretched across the street leading to Justice Hall. The street itself was long and wide by design. The Syndicate Corporation wanted those marched from the Marshals Station at one end to Justice Hall at the other to have some time to consider being remorseful. The watchful gaze of Lady Justice stood center stage in front of the hall, but unlike her historical counterpart, SynCorp's Lady Justice wore no blindfold. The alteration's message: SynCorp justice was all-seeing and absolute.

Now, as Adriana, Daisy, Edith, and their allies stood behind the barrier, the design of this walk of shame seemed shortsighted. There was a lot of open space between their position and the tall, white main doors of Justice Hall. The SSR defenders peppered them with fire from the windows now and then to remind the Callistans who still occupied the seat of power.

"How many are in there?" Edith asked.

"Two SSR companies at least," reported Commander Prapreet, the senior remaining officer in the Rabh Faction's security forces. "Maybe forty Soldiers?" Then, more grimly, "Standoff. We don't have enough to storm that place."

"Speak for yourself," an older miner said.

Turning, Adriana recognized him from Valhalla Station's labor council.

He faced Prapreet and spread his arms outward, indicating the several dozen miners behind him. *Samuels* read the badge on his jumpsuit. He'd always been mouthy on the council, Adriana remembered, and his bluster had annoyed the shit out of her. But now, she allowed, maybe mouthy was what they needed.

"I've got three-score miners ready to go in," Samuels said.

Prapreet started to say something, but Adriana spoke first.

"I appreciate your input, Mr. Samuels," she said, "balls out as always. But charging across that open ground would be suicide. And I need miners for Jupiter once we kick Cassandra's ass."

"They're back," Daisy said. She pointed overhead as the first camerabot dove into view. It was high up, only slightly bigger than a speck in the sky. One of the Rabh soldiers sighted in, then squeezed off a single round. The first 'bot abruptly changed course as a second one appeared. The shot missed.

"What are they doing with those?" Edith asked.

"Overwatching us," Prapreet said. To Edith's lack of understanding, he clarified, "Spying on our position."

Adriana reached into the substantial pocket of her farmer's coveralls and withdrew one of Estevez's stimulator hypos. A soft *phish* later, and the familiar, uplifted feeling like her power cells had just recharged swept through her. Estevez had been right. She needed the boost more often now. Like she was burning her candle faster, every time she lit up.

Daisy threw her a concerned look. Adriana ignored it.

"I say we go now!" Samuels said. He rounded on the hunkered-down miners. "What say you?"

A loud cheer went up. First singly, then as a group, they took up their Viking chant: "Hirst! Hirst! Hirst!"

In answer, a few shots rang out from the hall fifty meters distant. Most were conventional bullets, thumping into the barricade. A few, no doubt, were stunner slugs, so quiet when they hit, the bullets masked their impact.

"Quiet them down, please," Prapreet told Samuels.

"No, wait," Daisy said. She pulled her pistol and jerked her head skyward without looking up. Prapreet followed her lead, glancing subtly upward. The first camerabot had circled back and was flying lower, right over the chanting miners. Much lower than before.

Daisy cocked her piece.

The first 'bot circled ten meters over the miners' heads. The second did the same from a different direction.

Daisy rested her weapon in the palm of her left hand. She released her breath as a whisper.

"Hirst! Hirst! Hirst!" the miners chanted.

Crack! Then again, after she'd re-aimed. *Crack!*

The pistol shots were loud as cannon fire to Adriana's ears. Both 'bots lurched off course, then sputtered and spun to crash farther up the street.

"Good shooting!" Prapreet exclaimed.

Daisy's eyes shone as she looked from Prapreet to Adriana. "I have an idea..."

"If only we had jump packs," Edith said.

"Confiscated and sent to the *Freedom's Herald*," Krystin Drake reminded her. "Along with most of the armory and—"

"The *Pax Corporatum*, you mean," Adriana corrected her. "Let's get back in the habit of calling it that, shall we?"

"How much longer?" Samuels asked. "My people are restless."

Adriana scanned the miners crouching down behind them. Some carried automatic weapons; a few even carried stunners. Taken off dead Soldiers, Samuels had informed her proudly. Most carried hand weapons, the tools of their trade or farming implements from the hydroponics dome. Daisy and Prapreet had gone off with his augmented platoon to execute her plan. Adriana found herself missing their reassuring presence.

"Are you in a hurry, Mr. Samuels?" Adriana asked.

"To take back my home? You bet your lily-white ass!"

Adriana raised an eyebrow.

"Apologies, Regent," he sputtered. "I'm just anxious—"

"I appreciate your eagerness, Mr. Samuels," she said with more grace than she felt.

Samuels grinned. "You know what Cassandra's downfall will be? I mean, besides getting shot in the head or whatever finally kills the bitch?"

Adriana was intrigued. "Do tell."

"Assuming too much," he said. "Namely, that everyone feels about SynCorp like she does. What she didn't figure in? Three squares, lodging, profit sharing when the mining's bumper." Then, more softly, "You took care of us, Regent. You were like a mother to us."

"Really," she said. Despite her impulse to scoff at his sentiment, Adriana was surprised to find it pleased her. "Although I'd prefer you use the present tense, not the past."

"But it wasn't all good, either," Edith said.

Hold that thought, Edith. Yours is coming.

A single ping came over their shared comms channel.

"There's the signal," Drake said. "And there are the camerabots."

Two 'bots appeared overhead, right on schedule.

"Mr. Samuels?" Adriana said.

He nodded, turning. "Now, boys and girls! Get those lungs full of air and let it blow!"

Sixty-odd miners began slapping their hand weapons into their palms, a syncopated rhythm of deadly intent. Once the tempo was set, they added their battle cry.

"Hirst! Hirst! Hirst!"

As before, the 'bots swung around to capture the display, though they kept their distance this time.

Samuels smiled at Adriana, and it was so magnetic, she felt a smile of her own forming in response. Then he winked.

"Hirst! Hirst! Hirst!"

"Now, boys and girls!" Samuels said. "Like we talked about."

The miners stood up and spread out, pressing against the barrier to shift portions of it aside at either end.

"What are you doing?" Drake asked.

"Taking back our home," Samuels said. "For the Alabastered Bitch, yeah?"

No, Adriana thought. *You're only supposed to make noise, draw their attention.*

"Mr. Samuels, stop!" she said. "I order you to—"

Automatic weapons fire blasted from Justice Hall, drowning her out. Samuels, leading the charge, was one of the first to fall. But those still on their feet vaulted over their fallen comrades, shouting their war-cry and sprinting forward to engage the last of Cassandra's Soldiers on Callisto.

More miners went down. The fire from the hall was constant now. It was a race between the accuracy and ammunition of one side and the courage and speed of the other.

Edith was shouting her anguish at the loss of life. Part of Adriana wanted to tell her to shut the fuck up, that she wasn't helping a goddamned thing. Another, deeper part of Adriana wanted to join her. Far away, she could hear Krystin Drake shouting orders to the too-few members of their medical teams to ready themselves. They'd stayed to the rear, outside the range of the SSR's weapons.

Several miners reached Lady Justice and crouched behind the cover she offered. Half a dozen or so charged on, mounting the steps to the hall. Adriana expected to see them all cut down, but only two fell. The fire rate from the SSR was slacking off, becoming less coordinated—more sporadic.

Daisy.

The plan that was now on the shitpile had been simple. The miners were to demonstrate as they had earlier, drawing the attention of the camerabots and perhaps a rifle shot or two toward the barricade. Meanwhile, Daisy, Prapreet, and the veteran Rabh troops would storm the hall from the far side, surprising the defenders and taking them from the rear.

Samuels had changed that plan. And now dozens of miners lay wounded and dying on the streets of Valhalla Station.

Stupid, crazy sonofabitch. Stupid, willful, balls-out...

The miners that made it threw themselves against the reinforced main doors of Justice Hall. More gunfire erupted from inside the hall, though no miners fell. In a few moments, the reason for that was obvious.

"We've secured the prisoners." Daisy's voice crackled in their heads. "The ones still alive, anyway. Great job distracting them, Samuels!"

Adriana looked to the miner leader's body, a crimson pool still spreading around him. Edith Birch knelt next to him. Krystin Drake's voice barked over the shared channel, ordering the triage teams forward. They were all just blurred figures and distant voices to Adriana. The sight of Samuels dead on the ground had transfixed her, frozen her in place like Medusa turning her victims to stone.

Make it alabaster, Adriana thought, *for the Alabastered Bitch.*

Yes, she couldn't wait to leave all this behind. All this responsibility, all this burden, she thought, reveling in the guilt and self-pity it called forth.

She'd lived too long after all.

The butcher's bill was heavy. Eighteen miners dead, another twenty-five wounded. The dead were lined up in the grand foyer of Justice Hall, their weapons placed in one hand across their chests in the Viking style. To allow them entry into Valhalla, Drake explained. The wounded had been stabilized and moved to the warehouse now serving as an ad-hoc extension to the colony's infirmary.

"Now that I've retaken my home, we have some business to attend to," she said to Edith and the others. "Come here and stand on the SynCorp seal with me, all of you. Make a circle. Edith, I want you here in the center with me." Then, almost as an afterthought, she added, "Mind the blood."

They gathered, all of them, around the seal of the Syndicate Corporation engraved into the white marble floor of Justice Hall. Adriana thought the blood streaking the floor morbidly appropriate.

"I'll keep this short," she said. "I'm heading to the inner system to press the fight there. Daisy, I assume there's room in Fischer's death-mobile for me?"

It was obvious Daisy was hearing of Adriana's plan for the first time. After a slight hesitation, she nodded.

"Good. How long to reach the inner system?"

"With the refitted engines? Three days. We should get there about the same time as Galatz's corporate fleet burning from Titan."

"Perfect," Adriana said, turning back to the others. "Now, there's still work to do here—mopping up any remaining snake lovers, bringing collaborators among the colonists to justice, that sort of thing. Prapreet, I'm promoting you to acting head of Rabh Faction forces with the rank of colonel. You're in charge of restoring order under the double-bar-R of the Rabh Regency. Reconstituting our fighting force is also a priority. Understood?"

The Indian man's dark complexion appeared to darken further. "Yes, ma'am," he said. "Thank you, ma'am."

"Never thank anyone for a promotion," Adriana advised. "It just means you have to shovel more shit." Then more quietly, "Who speaks for the miners now?"

A woman with the name *Carlisle* stitched on her jumpsuit stepped forward. "I'm the junior representative on the council," she said. "So, I guess that's me." There was a grating sound to her voice. Adriana liked her already.

"Very good. Now, you're senior representative," she announced. "You'll need to appoint someone to your old position. I suggest it be someone who's not afraid to argue with you. But it can't be your husband."

The woman's eyes widened. "Regent, I'm not m—"

"It was a joke. Grow a sense of humor if you want to excel at leadership."

Carlisle smiled with teeth. "Yes, ma'am. I get it, ma'am. Now."

"What I'm about to say isn't a joke," Adriana continued, addressing everyone. "I have no heir. I have no distant family member I'd trust to sit the right way on a toilet, much less rule in my stead. So I'm drafting my counselor for the job."

She shifted her eyes to Edith.

It was like the air had suddenly been sucked from the room.

"What?" Edith said.

"I'm appointing you Regent of Callisto and inheritor of my faction—you now have the sole controlling interest. As do your heirs into perpetuity, with all the rights and obligations extending thereto." Adriana flicked her eyes to Edith's belly. "So take care of that one."

"Regent, I—this isn't what I want."

"And that's the best part for me," Adriana said. "But what you want is irrelevant. This is what Callisto *needs*—someone strong but with a conscience. The Company is too hard, too regimented. It needed to be that way to succeed, to help humanity survive in the early days—get all the people rowing in the same direction. Now it needs to be nurtured, its harder edges rounded off. And besides—you still owe me for that..." She paused knowing she didn't dare tell the others of Edith's betrayal. After the price of this victory, the miner's widow would be dead within an hour had Adriana revealed that. "...*indiscretion* we discussed before."

Edith's expression hardened.

Good, Adriana thought. *You're going to need that.*

"Will this make us even," Edith ventured. "Once and for all?"

"Once and for all," Adriana replied. "You have my word."

Prapreet spoke up. "Regent Rabh, is this legal? Not that I'm questioning your decision. I'm sure Ms. Birch would make a fine ... leader. But strictly speaking—"

"I make the law on Callisto, and because I say it's legal, it's legal." She turned to Edith, whose wheel of emotions had already spun through several iterations. From the look on her face, it currently rested on frightened. "And now that Regent Birch is in charge, she can make the law for Callisto. I'm sure there are a few policies that need ... modernizing."

Edith's eyes rose to meet hers. "I wanted to go home," she said, "to Earth. I wanted to make a life there. I wanted to—"

"If you think you can do more good there than here," Adriana said, "then go. I'll choose someone else."

Edith held Adriana's gaze. "No, here's my home, now," she said, as if discovering a truth for herself. "I'll stay here."

"Good," Adriana said. "I've already done the paperwork. The command codes for faction resources are already in your name. I recommend setting a strong password. The last thing you want is someone selling secrets to pirates or something." Edith gave her a look of *Really?* "Prapreet will brief you on the mop-up operation before dusk. Correct, Colonel?"

Prapreet snapped to attention. "Of course, Regent—Ms. Rabh."

Adriana nodded. "I also recommend you bring in a counselor who, as I advised Miss Carlisle, isn't afraid to argue with you. Krystin Drake seems a good candidate, but that choice is up to you." Drake's eyes had widened at the announcement that Edith was to be regent. Now her mouth dropped open.

Adriana pulled Edith aside, and they walked deeper into Justice Hall, away from the others.

"This is your karmic comeuppance for betrayal, Edith Birch," she said. The decades of a burden she'd never fully realized she was carrying had lifted from Adriana's shoulders. She was the older generation passing the obligation for humanity's future on to the young. She was the voice of an oracle warning of destiny. "You now have the power of life and death in your hands, my dear. And so," she said, holding Edith's eyes, "justice is served."

20

RUBEN QINLAO • LASKER COMPOUND, OLD NEW YORK CITY, EARTH

"Hey Frank," Strunk said, rapping on the inside of the filigreed door. "Can you come in here a minute?" He motioned for Ruben to step back. "No offense, Boss Man," the enforcer whispered, "but you're following me like a puppy. I need room to work."

"I can help," Ruben said, inexplicably offended by Strunk's tone. The ghost of a training session with his sister rose in his mind. Strunk had reminded him of Ming after he'd failed a maneuver she was trying to teach him for the third or fourth time.

"You can help by—"

"What do you need?" The voice was muffled by the wood between them.

"Me? Nothing. But Boss Man here needs a sedative," Strunk explained, eyeing Ruben. He waved at him to sit down, and Ruben complied. "Tony's conviction—it ain't sittin' well."

The filigreed door slid into the wall. Strunk stepped back respectfully.

A medium-sized man entered the room followed by another, bigger one. The Lasker operative named Frank walked past Strunk, his eyes on Ruben sitting in the chair.

"Look at him," Strunk said. "He's—" As Frank passed him, Strunk reached out with both hands and pulled him off his feet. With one hand gripping the back of the man's skull, Strunk rammed him face-first into the wall. He clutched Frank's hair, pulling his head backward, then slamming it once, twice, three times, driving it through the white plaster. When Strunk was done, a skull-sized hole rimmed in red gore gaped in the otherwise pristine period-piece wall. Killing Frank took less than three seconds. His body hung against the wall by the neck.

Lulled by a boring-till-now turn at guard duty, the second man had stood in the doorway and watched the kill happen, too stunned to move. Now, as Strunk turned toward him, the man quick-drew his stunner, aiming it squarely at Strunk's midsection.

"Guess this is it, Bernard," Strunk said to the second man. Ruben could see him tensing. Strunk must have misjudged because the distance between them was too great for him to reach Bernard. Strunk was a dead man.

"Guess so." Bernard put his finger on the trigger. "You did for Frank. Now, it's your turn."

There was a flash of porcelain through the air, a crack against bone, and the sharp cry of pain from the six-foot-and-more Bernard. The stunner went flying from his hand. The decorative ashtray Ruben had hurled like a discus smashed into pieces on the floor.

Strunk charged, catching Bernard off-balance. They crashed to the floor of the hallway outside the room, a pile of swinging fists.

Ruben moved too, grabbing up Bernard's stunner from the floor. They were the only three in the central hallway. But someone would have been watching those cameras. Others would be coming.

Bernard's fist came up in an uppercut between Strunk's legs. Strunk's whole body seemed to fold in on itself. Bernard twisted, coming to one knee, his fist drawing back to hammer Strunk's testicles again.

"Bernard!" Ruben shouted.

Lasker's man hesitated at the sound of his name, and Ruben shot him in the back. Bernard merely grunted with the impact of the stunner's slug. MESH. He was wearing MESH. He rose, rage on his face.

With a shout of furious effort, Strunk swept his leg from behind Bernard, knocking his knees out from under him. Ruben ran forward and, raising the stunner, brought it down across his skull. Once. Twice. And, when Bernard had finally fallen to his hands and knees, Ruben brought it down a third time. Lasker's man collapsed.

"I guess you really are feeling better," Ruben said, offering Strunk a hand. He took it.

"Most of me," Strunk replied, his voice half a register above normal. "My nuts? Not so much."

"There'll be more coming." Ruben was surprised they weren't surrounded already. Then again, the entire fight had taken less than thirty seconds. They'd probably thought Strunk was on their side. He'd been so good an actor on that score, he'd even fooled Ruben.

"Yeah. Give me that stunner. Grab Frank's. See if he has a trad pistol too. But hurry it up," Strunk growled, wincing as he knelt to search Bernard for other weapons.

Ruben returned from his own search with an 11-millimeter pistol and a spare magazine, along with a second stunner. Strunk had found a pair of brass knuckles on Bernard.

"Front door is this way," he said, putting them in his pocket.

"How do you know?"

"I paid attention."

Strunk halted. "In here." He placed his palm against the very modern biolock on the outside of a very period bedroom door. It didn't budge.

"Did you really think it would open?" Ruben asked.

"Fuck."

A man and a woman rounded the corner at a run, their weapons drawn. The other two *soldatos* from the previous night, when Matteo Lasker had taken them prisoner. Both were surprised for half a second, pulling up short.

It was enough. Strunk and Ruben raised their weapons. Ruben fired the pistol, taking the woman high in the chest. Strunk's stunner fire was dissipated by the man's MESH suit, but their impact made his own shots go wild. Ruben took an extra half second to aim carefully, and the second *soldato* went down with two bullets in his chest.

The echoes of gunfire died on the walls.

"You're pretty good with that thing," Strunk said, moving forward without looking back.

"Not really," Ruben grumbled, following. "They were close."

Strunk took the trad pistol off the woman and searched her for additional magazines. He found two. She warbled helplessly as his hands patted her down, the blood of a failing heart welling up in her throat and exploding over her shirtfront when she coughed. Her hands jerked reflexively. It was like she was looking for something to help her hold onto life. Her eyes pleaded with him to work a miracle.

"We should call for help," he said.

"Are you kidding?" Strunk demanded, frisking the male of the duo. He wasn't moving like his partner. He was half a step ahead of the woman in death. Strunk pulled another magazine out of the man's inner coat pocket. "We're on borrowed time. Mind on the mission, Boss Man. And here, I think this is yours."

Strunk rose and handed Ruben his katara dagger, then stepped over the woman, who reached after him. Then her hand fell slack. The blood trailing from her mouth stopped pumping. Only gravity made it flow now. Her eyes, still focused on Ruben, went dim.

"I'll do this with you or without you, Boss Man," Strunk called over his shoulder, still moving.

Ruben blinked, stowing the dagger and following. He stared forward after Strunk, trying to rinse the image of the dead woman's eyes from his memory.

"We need to ditch these clothes," Strunk said, glancing down at his marshal's star. Once outside the Lasker Compound, they'd quickstepped for a hundred meters or so, their weapons cache stowed under clothing. Now, they walked almost leisurely. "Lasker will have put out the word already."

"He wouldn't risk that," Ruben said. A woman with a baby carriage strolled by. He smiled sociably at her. She flashed a quick, respectful grin in return, her eyes darting quickly away. Had her step sped up as well?

"Not officially," Strunk said. "But he'll have back channels all over the city. The families strike deals when it's mutually profitable. Information is currency. They've got eyes everywhere, and I don't just mean cameras."

They'd reached a small town square with shops and stores.

"Let's duck in here a minute," Strunk said. He waited till the eyes that had noticed two marshals walking down the street became elsewise occupied, then slipped into the alleyway between shops. "Keep watch."

From the shadows of the alley, Ruben observed the town square. The small borough of Annadale was coming to life, its daily routine kicking into gear. A few people sat sipping coffee and tea at outside tables.

"Chrysler Building," Strunk said. Ruben turned with a quizzical look and found Strunk refocused on their surroundings. Now well beyond Matteo Lasker's dampening field, Strunk had been accessing his sceye.

"What?"

"They're holding Tony in the Chrysler Building. It's not far from Cassandra's UN compound. And built like a fucking fortress."

"Okay," Ruben said, suddenly remembering their newest asset. "We should ping Gregor. Let him know—"

"No," Strunk said, moving to stand beside him. The enforcer cast his eyes around the square. "I know Erkennen said it was secure, but we have to be sure—stay off the grid. If somehow Cassandra knows we're coming..." His cautious tone said he'd already done the math. "This is going to be hard enough as it is."

Ruben considered the alternatives, then deferred to Strunk's expertise. "What about Junior?" he said.

Strunk regarded him. "What is it with you and your conscience? First the woman who would've plugged us without thinking twice. Now the kid who put us in front of her barrel in the first place. You aren't cut out for this business, Boss Man."

Ruben considered that revelation almost a compliment. It was the inverse of what Ming had said to him before she died. A moral man, she'd called him then. Then, it had almost felt like she was identifying a weakness in him. Now, it felt like a strength. In his own way, Strunk had just confirmed that judgment.

"Lasker thinks Tony Junior's the Golden Goose that craps opportunity,"

Strunk said. "And who knows how this will end up? He could be right! In any case, they'll protect him."

Again, there was that quality of knowledge born of experience in Strunk's voice. Ruben took it at face value.

"The Chrysler Building, then?"

Strunk rumbled, "We have to get there first. That section of Manhattan is forty kilometers from here." He jerked his head across the street where an aircar was touching down in front of an open-air restaurant. "We need one of those."

"Okay," Ruben said. "How do we get one?"

"One guess," Strunk muttered under his breath.

Strunk parked their stolen aircar in a garage in Little Italy on the southern side of Manhattan Island. Boosting the ride had proven easy and refreshingly free of drama. Now, at least, they were in the right section of New York.

Morning was in full bloom. As it had been for centuries, New York had been one of the primary coordination nodes of the Company economy on Earth. The central distribution port for the raw crops reaped by Kisaan Agro's farming collectives in the Eastern United States. The primary coordination hub for the Rabh Conglomerate's never-ending efforts to diversify and enhance the Company's bottom line. The sidewalks were alive with a million voices, a million bodies moving, each a clicking cog in the clockwork of SynCorp's machinery.

Corporata Machina Omnis Est.

The Company's slogan made real, Ruben thought. The corporate machine really *was* all, just like the Latin said.

"You coming?" Strunk said.

"Cassandra is getting the whole economy back on its feet," Ruben said admiringly. "It's not just the ag farms. Everything's ramping up."

The enforcer mumbled something inarticulate and vile as they stepped into the busy stream of humanity outside the parking garage.

And speaking of vile...

"What's that smell?" Ruben asked as they walked. It came on strong and thick, like the air molecules around them were bloated with it. Then the wind would change and carry it away again. It smelled like meat rotting. Worse, it smelled like—

"Death," Strunk said. "That's what death smells like after it's been baking a while." Without stopping, he nodded toward an apartment building across the street. "Over there."

Out front, a vehicle was hitched to a flat trailer with high walls. The trailer was intended to haul several tons of garbage at one time. A conveyor belt crawled slowly upward from the ground to the top of the trailer's high side, where it looped over and came back down again. A team of two men exited the building, an anti-grav gurney floating between them. The gurney's contents were covered by a sheet. Busy pedestrians made a wide path around the men as they guided the gurney to the trailer. One of them pulled the sheet off, and Ruben stopped in his tracks.

Three bodies, one piled atop another, lay motionless on the gurney. The men each grabbed the head and feet of the first body. They heaved it onto the conveyor, and the corpse was dragged upward until it dumped into the trailer. It made a hollow, mechanical sound even at this distance. The second body followed, then the third. The team took the empty gurney back into the building.

"Jesus," Ruben said. He held up a hand to stop a random stranger. "What's happening over there?"

The stranger glanced anxiously down at the badge on Ruben's chest. "Don't you know?"

"I'm new to this sector. Just transferred in."

"You mean it ain't like this where you're from?"

"No," Ruben said, trying to cover. "Not exactly. Is there an outbreak? Or—"

"Sure, if that's what you want to call death by 'scaping," said the man. A second team exited the building, carrying two new bodies on the anti-grav. They repeated the ritual Ruben had just seen. "Whatever you can say about SynCorp, it wasn't like this."

"What do you mean?" Ruben asked, pulling his eyes away from the scene across the street.

Strunk had doubled back. "Hey, Boss Man, we're on a schedule, you know."

"I know people said things were bad," the man said. "And maybe they could've been better. Tony Taulke was a profit-grabbing sonofabitch—no offense, Marshal—but this... This is worse. I probably shouldn't say this..." He leaned over and whispered, "But I voted to let him live."

"That—" Ruben began, halted by a look of caution from Strunk. "That was kind of you."

The stranger stared. Then, "God, the buildings stink with it. People dying in their own dreams—everywhere! And the cleaning teams ... what heartless assholes they must be, huh? It's like they're taking out the fucking trash!"

"Boss... Deputy Marshal," Strunk prompted.

"Can I go, Marshal? I'm late for the desk," the man said. "I don't want to lose energy credits. It's gonna be a hot summer."

"Of course," Ruben said. "And ... thank you for your time."

The man waved absently behind him, redoubling his gait.

"Jesus, Strunk," Ruben said. "It's like the Black Plague in the Middle Ages. Corpses thrown on carts like refuse, buried in mass graves—"

"Unless you want us to be two more dead bodies thrown on the pile, we need to get moving."

"Moving," Ruben repeated, trying to shake off the sight that seemed to repeat, like a ride from a dark carnival, across the street. "Moving where?"

"I think I know how to get us into the Chrysler Building," Strunk said.

21

STACKS FISCHER • ABANDONED ERKENNEN LAB, THE MOON

I'd out-Armstronged ole Neil himself hip-hopping back to Erkennen's abandoned lab.

What I'd learned from Minnie required discretion—so, no unsecured comm traffic. I needed to deliver this news to SynCorp leadership, and fast. Bekah was already talking with Masada Station as I took my vac-suit's helmet off, and I filed that fact under lucky happenstance. I waved to get her attention, but she stuck a finger in the air. At least it wasn't the middle one. I'd known a nun like Bekah. Different religion, same shut-up index finger.

"Beyond the ninety-fifth percentile!" Daniel Tripp's voice said. Onscreen, he wore a half-moon smile.

"That's great, Daniel!" she said.

Standing beside Tripp were Milani Stuart and the Traitor of Mars, Kwazi Jabari, who was supposedly doing God's work now for Gregor Erkennen.

"Ladies and gentlemen, we have a closing window." Erkennen's voice was offscreen but unmistakable. "Brief her—*briefly*—on what you've found, Dr. Stuart."

I stepped into camera view. "Bekah, I need to—"

I got the finger again.

"With Kwazi's help, we've added a qualitative dimension to our study of the Dreamscape algorithm," Stuart explained. "Basically, we pulled apart the code to determine Dreamscape's true purpose."

"Okay." I could tell Bekah wasn't sure what Dreamscape had to do with her or why the home team was taking time off the clock to explain it to her. I was definitely on Team Get-on-with-it.

"*Briefly*, Doctor."

"Sorry, Gregor," Stuart said. "The upshot is this, Ms. Franklin: it's a segmentation protocol. It determines who among the user population has a mutation in the HLA gene complex and who doesn't."

"The same mutation we're targeting in Cassandra?" Bekah said. "That's not a coincidence."

Stuart took a breath and glanced at Kwazi. He put a hand on her arm and said, "No, it's not. Fantasy fulfillment is just the lure to get the fish on the hook."

"And once the user is hooked, the program tags them as having the mutation—or not," Stuart said.

"To what end?" Bekah asked.

"Doctor, if I may?" Gregor Erkennen stepped into view. "Bekah, our working hypothesis is that Cassandra is tagging users who don't have the mutation for ... elimination. There's a genetic bomb in Dreamscape—setting it off will create a cascade effect decoupling the chain-like network of the user's genome. This genetic bomb is tied to the HLA mutation and ... it only affects those who don't have it. Those who do—"

"—are able to assimilate Cassandra's synthesized DNA with their naturally occurring DNA," Bekah finished. Her eyes widened. "Become a hybridized form of human?"

Gregor nodded. "Just like Cassandra."

"Weeding out the chaff," I said, surprising myself that I'd followed the geek speak. "She's killing off the ones who can't become like her."

"Evolving the species," Gregor said, "in her own image."

"Jesus," Bekah breathed, looking at me. "That's potentially billions of people."

"I hate to interrupt, but I have news of my own," I said, remembering Minnie's intel.

"Mr. Fischer, we have limited time—"

"Exactly my fucking point! Those signals you were picking up from the basin? It's a second SSR fleet, preparing to launch."

A few precious seconds ticked by.

"Are you sure?" Gregor said.

"My source is solid. They've been assembling a second fleet, like the one Galatz beat up near Pallas."

Gregor leaned offscreen, listening to someone I couldn't hear. "We're approaching the security threshold for time," he said. "We'll analyze your theory, Fischer—look at the communiqués and see if we can see a pattern that bears it out. If so, I'll pass along the intel to Admiral Galatz. Masada out."

The screen went dark.

"Analyze my theory?" I said. "I just told you..." I shut up when I realized I was only talking to myself.

"A second fleet," Bekah said. "Does the Company have the ships to deal with that?"

I blew out a breath. "Probably not. But that's not our problem right now."

"Right."

"Project Jericho—is it done?"

Bekah lit up. "It is! Daniel validated the final code while you were away. Using the Cassandra-Prime base code as a way in, we can introduce the virus directly into Cassandra's cells."

"Good news, then. And—I'm almost afraid to ask—how does it work again? In case..." I'd decided I needed to know the details after all. "In case anything happens to you, and I need to pull the trigger or ... whatever. And keep it elementary, Dr. Watson."

Truth was, if anything happened to Bekah Franklin, I'd already be dead. Because it wouldn't be happening to her if I was still alive. Still, every contingency...

"The HLA mutation you heard us discussing—it's why Cassandra exists. The mutation is what enabled the Cassandra-Prime mainframe to mesh its synthesized DNA with Elise Kisaan's human DNA thirty years ago. Using a CRISPR enzyme ... oh, CRISPR stands for—"

"Don't bother," I said, both hands waggling. "My eyes are starting to glaze already."

Bekah took a moment to think it through, trying to dumb it down for me. She seemed a little sad at having to do so. I get that a lot.

Ping!

A light flashed on the comm panel. Masada Station, calling back already? We'd just gotten a lecture from Erkennen on the need to cut the connection for the sake of security.

"Do you need to get that?"

"It's probably just Daniel with more validation data," she said. "Anyway, when Kisaan became pregnant, the embryo became the beta test for this new version of human DNA—the amalgam of Cassandra-Prime's synthetic DNA fused with the combined DNA from Kisaan and the baby's father. That genetic fusion became the woman we know as Cassandra today."

"I'd debate you that *it* is a woman but go on."

With an expression that reminded me a lot of a middle finger, Bekah continued, "Scientists have been adapting genetic structures for centuries, now. Breeding mice with ears on their backs, for example. Remember when they eliminated sickle-cell anemia in African Americans last century? That kind of thing."

"Okay. I still don't know what this kill code you and the others made is. What it does."

"You know why we call it Project Jericho, right?"

"Not a clue."

"Do you know the biblical story of Jericho?"

Of course I did!

"Of course I do!" I *do* read a lot, after all. "Somebody blew some horns and some walls fell down. God on the side of the righteous and all that."

Okay, I'm more of a summary guy.

"It's from the Book of Joshua, yeah," Bekah said. "The story goes that the Israelites marched around the walls of Jericho, blowing their trumpets —the trumpets represent the power of God supporting the Israelites conquering Canaan. Jericho's walls fell, allowing the Israelites access to the city. Cassandra's HLA mutation is the wall. The contents of this hypo—" Bekah held up said hypo for emphasis— "are the trumpets. Once injected into Cassandra, her HLA mutation will ... mutate." Bekah must have seen the look on my face. "Her genetic bridge will collapse, breaking the bonds between her synthetic and human DNA."

"So, it's our own version of the gene bomb she put in Dreamscape," I said.

"Much more focused genomically speaking, but yeah."

I got a mental image. "You mean, she'll melt into the floor like the Wicked Witch of the West?"

"I don't know who that is, and no, she won't melt into the floor, Stacks. But it should ... it *should* kill her by breaking the hybridized connection and compromising her cellular structure. And neutralize the programming behind it—permanently."

"Well okay then," I said. "You could've just said that."

The stare she gave me definitely had a middle finger quality to it.

Ping! Ping!

"Would you please answer that?" I said. "I've already got one headache from all the tech talk."

What I wouldn't have given for half a bottle of scotch right then.

Bekah glanced at the panel. "It's just text..." Her voice said it wasn't just Daniel with updated numbers. I could tell it wasn't good news. Again.

She moved aside, pointing at the screen. The message was simple and fronted by Erkennen's old epsilon brand.

EVACUATE! SSR FAST-MOVERS INBOUND. ETA: TEN MINUTES.

A warning from Masada Station. The data we'd sent them monitoring local comm traffic was paying off for the narcs who sent it—in a bad way.

"That second fleet?" Bekah said. "*Now* it's our problem."

Fast-movers from the basin? How the hell did they even know we were there? Had Minnie flipped on me? Had I been followed, hippity-hopping home from Darkside? Or Maybe Minnie's influence over the fleet captain wasn't as airtight as she'd thought. Maybe the SSR had come back and closed her other eye—both permanently.

I fought the sudden impulse to Armstrong it back to the Arms. Sorry, Minnie. I hope you're okay, but I've got faster-moving fish to fry.

"I'm setting a countdown clock on my sceye," Bekah said, "allowing for the delay in reading the message—we've got nine and a half minutes."

My brain kicked into high gear. "You've got what you need, right?"

Bekah nodded, holding up the hypo again.

"Store that some place safe," I said. "Get into your vac-suit. I'll wipe the drives."

You always wipe the drives, right?

"Okay," she said, sliding the hypo into a side pocket.

I wracked my brain, trying to remember how to wipe a hard drive. It'd only been a few thousand years.

Command Line: check!

Format All Partitions: check!

Bekah slammed into the lower half of her vac-suit and grabbed the rest. I carried her helmet. We had four floors and an umbilical to navigate, not to mention that Bekah somehow had to fly the *Coyote* away from here with bad guys on the horizon.

It was a bad day getting worse.

By the time we reached the vator, Bekah had shimmied her way into the upper half of her vac-suit. The ascent took forever and felt destined to end suddenly—in fire.

"Six minutes, fifty seconds," she said as we stepped onto ground level.

"Helmet," I said.

"Thanks."

It took a bit for the suit systems to check the seals. All green. Bekah gave me the thumbs-up, and we began the skip-walk up the long corridor toward the anteroom and all those bodies. The fritzing lights came back to life when we arrived. They were the only thing that did.

The woman-corpse at the console, the one who'd reminded us both of Carrin Bohannon, was still at her station, of course.

"Bekah, we don't have time," I said, tinny over comms. She'd paused next to the body.

"I said I wanted to come back here."

"I know."

"I meant it," she said.

"I know. But we need to go. Time?"

The data request seemed to snap her back to reality. "Four minutes, twenty seconds." Bekah moved back to the door we'd just come through and began pressing her gloved fingers to the locking panel. The door slid shut, sealing us into the anteroom with the dead.

"Limiting the explosive decompression," she said, then hopped across the room to the outer door. "Hold onto something, Stacks."

I did what I was told. If we wanted to avoid being blown out onto the lunar surface, Bekah needed to bleed off the atmosphere from the anteroom a little at a time. Okay, a lot at a time—we didn't have time for textbook procedure. She tapped the decompression sequence. The security lock phased from green to red. Slowly—by the book—the atmosphere began to vent. She slipped her lighting port drive into a slot and tapped in an override sequence.

Whoosh.

It wasn't anything close to sweeping us out, but I could feel the air evacuating the room.

"Time?" I asked.

"Two minutes, thirty."

The atmo meter dropped from green to red in about fifteen seconds. Opening the door to the surface, Bekah snagged the tether she'd rigged when we landed and pulled herself along. By the time I'd reached the *Coyote*, she was already dropping into the cockpit.

I swore I could see a drive plume on the lunar horizon. Then another. The fast-movers, approaching for what I assumed was a bombing run.

"Time?"

"Not enough!" she yelled. "Get your ass aboard!"

I'm slow but not stupid. Three quick-draw pulls of my arms and a silent thank-you to the lack of lunar gravity, and I was struggling into the cockpit.

"Hurry up, Stacks! I can't work these controls for shit in these gloves."

I dropped in. Before I'd even lit on my feet, the hatch was closing behind me.

"Can you outfly those guys?" I asked, not really wanting to hear the answer I already knew. Even an experienced pilot with a working nav interface would need God's grace to do that. Bekah Franklin was neither experienced nor did she have a working nav interface. God's grace? Maybe.

"No," she said. "But Gregor designed this prototype with state-of-the-art stealth tech, remember? Now, quit distracting me!"

I shut up.

"Repressurizing the cockpit," she narrated like she always does. Doing that reassures some people they're in control when they're not.

The air pressure filled in around us.

"Come on, come on, come on," Bekah said. Then she hissed in pain, and I saw why. She'd started removing her gloves so she could work the keyboard, but the heat in the cockpit was catching up with the air. It wasn't deep-space freezing anymore, but it was far from comfortable. Bekah tapped out our escape route.

"I'll pop us off the surface with a quick burst of thrusters, then let us drift for a while. Remember the *Earn*? The ag freighter?"

"Sure."

"If we leave the surface and power drift in the direction opposite the Moon's rotation, we can get some distance. If we're lucky, they won't see us. Like the *Earn*."

"Okay."

The *Coyote* shook as Bekah tapped the thrusters. The stars moved in their courses through the forward window. Our pitch angled a bit, and the Moon's surface reappeared. Were those drive plumes again? They seemed a lot closer. My imagination, surely. Space is vast.

"Our momentum has us moving away from the lab," she said, relieved.

"Fire the thrusters again?"

"No need," she said, massaging her fingers. "Not yet, anyway."

The *Coyote* stabilized as it drifted outward. Below us, the old lab-tomb with its cracked outer dome rotated into view. The sensors pinged a warning like they had with the *Earn*. The fast-movers were close enough I could see them with my own eyes.

"Fire the thrusters," I said. "Just once."

"It's a risk," Bekah said. "They might see."

"Trust the tech!" I said, not believing I'd actually said it. "Do it!"

She reached forward and pressed a button. The *Coyote* jolted. After a couple seconds she killed the burn.

The fast-movers stayed on target. The SSR had sent two of them. The first one launched a missile, followed by its wingman doing the same.

The missiles impacted, consuming the facility in a silent inferno. The lab's atmosphere fed the flames, which exploded outward. It wasn't long, but it took a few seconds for them to start guttering out. The fast-movers banked in a long, lazy arc, likely observing the results of their attack, making sure the missiles did their job. We'd been far enough out to avoid any damage from the blast and let our momentum carry us farther. The two SSR ships headed for the quarter they'd come from. Mission accomplished.

"Well done," I said, unsnapping the helmet of my vac-suit.

"Goodbye," Bekah muttered, seeming not to hear. Her eyes were cast downward at the destroyed lab.

22

TRACE ANDERSON • UN BUILDING, OLD NEW YORK CITY, EARTH

Songbirds invaded his dream, but Trace fought against them. He didn't want to let the dream go.

It was the comm dragging him into wakefulness, not birds. When he swiped the display, Trace knocked the paperback of *Huckleberry Finn* off the nightstand. Elissa Kisaan appeared.

"Did you fall asleep?" she asked. "It's almost time for dinner."

"Okay."

"You'll need to hurry. Cassandra requires dinner *precisely* at seven—"

"*Okay*," he said, rising to a sitting position. Bandit's head popped up from the foot of the bed.

"I'll see you shortly." *The Real Story*'s looping recap of Tony Taulke's trial replaced Elissa's image. Trace muted the sound.

The dream had been gloriously real. Bittersweet and touchable. He and his mother, working side by side in the Pennsylvania fields, the white noise of the mechanical reaper humming nearby as it plucked plants from the soil. The soft warmth of his mother's voice in his ears as she quizzed Trace on the etymology of plant names. Once you had the name of a thing, she'd taught him, it could never again be as deep a mystery to you. Her smile when he got a name right felt like sunshine on a cool, spring day. And then, after work, they were back in their FAMS—the spices from her home cooking hanging in the air, twisting together around him like a blanket of warm memories.

But then Elissa interrupted, and the tremendous weight of his mother's loss settled back onto Trace's heart. The dream's details were already fading.

"No, don't leave me again," he said, tears on his cheeks.

Bandit roused from his resting place on the bed. *I'm here,* the dog seemed to be saying, panting his always-smile. *How can I make you feel better?*

Was that what Dreamscape was like? Trace wondered. Calling your fondest wish into existence and then living inside it forever? He could see why his mother had totally surrendered to it.

"She missed Dad so much, she..."

The monitor fritzed with interference. The SSR commentator talking over courtroom soundbites bent and froze. *The Real Story's* high-def broadcast was replaced by jerky, indistinct images from high in the air. A camerabot, flying over the countryside. Could have been Pennsylvania, Trace thought, though it might have been anywhere—a field covered by a semi-cloudy, gray sky. Reapers like the one from the dream worked the fields far below; dozens of them. The image made him homesick for his dream.

But the reapers weren't working row by row. That was weird. Instead, they were moving toward the center of the field from a highway, where large trucks sat idling. From far away the reapers appeared to be harvesting squash. Butternut, maybe, by its pale, camel color. Not quite the bright yellow of ripe spaghetti squash. But that didn't make sense, either—you harvested butternut squash in the fall. Not late spring.

The drone dived. Trace blinked as it zoomed in. He reached forward to swipe up the volume. A banner appeared at the bottom of the screen.

SSR BURIES DREAMSCAPE VICTIMS IN MASS GRAVES

"Cassandra murders millions and buries them in the empty fields of the American Midwest," a deep, sorrowful voice said, *"scapers and hackheads, interred together in this final, horrible resting place."*

At the center of the screen was a deep hole gouged into the green verge of the countryside. The trucks, some drawing refuse trailers behind, waited in a long line to unload their grisly cargo for the reapers to pick up.

Screeching hydraulics dumped bodies, and the corpses tumbled over one another, their limbs pinwheeling. Hands and feet—what Trace had taken for squash before—lolled and jerked, loose and lifeless. The reapers picked them up, then turned and carried them to the corpse pile. Automated bulldozers moved inward from the edges of the pile, scooping dirt and cadavers together to compact them in the earth.

"Bandit—" Trace whispered. He tried to process what he was seeing. It seemed ... unbelievable. The machines moved with cold efficiency, lifting and herding and dumping and burying the bodies like garbage.

"Cassandra Kisaan promised freedom," the voice said. *"And here, for the victims of Dreamscape, is what freedom means."*

The victims of Dreamscape?

So, Tony Taulke told the truth...

The screen fritzed again. In place of the horror, SynCorp's old "signal interrupted" pattern appeared.

The door chime sounded.

"Trace," Elissa called through the door. "We're going to be late for dinner."

His mind took a moment to register her voice. If what he'd seen was true...

"Trace?" Elissa rapped on the door with a knuckle.

"Coming," he whispered. Then, louder, "Coming. Just a second."

"We're *late*."

"Just a second."

Onscreen, *The Real Story*'s coverage of the trial had returned.

"They can do anything with vids these days, folks," the commentator said, somehow sounding outraged and amused at the same time. *"Sometimes you can't believe your own eyes."*

"Monitor off," Trace said. His hands held fast the bedcovers to his chest.

"Trace!" A fist, pounding this time.

He released the covers and scrambled out of bed for the clothes he'd worn at the trial.

"I'm coming!"

Bandit barked as his master stumbled out of bed.

"Quiet, boy!"

Still tucking in his shirt, Trace was surprised when his door opened. "I had to override the lock!" Elissa said, advancing into the room. *"Sorry."*

She took a breath while he put on his jacket. "Is everything okay?"

"Yeah," he said without hesitation. "Why?"

"Nothing ... you look flushed."

Bandit hopped down from the bed and padded to the center of the room. Shrugging at Elissa, Trace pushed past her into the corridor. She followed, and the door slid shut, leaving Bandit behind in Trace's bedroom. Good. He didn't want his dog anywhere near Elissa Kisaan. Especially now, after what he'd just seen on CorpNet.

"I fell asleep reading my book again," he said, which was true as far as it went.

"And?"

They began walking together.

"Something Huck says, when the people in the town tar and feather the king and the duke and run them out of town. About how cruel people are to each other. I keep thinking of the word he uses: *dreadful*. How dreadful people can be."

But it wasn't the image from the book Trace thought of when he said that word.

"That's precisely what we're trying to remedy," Elissa said. "To push the best of what we are forward and leave the worst behind."

"Bury it, you mean," Trace said, his words precisely chosen. Despite the fear squatting in his head, he felt bold and angry. He felt like Huck Finn, hands thrust downward in fists at his side, a scowl on his face as he'd observed the inhumane treatment of the king and the duke.

"Yes," she said. "Exactly."

Down the hallway, the old UN formal dining room waited. It was where Cassandra took her formal meals. Tonight's dinner was a pre-celebration of victory over Tony Taulke. Tomorrow would see the final vote tallied.

To their right passed a large room, brightly lit beyond the tall glass windows that sectioned it off from the hallway. Trace was startled to recognize it, if only from a distance—it was the room where Cassandra gave her speeches. A raised seat sat at the back of the room not unlike the one he'd sat in for the trial. At the base of the short stairs leading up to it, the head of Elise Kisaan rested on its pike in all its horrific, slagging decay.

Dreadful.

"Why aren't you mad at Cassandra?" Trace asked, his boldness growing.

They walked a few more steps before Elissa stopped and turned Trace toward her. "What do you mean? Why would I be mad at Cassandra?"

In his head, Trace pictured the reapers dropping bodies into the hole and the bulldozers shoving dirt over them.

"She killed your mother," he said, wanting but not daring to add ... *and mine.* "Why don't you hate her?" ... *too?*

Elissa squeezed Trace's shoulder. She was making that same effort toward empathy he'd seen in Cassandra's eyes after his mother's funeral.

"I loved my mother," Elissa said. "All of us did—my sisters, Elaena and Elinda, and I. But our sister Cassandra's vision was greater, more important than any one life. Than our mother's life."

"Cassandra ... she's your sister?"

Elissa was surprised. "Of course. You didn't know that?"

"No," Trace said. "No, I don't think..." Had he known? He felt all mixed up. There was a giddy kind of detachment spinning up inside him. He half-thought maybe he was still dreaming... "What could be more important than your mother's life?" Trace asked.

Elissa smiled. "The life of the children I'll have one day. Your life, and the lives of all our children."

Trace's confusion deepened, became a solid thing. Everything felt foreign, made distant and unreal by what he'd seen on CorpNet. He missed his mother. He missed their shelter with its scents and dust bunnies and memories of their life together. He missed afternoons reading under the magnolia tree.

"All births happen in pain and blood, Trace. We had to shed the blood of our mother to prove ourselves worthy to write the history of the future. Do you understand now?"

He tried not to sway on his feet from the feeling of being disconnected, of floating in loss—of feeling untethered from a universe that made any sense at all.

"Sure," he lied. "I guess."

Elissa regarded him a moment longer, then prodded him along with her hand. "Well, Cassandra's waiting."

They entered the dining room, and Trace found something new to distract him: a long table covered with sweet-smelling, luxurious meats, steaming vegetables, and breads of all kinds. There were even desserts prepared and waiting, and Trace's eyes lingered on those. He'd never seen so much food in one place in his life, not even at the largest celebrations when the clique had reaped an especially bountiful harvest. All this was for just the three of them?

Cassandra stood up at the far end of the table.

"I'm sorry we're late—" Elissa began.

"It was my fault," Trace offered. Elissa moved to stand before the chair at Cassandra's right hand. When Cassandra motioned to the seat to her left, Trace took his place there.

"Nonsense, it's been a long and momentous day," Cassandra said, indicating they should all sit. "A little play in the schedule? I think we can accommodate that." She gave Trace a matronly smile, but her overpowering presence, her terrible beauty no longer fascinated him. Hadn't for a while, he realized. Now he saw only the author of Dreamscape and his mother's death. The digger of mass graves in the deserted countryside.

He sat down and picked up a crystal water glass. The ice cubes were half melted.

"What of your sister?" Cassandra asked.

Elissa cleared her throat. "*Our* sister disembarked from the *Freedom's Herald* when it arrived earlier, per your orders."

Trace watched the women over the rim of his glass. Cassandra's iced tea hung halfway to her mouth. After a few heartbeats she took a sip, then set it back on the table.

"I was just telling Trace that we're all sisters," Elissa said. "And why it was necessary that you ... that Elise, our mother, had to die."

"Indeed," Cassandra said, holding Elissa's eyes.

"Like Mr. Taulke has to die?" Trace said.

Cassandra picked up her napkin and placed it on her lap. Elissa did the same.

"Symbols are important," Cassandra said, reaching for a platter of roast beef. She forked a first, then a second piece onto her plate. "Symbols resonate in the consciousness of the people. When they share an experience—voting a tyrant from his throne, for example—it binds them together in common cause."

Trace took the platter and forked roast beef onto his own plate. He had no appetite, no intention of eating it. The bloody sauce in his plate threatened his stomach with somersaults. He spooned something green and stringy next to the meat.

"Was he lying?" Trace asked.

Elissa took a bite of bread.

Cassandra picked up a decanter of wine and poured herself, then Elissa, a glass. "About?"

Trace speared some of the thin vegetable and put it in his mouth. He chewed it more than necessary. He was gathering his courage.

"Dreamscape," he said.

Go on—tell me it's just stories made up by Tony Taulke's friends. Lie to me. I dare you.

Turning her head curiously, she said, "No." Then, taking a sip of wine, she added, "That was one of the few truths to come out of Tony Taulke's mouth, in fact."

Trace picked up the knife.

"Dreamscape killed my mother," he said, staring at the roast beef on his plate surrounded by its halo of blood. He speared it with the fork and applied the knife.

Hold. Saw. Cut. Set the slice aside.

"I'm sorry about your mother, Trace," Cassandra said. The right words but hollow—without empathy.

"I saw the footage on CorpNet," he said. He could feel his throat tightening, the fear in his belly hardening into something else. Something blacker. When he cut the next piece of meat, his knife screeched against the china.

Hold. Saw. Cut. Set the slice aside.

"What footage?" Elissa asked.

"The giant hole in the field," Trace said, focused on the knife blade. "The bodies."

There was only the sound of his heavy knife sawing meat. Scraping china.

"Trace," Cassandra said softly.

He'd begun segmenting further the pieces he'd cut before.

Hold. Saw. Cut. Set the slice aside.

"*Trace*."

Cassandra placed her hand on his wrist, and there was the harsh sound of silverware and china clashing.

"Your mother and my mother—both died at my hand."

"Necessary sacrifices—" Elissa began, then stopped when Cassandra's golden eyes found her.

"Trace."

Holding the knife tightly, he brought his gaze up to meet hers. His hands were numb. His whole body was numb. He couldn't tell where his fist ended and the knife began. "Your mother died the most merciful death I could offer her. As did the others. They couldn't live and we still move forward as a species. All progress happens at a price. Sometimes a terrible price. But I can be your mother now. I can be the mother to all the future."

She wouldn't be his mother. Not now. Not ever. And as for the future...

"Eat your dinner," she said, releasing his arm. "Tonight is a night for celebration. Tomorrow, the people of Sol render judgment on Tony Taulke. And the springtime of humanity begins."

Cassandra lifted her glass and touched it to Elissa's. They held them in the air until Trace understood that they expected him to join them in the toast. He set down his fork and picked up his water glass and held it to theirs.

"To the future," Cassandra said, clinking their glasses with hers.

"To the future!" Elissa echoed.

Trace took a deep breath but said nothing.

And as they drank, he slipped the steak knife beneath the napkin on his lap. Then he finished his meal, eating every single bite of the bloody red meat.

23

ADRIANA RABH • APPROACHING THE CORPORATE FLEET

"We're here."

The words resonated more in Adriana's consciousness than her ears. They contained a Doppler quality, a leading edge followed by the slow drop of intonation. Her body felt tied to the same descending arc, pulled downward by time and Wellspring's failure.

"Adriana?"

"Yeaph." Cottonmouth. As saliva began to flow again, Adriana flexed the arthritic stoniness from her fingers and focused on the pain as proof she wasn't dead yet. The upside, as it were. Her mouth tasted like shit.

Daisy groaned, not without her own physical challenges, the lingering effects of her neurological damage suffered in Adriana's service on Pallas. Another Lazarus risen miraculously from the dead thanks to Gregor's med-tech genius. They made quite the pair.

A sensor alarm blared.

"We're approaching the night side of Mars," Daisy said, her hands working the Hearse's controls with effort. "I'll ping Galatz when we're closer."

"Why not now?" Adriana asked, impressed she'd gotten all the syllables out.

"Less satellites to hop across, less chance of interception," Daisy said, distracted. "There, that's good for now." Adriana heard her sigh back into her seat. "The drag-bends should get easier from here."

As they closed on the fleet's location, their decel burn would slow them down, and gradually the drag-bends of heavy thrust gravity would decrease. Newton and his fucking force-from-acceleration would stop trying to pinch off the veins in her skull. But anyway, she'd managed to conquer the undiscovered country of reaching the inner system from Callisto in just three days. With a little help from her friends.

Three of them rested in her right thigh pocket. Doctor Estevez's potion was bolstering her system with iron and calcium and a cellular nutrient cocktail she couldn't begin to understand, reducing the geometrically accelerated progression of cell degradation now that Wellspring no longer worked. She should have given Estevez a bigger grant. Maybe, if she didn't forget the notion five or ten seconds from now, she'd make that suggestion to Edith when this was all over.

Daisy was moving more freely now, and Adriana found herself absurdly jealous, like a grandmother who begrudges her own grandchildren their turn at being young. She stretched her legs in their foam supports. There was pain in her knees and hips, but it was manageable.

"How long till we rendezvous?" she asked, aware of the rumbling grumpiness in her own voice.

"A few hours," Daisy answered. She turned to Adriana. "I'm feeling like shit. I can only imagine—"

"Kiddo, I haven't felt this good in years," Adriana lied in her best negotiator's voice, the version she used when her opponent was in the stronger position. "Smart, that Galatz," she said, "using Mars as cover." Changing the subject avoided the conscious effort lying required.

Her praise for Galatz was also genuine. He was an innovator in tactics, as she was in business. Hiding his fleet by taking advantage of Earth's orbital position between Mars and the Sun was a good example—being in opposition, the techies called it. It meant Earth was just under sixty million kilometers from Mars, and *that* meant Galatz could reach Earth in less than a day at hard burn. That was about as close to sneak attack range as you could get in the inner system, if the Moon wasn't an option. And it wasn't. It was still considered enemy territory.

"I was worried about you, you know."

Adriana had to replay it to realize Daisy had spoken to her. Knowing she needed to say something, she switched gears. To say nothing would be rude.

"Okay," she said. Then, "I thought I'd lost you. When Fischer came back..." She found anger stirring inside again and embraced it, like she had the pain of arthritis. More proof of life. "That sonofabitch should have checked closer. He should have stopped for five seconds—"

"It wasn't Stacks's fault," Daisy said. "I told him to go. You needed the intel. And Galatz's bombs had the place coming down around our ears... I mean, priorities, right?"

Adriana didn't know what to say to that. Then, "Right."

"The Birch woman," Daisy said. "She seems meek to me. Yours isn't a meek business."

Releasing a small breath, Adriana wished she had a mint. Or anything that wasn't shit flavored.

"No business is a meek business," Adriana said. "She'll do all right. She's got more backbone than first impressions suggest." A mournful feeling tickled her belly, then dissolved into acceptance. "And she's a bean counter, which is practical, and ... she has the willingness to do what's necessary when the chips are down."

Daisy was silent. Maybe checking sensor returns. Maybe not. "All right, then," she said.

"Three hours, you said?"

"Yep."

"In that case, I think I'm going to take a little nap." Adriana sighed, trying to relax. "Not that I'm not enjoying our conversation."

"Sure," Daisy said, something knowing and sad in her voice. "I'll wake you when we're on approach to the *Sovereign*."

"Wake me a few minutes before that." On her right side, the side opposite Daisy, she put her hand on the three remaining hypos from Estevez. Just a little reassurance. "Gives me a little time to spin up before I have to play civilian authority to the good admiral's chestosterone."

"I understand if you have to hurry off, Ms. Brace," Matthias Galatz said. He turned to Adriana. "Are you sure I can't persuade you to remain aboard the —" He couldn't bring himself to say the name of Fischer's ship, Adriana thought. Such a proper military man. "—shuttle? It will get quite hot up here soon, I think."

"I'm here representing the Board of Directors," Adriana said with all the rich-born, self-important authority she could muster. "But thank you for considering my welfare, Admiral."

Galatz's look remained tolerant and taciturn. A tribute to his training, no doubt.

Daisy cleared her throat. "Me, however—I have a mission to fulfill." Her delivery came across as somehow supportive for Adriana's remaining behind. "Admiral, thanks for having your maintenance crew check over the Hearse. The flight here was rigorous. And thanks again for saving my life on Pallas. I still owe you."

Despite his obvious desire to be rid of both civilians, Galatz bowed his head in polite acknowledgment.

"Adriana, a word before I go?" Daisy suggested, already moving off from the admiral. Then, whispering, "Sure you'll be okay here with him?"

Adriana was touched at the genuine concern in her voice. "My dear Daisy, I've been chewing up and spitting out men like Matthias Galatz my whole life. Even with these teeth, I'll be fine."

Daisy laughed lightly.

"What about you?" Adriana said. "Chasing after Fischer… Wherever that man goes, Death seems to sharpen his sickle."

Sobering a little, Daisy retained a wistful smile. "Fischer's good—the best, really. But he's not a spring chicken," she said. "He's more like a winter goose."

"Aren't we all," Adriana said.

"You know what I mean."

"I absolutely know what you mean."

Daisy let her eyes roam the military efficiency on display around them. "We have to win this fight, Adriana, no matter what it takes. Fischer needs me to make sure Jericho takes Cassandra down."

"No matter what it takes. Agreed."

"And on that score..." Daisy said.

"Yes?"

"Take it easy on the drugs."

Adriana wasn't sure she'd heard right. "Drugs?"

Looking her in the eye, Daisy said, "You have a lot to learn about covert ops, Adriana. Estevez's extension drug. I saw you pop another hypo after I hailed the *Sovereign*."

Adriana pushed down the impulse to reprimand Daisy about over-reaching her station. "Oh, that," she said, flicking her fingers. "Don't worry, dear daughter, I'm not abusing it. I promise not to become an addict like those hackheads on Dreamscape."

Daisy's eyes narrowed. "Did you just call me 'dear daughter?'"

"Figure of speech," Adriana said. "You're starting to sound like a concerned child, wondering if it's time to put mother in a home."

"Not that, no." The thoughtful smile returned. "But always concerned. It's my job, you know. To protect you."

"Not anymore, Daisy Brace," Adriana said, raising her chin. "Go protect Fischer. And the future." She was surprised to find her own arms open and Daisy moving into them. The younger woman's embrace was so fierce it hurt her ribs.

"Take care of yourself, old lady," Daisy said. "You only get to come back from the dead once. Trust me, I know."

"Not true," Adriana said into her hair, hoping Daisy could feel the curve of the smile against her cheek. "I've got two hypos left."

The bridge of the SCS *Sovereign* was a hive of curt, practiced efficiency. Orders given, and the brevity in its expression. Quick nods and salutes, acknowledgments for duties accomplished.

"You've confirmed this?" Galatz asked. Gregor Erkennen nodded from the forward screen. He looked tired to Adriana. They were all tired.

"A second fleet, yes," Gregor said. "Launch ready from the far side of the moon, already mobilizing based on the uptake in comm traffic. Cassandra must have been working on this fleet in tandem with the one at Pallas. We exposed her plans there early. But now—"

"—we face two fleets," Galatz finished for him.

"Da. One new and unknown in strength," Gregor said. "The other severely crippled by you but still viable."

Adriana knew Gregor well enough to know he was scared. The human animal reverts when afraid, falls backward into the familiar to feel secure. Gregor's particular remedy was to slip back occasionally into his family's mother tongue.

"Timetable for launch?" Galatz asked.

"Communications are coded and complex, of course," Gregor said, "but we're running decryption algorithms on them now. If I had to guess?"

"Please."

"A day, maybe two. But launch for what purpose, we don't know."

Galatz grunted. "Once Chairman Taulke is dead, they'll need to bring the outer system back into line, and quickly," he said. "Cement their inner-system gains and extend them."

"And we don't know the size of this new fleet," Gregor said.

"In the eighteenth century, the Spanish controlled the Caribbean with a single frigate at times," Galatz replied.

"If there's no fleet to oppose it," Adriana reasoned, "their fleet doesn't have to be that big. It just has to have more firepower than your defenses on Titan. As far as Callisto is concerned, Rabh Regency Station is destroyed. Valhalla Station is still stabilizing, guarded only by a skeleton crew of loyalists vulnerable to orbital bombardment."

"Understood," Gregor said. "We need to end this transmission. We're nearing our time threshold."

"Thank you for the intel, Regent Erkennen," Galatz said without delay. "*Sovereign* out."

Adriana watched the image fade. "So we're the shit in the shit sandwich."

Galatz addressed the *Sovereign*'s commanding officer. "Captain Atreides, best time to Earth and weapons range of the SSR's first fleet? Since there are two now, we'll name her that."

Atreides leaned forward in his command chair. "Castro?"

The ship's navigator made some calculations. "Hard burn from our present position? Half a solar day. We can leverage some momentum sling-shotting around Mars."

Galatz nodded.

"What are you going to do, Admiral?" Adriana asked. She wondered if it was prudent to ask him that here on the bridge. If it might be breaking some kind of military protocol or something.

"Captain?" Galatz said, inviting suggestions.

"There are two fleets to fight now," Atreides said, lining up his facts. "One badly damaged and weak. We've suffered losses too, of course."

Galatz said, "Go on."

"We have no intel on the second fleet. They're a phantom, a rumor."

"A phantom fleet backed with Gregor Erkennen's covert intel and best guess," Adriana said. "That's more than mere rumor."

"Yes. But as Regent Erkennen noted, we don't know their strength," Atreides continued. "Best guess of my own? Planners follow patterns. We were pretty evenly matched against the First Fleet, but we caught them by surprise. At worst, I'd guess we're facing a carbon copy of that in the Phantom Fleet. A few heavy ships, mostly lighter vessels. Frigates for drawing fire and maneuvering."

"Can we deal with two fleets at once?" Adriana asked. "I mean, with any hope of victory?"

"Their crews are green ... ours have years of training," Atreides said. He seemed to be trying to convince himself of something.

"No," Galatz said. "The answer to your question, Regent Rabh, is no."

The members of the bridge had subdued the hubbub of military activity out of respect for the debate. The noise quieted further now.

"Then, what—" Adriana began.

"Captain, if I may?" Galatz interrupted.

"The bridge is yours, Admiral," Atreides said.

"Keep your seat." Galatz held up a hand. "Navigator, plot a course for Earth at hard burn, slingshotting Mars as you suggested. Pass the word to all decks and all ships to prepare to match course and speed. When we arrive, I want a ten percent tighter formation than safety thresholds mandate. We'll form a goddamned spear in space—hit them hard and fast. We spin up in an hour."

"What are you doing?" Adriana asked. She was curious, not scared. Fact was, there was energy passing around the bridge, and the current had caught her too. Potential energy readying to become action.

"We have two enemies to fight," Galatz said. "Right now, they're apart. I'd rather fight them that way, starting with the First Fleet over Earth. It's already weakened—kill that first, then we'll address the stronger threat."

"Okay," she said.

"We'll be spinning up to hard burn soon, Regent," Galatz said. Onscreen, the Hearse arced up and away from the *Sovereign*, headed for Earth. Its trajectory predicted their own. "I'll assign you quarters in the ship's interior, the best-protected part of the ship, before—"

"No," she said.

"—the close action begins. We'll..." Galatz had kept on talking. His ears weren't used to hearing his words confounded. "All respect, Regent, what did you say?"

She hadn't corrected his use of her old title earlier, and she didn't now. The news that Edith Birch was Regent of Callisto had been kept to the few people standing in Justice Hall—by design. She had one more service to render the Company, and no one, not even the admiral in charge of the Corporate Fleet, was going to stop her.

"I said *no*. If the *Sovereign* dies, I don't want it taking *two* of SynCorp's leaders with it. Imagine the public-relations coup for Cassandra."

"Ms. Brace is already on her way. Perhaps you should have—"

"No," Adriana said again, and this time it registered because Galatz stopped speaking. She considered adding *with all due respect* for the sake of the crew. Then she decided, no, with men you had to hit them in the forehead with a two-by-four, not offer subtle hints. "I need to be embedded in this fleet. As a witness. As a member of the Board of Directors. I need to be seen fighting." To Galatz's dubious expression, she said, "Optics, Admiral."

His face pinched, like she'd just passed gas on his bridge. Loudly.

"Then, what do you suggest—"

"There's a frigate in your command, the *Sun Tzu*. Perfect for me, right down to the name. Install me aboard her, and I promise to stay out of your iron-gray hair."

Atreides cleared his throat to cover what might have been giggling from a junior officer.

"As you wish, Regent," Galatz said cryptically. And then, so only she and possibly Atreides could hear, "And with all possible speed."

24

RUBEN QINLAO • OLD #4 LINE, NEW YORK SUBWAY, EARTH

"It smells like shit down here," Ruben said.

Strunk made a clucking sound. "That's because there's shit down here."

The graffitied sign over the stairwell leading down into the New York Subway system's Broadway-Lafayette Street Station advertised connections to the B, D, F, V, and Downtown lines. Ruben wondered if any of those lines were still active. So much flood damage over time had forced the city and later SynCorp to prioritize lines for repair. Most of the east-to-west lines made the cut because they ferried goods and crops from the inner country to New York's coastal distribution nodes for off-world transport. Several of the north-to-south lines had been abandoned entirely. Decades earlier and despite its major artery-like service history across Manhattan Island, the #4 Line was deemed too compromised to rebuild.

Strunk led the way down the narrow stairwell. The concrete steps were slick and pitted by time and neglect, still marked by old flood damage. Ruben had the distinct impression of descending into a first level of Dantesque hell. Leaving the morning light behind them felt like leaving civilization itself behind. The smell was only part of it. The shadowed tunnel below seemed to deny the light access to the Underworld.

At the bottom of the stairwell, Strunk held up.

"Let your eyes adjust to the lower light. Open your ears."

"Okay." Ruben inhaled and regretted needing to breathe. "What am I listening for?"

Strunk's answer was silence.

Ruben took the hint. He closed his eyes to hurry their adjustment to the low light. He tried focusing his ears more on the environment around them. There was the rhythmic *drip ... drip ... drip* of water somewhere close. There was a slight breeze, barely perceptible if you weren't feeling for it, that carried the stench of human waste along with it—and decay and mold. It was the smell of failure. Abandonment.

Ruben opened his eyes. The signage announcing the station's designation remained partially evident: "Br dw y-Laf y tte St."

"Come on," Strunk said.

"Where are we going?" Ruben whispered.

"Grand Central. The subway used to run right underneath the Chrysler Building," Strunk explained. He walked slowly. He seemed a man wary his next step might drop him off a cliff.

"How far?" Ruben asked.

"Couple miles or so."

The farther they walked from the stairwell, the less light showed the way forward.

"You sure we can still get there?" Ruben said. A short distance ahead: what appeared to be a rockfall blocking the tunnel. Not a rockfall—rubble from the old station's walls. Quake damage? Or maybe the floodwaters had carried so much force they'd broken through the concrete.

"Nope," Strunk said. "And, Boss Man, quit asking questions. Minimize the noise—" His hand came up then, holding a stunner taken off one of Lasker's crew. "Hold up," he whispered. "We ain't alone."

Ruben squinted ahead, saw what had given Strunk pause. A sputtering light near the pile of rubble—orange, not silver from one of the old LED tubes, had there been electricity to power them. Firelight.

"Use your stunner," Strunk whispered. "Keeps the killing quiet." He moved to the edge of the platform and crawled quietly down into the channel that had once carried subway trains.

"Weren't these trains powered with electricity running through the tracks?" Ruben asked quietly. He hopped down, careful to avoid touching the rails. A rat squeaked next to his feet, then skittered away.

"Third rail, yeah."

"How do we know—"

"Last question, Boss Man," Strunk hissed. He bent over and picked the rat up. It struggled and screeched, its tail whipping frantically. There was just enough light from street level for Ruben to see its beady, red eyes. "Let's test your concern."

Strunk held the creature at arm's length, then dropped it onto the thick center rail. The rat squeaked when it hit the rail, then scrambled over it and away.

"Confirmed," Strunk said. "Electricity is off."

"Okay, then."

"Come on. Let's see if we can get past."

They walked inside the rail channel, keeping the platform at shoulder height and on their right. The flickering firelight drew closer at their two o'clock, as did the pile of crumbled tunnel architecture. Ruben could make out the sound of running water. More than the slow drip from earlier—this had a current to it. Other orange flickering appeared from the darkness, moving toward them through the shadows.

"Hold your piece with both hands," Strunk growled. "Shoot for center mass. Remember we're five feet lower than—"

"Now, that ain't too friendly," a man's voice said. The light flared a bit as several torches converged. In the glimmering spotlight they created, a large black man appeared. "Y'all oughta lower those electric boogaloos and come on up outta there. The rats are hungry."

"Already introduced myself to King Rat," Strunk answered, keeping his voice neutral but full of baleful resolve. "He and me? We've got an understanding." Other shapes, indistinct and freakishly tall, hovered at the edges of light surrounding the first man. Ruben reminded himself they were standing a level higher. "And I'm guessing those rags you're wearing ain't MESH," Strunk went on. "So I'll just keep aiming my piece at your fun bits."

The man smiled, and it almost seemed genuine. There was a thin line of beard running from one ear to the other, lining his jaw and chin.

Without a mustache, it framed his African face like the sidepieces of a Roman helmet. The tightly knitted dreadlocks encasing his head added to the image.

"Here's the thing, bro," he said, "y'all can't even see all of us. Whereas, we can see both of y'all. So—y'all might kill some, me even, but then you'd be fallen upon like the aforementioned rats on a fresh corpse. In this analogy, y'all are the corpses. There are few more horrific things, if you've never seen it. It's like the reverse of rats fleeing a sinking ship. Who knew the human body could hold so much blood?"

Ruben's palms were moist on the grips of his stunner. Strunk seemed to be considering his options.

"Name?" Strunk said. "Affiliation?"

"Bryce Kenneth Paré," the man said without hesitation. "I run the Lafayette Pirates between B&L Station and the L-Line."

"Never heard of you," Strunk said.

"That's how we like it," Paré said. His shrug in the half light felt unnecessary, part of a welcome ritual he'd practiced. I'm nobody to fear, it promised. "A pirate with reputation is a pirate with problems, eh?"

"Your naming yourselves pirates isn't motivating us to lower our weapons," Ruben said with a glibness he didn't feel.

Paré shrugged again. "I could call us the Schoolteachers Association of Lower Manhattan, but I don't think you'd buy it. And I was hoping y'all were intelligent and would be motivated by a half-dozen weapons pointed at you."

Paré stepped closer to the edge. Ruben felt Strunk tense next to him. He adjusted his sweaty grip on his own stunner but maintained trigger discipline.

"Y'all marshals?" Paré said. His tone sounded narrow, like eyes trying to make out something mysterious.

"Used to be," Strunk said before Ruben could speak again. "Before the Company got knocked on its ass."

Paré made a sympathetic sound. "We all used to be something before then. Times are tougher now. Gotta go where the opportunities are."

"Yeah," Strunk allowed.

"Well, y'all come on up outta there," Paré said again, stooping and offering an arm up. "We'll get our business done and even escort you to the L. You're the GCB's problem after that."

"What business?" Ruben said. "Who's the GCB?"

"The Grand Central Boys. They control from the L-Line to the hub station. As for business—y'all give us what you got," Paré said with that practiced quality to it. "Leave with your lives. I'll throw in safe passage to the L."

Strunk made a sound that might have been laughter. "How about we keep what we've got. And let you leave with *your* lives."

On the platform, a pistol cocked in the darkness. Feet moved. The torches wandered a bit.

"Well, now, that would be unfortunate for us, I suppose," Paré said. "But we have the numbers. And the high ground. So let's keep everyone's blood bagged, shall we?"

There was a squeak-squeak next to him. Another rat. Ruben side-eyed Strunk's position, but the big man had vanished.

"Where you gone to, hoss?" Paré asked. His tone suggested things were taking a turn that was testing the last of his patience. Two of the torches began to move on Ruben's left, searching for Strunk. In their glare a shotgun appeared in Paré's hands.

The squeak became a squeal. Tiny feet scratched across the concrete platform. The torches bobbed, looking for it.

"It's just a goddamned rat," Paré said. "Ignore it. Find the loudmouth."

Punk!

At the sound of Strunk's stunner, Ruben dived for darkness. He heard cursing in Paré's southern baritone. A torch hit the platform, showing the rat's tail whipping left and right as it fled.

"Shouldn't'a oughta done that, hoss," Paré said, lost in the shadows. His voice echoed now in a way it hadn't before. "All we need's your heads. Coulda left 'em attached."

Ruben scuttled along the channel deeper into the tunnel. He turned, braced his stunner on the lip of the platform and squeezed off two shots.

Punk! Punk!

Another torch fell. Ruben levered himself onto the platform and lay prostrate, waiting for opportunity.

"Drop those spotlights, morons!" Paré shouted. He'd moved too. "They're tracking you!"

Boom!

A shotgun blast lit up the tunnel. Dozens of tiny shot from the shell scored concrete. Metal rang, reverberating around the wet platform. Paré was taking a sounding with that shot, Ruben figured, trying to connect.

Boom!

A second blast was followed by the horizontal rain of impacting buckshot.

How many of the pirates were left? Ruben had counted half a dozen torches before, so that suggested four but assumed every pirate was holding a torch. And Paré had seemed to confirm that number when he'd threatened them with *motivation*. But there could be twice that many, three times for all Ruben knew. He rolled to his left and slammed into something solid. Subway car, lying on its side on the platform.

Opportunity.

"Still with us, Strunk?" Paré teased. "Didn't get y'all with that side-by-side, did I? All we need's the heads, boys!"

Silence from Strunk, assuming he was still alive. Ruben worked himself around the overturned Pullman car, away from Paré's voice. With the car for cover he found a handhold and began to climb. It dawned on him suddenly that Paré knew Strunk's name.

There was a hard, smacking sound from below. A fist smashing into a jaw, followed by the thick, staccato sound of a stunner.

Punk!

"That answer your fucking question?" Strunk called.

Relief flooded through Ruben.

Boom!

Another shotgun blast in the direction of Strunk's voice.

"How about now?" Paré demanded.

Boom!

"How about *now*?"

Two fucking bulls, Ruben thought. *Both too fucking stupid to fight in silence.*

"Throw those torches over there," Paré ordered his men. He was so close, Ruben could hear him shucking shells and reloading. The shotgun barrels snapped back into the stock. "Time to bag these sumbitches."

Ruben lay flat on the side of the Pullman car, the cold metal slippery-slick from years in the tunnel. Three torches were briefly hoisted, then tossed at the blast marks left by Paré's shotgun. In the spatter of firelight, he saw Strunk jerk back into the shadows.

Boom!

The noise was so deafening, Ruben's ears rang. The blast from the end of the barrel reflected upward on Paré, his grin wide, eyes alive with a feral desire to kill Strunk.

Opportunity.

Ruben aimed. He fired.

Punk! Punk!

He missed.

Boom!

The wind from the buckshot sped past. Something seared his left cheek as he rolled away from the blast.

"Found the pretty one, boys!"

Ruben's hand came away slick when he checked the side of his face.

Fuck this shoot-out bullshit.

Stowing the stunner, he pulled his katara dagger. Below, someone yelped and then had their airway abruptly interrupted. Strunk, still vertical and killing.

Boom!

Leaping from the Pullman car, Ruben aimed for the flash of the shotgun blast.

Boom!

The second shot went wild as Ruben slammed into Paré from behind. The bigger man tried to turn, but Ruben wrapped his legs around Paré's torso, then encircled his head with one hand and dragged the knife from one side of his thin beard to the other. A brief cry of pain became desperate and wet. Paré's blood gushed onto his shirtfront. His knees gave way, spilling them both onto the platform.

"Your boss is dead!" Ruben shouted, rolling off the still-struggling Paré. He kicked the shotgun out of reach.

"Y'all stick around and join 'im!" Strunk added from the darkness, mocking Paré's accent. "We're just gettin' this here party started!"

There was the sound of running feet, dashing away. The only noises left on the platform were the distant sound of rushing water and Paré's final death throes.

"Nice work, Boss Man," Strunk said. He'd picked up a torch and took a moment to examine Ruben's handiwork. "I see you got sliced."

"Paré's shotgun."

Strunk grunted, sounding half impressed, half incredulous. "You got lucky, then."

"Yeah."

"Here, give me that knife. Hold this."

Ruben exchanged his katara for Strunk's torch.

"Hold it over here, where I can see." Strunk knelt next to the motionless Paré. "Goddamned blood everywhere... And watch our backs."

"What *was* this?" Ruben asked. "How'd he know your name? How'd you know he wasn't on the up-and-up—"

"I didn't." Strunk's voice took on the quality of physical effort. "But I wasn't about to give up our guns. It was an ambush, I think. The Laskers, likely putting out the word to the street gangs like we thought. Above and below ground, too."

Ruben flinched. In the firelight, he could see Strunk's arm making sawing motions. "Is that absolutely necessary?"

Strunk paused. "The neckbone's the hardest. Ever eat a chicken neck? You can gnaw it for a week and you won't get all the way through."

"Is this *necessary*?" Ruben repeated.

"If you'd rather carry this big motherfucker the whole way, I'll stop," Strunk said. To Ruben's silence, he continued, "It's an offering. You heard Paré mention our heads—proof of death for Matteo Lasker. Tables are turned now." More grunting, more sawing. "This is *not* a good knife for this kind of work."

"An offering? To who?"

"The Grand Central Boys." The sounds of sawing ceased again. "The pirates who ran will do some dick measuring—personal combat, or maybe they'll pull stones from a fucking hate—to take Paré's crown. We need to beeline it to the L-Line border. Maybe the GC Boys'll be grateful we took out the leader of their neighboring competition."

"Maybe? What's to stop them from pulling the same shit? The Laskers are probably offering a fortune for us."

"Yeah," Strunk said, resuming his exertions. "It is what it is."

Ruben sighed, but it wasn't a defeated sound. "You know, Strunk, I'm getting good and goddamned tired of being jerked around like a goddamned puppet on a goddamned string. Hiding and running in the shadows. When we walk across the L-Line, we'll deal with the Boys from a position of strength."

"That was where my head was at," Strunk said. "Or his, anyway." There was a muffled clunk. Paré's head, hitting the platform. Illuminated by the torch in Ruben's hand, Strunk looked up. "But you were right about the same shit maybe happening. How you gonna motivate the GC Boys to think outside the box, Boss Man? Point guns at 'em like Paré? We're a little light on that front."

Ruben raised the torch. Framed in matted dreadlocks, the open-mouthed head of Bryce Kenneth Paré stared back at him. Ruben shifted the torch and his hard eyes to Strunk.

"I'll make them an offer they can't refuse."

25

STACKS FISCHER • APPROACHING OLD NEW
YORK CITY, EARTH

The Earth is spectacular from a distance. I'd been away long enough that seeing its blue-green surface and wispy clouds tugged a bit at an old man's heartstrings. The terraforming on Mars is impressive, and that people can exist at all on Callisto and Titan is a tribute to man's ability to carve life out of dead places. But there's no place like home, Dorothy.

I'd had a handful of hours since leaving the Moon to worry about Minnie. How had the SSR known to target the lab? Distracted by the import of the intel I had, maybe I hadn't been careful enough making my way back there. Maybe Cassandra had broken Erkennen's super-secret channel-hopping protocol. Or maybe the simplest answer was the likeliest answer, and Minnie had given me up under duress. That didn't explain how they knew to target the lab, though, so maybe it really was that I hadn't been careful enough. For Minnie's sake, I hoped so.

"Approaching New York airspace," Bekah reported.

We dropped fairly quickly and without incident through the atmosphere. I got a little antsy when all I could see were those wispy clouds around us, but Bekah never lost focus. Pretty soon we were gazing at the patchwork countryside on the horizon, the deep blue of the Atlantic stretching away in every direction below us. Then, signs of industrial life— the old dockside facilities of New York Harbor, now modernized for freighters like the *Earn*. Aircars jotting through the new morning sky. The former coastline of Old New York, drowned by flooding in the middle of the last century, skeletal girders and washed-out walls still visible.

"Thank God and Gregor Erkennen," Bekah said.

"Yeah?"

"I'm monitoring local air traffic control," she said. "No one knows we're here."

"Excellent news."

We flew over the still-habitable areas of Long Island, a high-tech ghost passing overhead. People looking up could see us, of course, but to them we'd just be one more—if butt-ugly and boxy-shaped—vehicle cruising the airways.

"There's the UN Building."

I took a deep breath and stretched. The last couple of days in unregulated lunar gravity followed by the three-hour hop to Earth had made my lazy bones lazier. My left knee began its whining early.

"Hey, Stacks, look," she said. "Isn't that—"

The nostalgia at seeing Earth again flushed out of my brain. I forgot my worries over Minnie. Even my left knee shut up.

"The Hearse!"

On the rooftop below sat my own best girlfriend in all her sleek, slightly dinged-up beauty. I couldn't believe it! But the pleasantness of the surprise wore off quickly. If the Hearse was here, that meant Daisy Brace was here, too.

"Get us down there," I said to Bekah.

"Well, yeah. That was the plan."

I could see the Hearse wasn't alone. There was a body—make that two —nearby, both unmoving. I flashed back to Pallas and that flight deck where I'd left a disabled Daisy behind—one of a handful of lifelong regrets I'd always have. By the time Bekah brought the *Coyote* to rest on the roof, I could see neither body was hers. They were SSR troopers.

Ignoring my achy muscles, I stripped the vac-suit quickly, snagged my longcoat and hat, and double-checked my weapons.

"Stacks, wait, we have to be careful."

"You're right, you do," I said. "Wait here till I signal."

"Signal how?" Bekah said, starting to unstrap from the pilot's seat. "You don't have an implant!"

"I'll manage."

"Stacks, wait!"

Protests from my left knee were lost in a chorus of similar complaints from other body parts as I made the short jump down from the ship.

I quickly examined the Soldiers. Each had a mortal bullet wound. That was Daisy, giving me intel. The fact that she hadn't used stunner tech to kill the troopers suggested they were likely wearing armor reinforced with MESH. I'd be relying on my .38. Then again ... I snagged an M24 automatic rifle and slung it on my back, along with extra magazines from them that didn't need 'em anymore.

"Stacks!" Bekah called. She hopped down from the *Coyote*. "We need to be cautious."

"Daisy's in there," I said, pointing at the roof's access hatch. The cover was lifted, propped open. Hanging over the lip—another unfortunate SSR recruit. I bent down and picked up a sidearm and an extra magazine from the Soldier at my feet.

"But you don't even know where she is," Bekah said.

"I'll just follow the trail of dead Soldiers."

Bekah put her hand on my arm. "Stacks, Daisy's not the mission. Cassandra is the mission."

I almost barked back. I almost cursed a kid for not knowing me better than that. But I didn't because Bekah was absolutely right. Well, mostly right.

"You're mostly right," I said. "But Daisy will be where Cassandra is. We're all on the *same* mission, right? Find Daisy, find Cassandra."

Bekah sighed. "Okay."

I handed her the 11-millimeter pistol and magazines I'd taken off the dead trooper.

"For comfort?" she said.

"And killing. Come on."

I made for the access hatch.

"I'll scan CorpNet, see if I can find out what's happening inside."

But I knew that info wouldn't be on CorpNet. It was need-to-know. The real-time info I needed would only be on a military frequency. We'd be flying blinder here than in the *Coyote*.

"Hey! Tony's still alive," she said.

"Good to know," I said. "Now, keep the talk to a minimum."

We found another breadcrumb of a dead body at the bottom of the stairs. I held my revolver in a tight, greasy grip while I reconnoitered the next level down. Maybe I was still smarting over what might've happened to Minnie. Or maybe I was loath to admit that Daisy, alone, had no chance against a building full of snake troops. Maybe she was already dead.

Stop that, Fischer. Stop that right now.

"One more level," Bekah said.

"What? How do you know?"

She tapped her temple. "Building plans are online."

I could feel my forehead wrinkle up. That didn't make sense—the floor plan for the lair of the Snake Queen was online?

"Remember, this is a historical building now, a tourist thing," Bekah said, smiling. "If you want, I can get us to the gift shop."

"Maybe later. One more set of stairs?"

"Yeah, and then we're at the top floor of apartment suites. Cassandra's home, if you believe the vids."

Worked for me. That seemed as reasonable a place as any to start looking for Daisy.

I started to round the corner of the stairwell.

Punk! Punk!

What felt like fists hit my longcoat—the slugs fired by the stunner. My ribs took the impact. I stumbled on the stairs, surprised, and Bekah Franklin grabbed the lapels of my coat and pulled me back into cover.

"Maybe I should rethink this barrel-forward strategy," I said, rubbing my ribs.

"You think?"

We were stuck. The enemy—I assumed there was only one—had used a stunner. As long as he didn't aim for my feet or head, my longcoat should protect me from my life coming to a shocking end. I figured I had one more shot before he wised up and went old school on me with an automatic weapon.

More to the point, we were cut off from Daisy. She was down below somewhere and maybe being flanked by this guy's buddies. If she was even still alive.

Shut that shit up.

Nothing for it but to go for broke.

"You stay back," I said, "and keep that hypo safe. Even beyond your own life, Bekah."

"Whatever it takes," she said. "I've known that since Masada."

I nodded at her and unslung the M24 from my back. "I need you to fire this thing."

"I don't know how to use one of those!" Bekah protested.

Punk! Punk-punk!

The enemy below, reminding us he was there.

"You don't have to. Just don't shoot me in the back. I'm going to lay down cover fire for myself, then move down the stairs. I can't move as fast as I used to, but if you can shoot into the air while I'm moving, it should keep any heads down."

She stared at me. Then, "Okay."

Punk-punk!

Kneeling, I brought the barrel around the corner of the stairwell and fired.

Bracka-bracka-bracka-bracka-bracka-bracka-bracka!

My shoulder was numb from the kickback. I handed the M24 to Bekah, darted my eyes at the ceiling, and went around the corner, my .38 in my unnumbed hand. I was three steps down, my knee screaming, when Bekah fired into the ceiling.

Bracka-bracka-bracka-bracka-bracka!

She was screaming too, and I didn't know if it was for effect or because she was terrified.

I swung around the base of the stairs and—shit!—found *two* Soldiers ready to rock. My .38 came around, taking the first one in the forehead.

Crack!

His buddy brought up a stunner. I turned aside, bracing my longcoat with my empty hand like a shield.

Punk-punk!

The slugs hit my coat, the force of their impacts making me stumble again.

Bracka-bracka-bracka!

That was Bekah upstairs, still firing. I barreled forward at the Soldier, landing on top of him and knocking the stunner aside. He was young like those kids had been on Masada Station, and I could see the fear in his eyes —fear that his training wasn't enough, that his friend was dead and couldn't help. I pinned his shooting arm to the floor, wedged my .38 under his chin, and pulled the trigger.

Crack!

The kid's brains painted the white wall. The noise rang in the empty stairwell. When my ears began to clear, I could hear another firefight, farther in.

Daisy.

"Get down here!" I called to Bekah. "Hurry!"

I was surprised to find the corridor beyond the access door empty. I reconnoitered as I reloaded my revolver. Bekah knelt beside me, close enough that I could feel her trembling.

"I think I might be sick," she whispered, her gaze focused on the slow creep of brain matter trailing down the wall.

"Hold it in," I said through gritted teeth. Daisy was through that door. "There'll be time for that later."

"Okay," Bekah said. "Here, take this back. Please."

I stowed the .38 and took back the rifle, replacing its empty magazine.

Inside, gunfire blasted.

I turned to Bekah. "Do what I say. This is my business, now. Understood?"

"Yes."

I pushed through the door. There was blood on the floor. The room was large, with half a dozen wide columns running along both sides. On the other side of the room, a large window overlooked the city, floor to ceiling. Against the back wall, a raised platform, the "throne" everyone in Sol had seen by now, Cassandra's perch for all her broadcasts. In front of it—what remained of Elise Kisaan's head on its pike. Three dead Soldiers littered the floor. More of Daisy's handiwork.

Somehow she'd made it to the second column along the near wall. Her back was against it, her legs splayed out in front of her. Each hand held a pistol, one of them empty, its slide sprung. She looked ashen, and I found the source of the blood streaking the floor. It made a trail all the way from the doorway to the stomach of Daisy's soaked-through bodysuit.

Shit.

I wasn't about to let her almost-die on me a second time.

From behind Cassandra's throne, a rifle barrel appeared, peppering Daisy's column.

Bracka-bracka-bracka!

Suppression fire. She shrunk away, her hands moving lazily. She'd lost a lot of blood. From the column opposite her position, another rifle fired.

Bracka-bracka-bracka-bracka!

Hemming her in. Eventually, she'd give up too much cover, left or right.

"I can't leave you here," I told Bekah, "but Daisy's cover isn't big enough for three of us. Follow me to the first column. I'll plant you there and see to Daisy."

"Okay."

The SSR troops hadn't seen us yet. I quick-stepped from the access door to the first column. When I was there and set, I motioned for Bekah to join me.

They saw her when she moved from the door.

Bracka-bracka-bracka!

Bullets pocked the wall behind her.

"Keep moving!" I shouted. "Don't stop!"

I aimed around my own column and returned fire.

Bracka-bracka-bracka-bracka-bracka-bracka-bracka!

Bekah collapsed next to me.

"Are you hurt?" I asked.

"No."

"Good. Stay here." I was already on my feet and moving to Daisy's column before the enemy brought their heads back up.

Bracka-bracka-bracka!

They'd aimed for where they thought I was—Bekah's column. She'd be safe, as long as she stayed hidden.

"You're late," Daisy said. Her eyes smiled, but her voice was weak. Barely audible amid the echo of automatic weapons fire.

"What do you mean, coming in here alone?"

"Looking for you," she breathed. "Jericho..."

"You're a fucking idiot," I said. "But I'm here now. Better late than never, huh?"

"Maybe," she whispered.

"Stop talking like that ... Daisy?"

She'd passed out. I needed to field dress her wound, but I had nothing, *nothing* to work with.

Bracka-bracka-bracka!

The SSR, testing our resolve. I couldn't shoot *and* dress Daisy's wound.

One thing at a time. I took the pistol with the sprung slide and pressed it against her gut. Daisy stirred, moaning with the pain of the pressure. I took off my belt and wrapped it behind her, binding up her midsection and the pistol to the wound. It was a poor substitute for what she needed.

Feet were moving—the SSR trooper behind the half-breed's throne getting brave. I showed him the error of his ways.

Bracka-bracka-bracka-bracka-bracka-bracka-bracka-bracka-bracka!

His Kevlar caught most of it, but I'd gotten lucky, too. He went down. Two more rifles opened up from across the room from two more columns. Enemy reinforcements had arrived.

"Stacks!"

Bekah, loud and clear, like a pistol shot. I turned and found my worst nightmare staring back at me. Cassandra, the Snake Queen herself, flanked by two SSR troopers. They'd come in through the same door we had, probably to flank Daisy.

"Cease fire!" Cassandra said, victory spreading across her face. The room went quiet with the ringing absence of gunfire. I half-considered going for broke again and mowing Cassandra down right then and there. But I'd have to kill Bekah to do it, and maybe that's exactly the price that needed paying. I looked down—Daisy was still unconscious, my poor excuse for a tourniquet doing little if any good.

"Throw down your weapons!" Cassandra ordered. She held Bekah around the throat, one hand squeezing, Bekah clawing at it. Cassandra held

Bekah's other arm pinned behind her back. "This is over. You'll die next to Tony Taulke, Eugene Fischer. Another old symbol of the old regime, uprooted and discarded."

"Whatever it takes!" Bekah shouted. "Do it, Stacks!"

Around the corner of the third column to my right, one of the Kisaan clones appeared. She held an M24 on Daisy and me. I looked back to Bekah.

"Do it!" Bekah said.

Cassandra's golden eyes dared me to be so bold.

"What's happening?" Daisy asked, roused to semi-consciousness. She saw me put down the rifle and began shaking her head. "No, Stacks, no..."

"We can't win if we're dead," I said. She kept shaking her head, but it was more willpower to win than real belief that we could. I lifted my hands and stood. "All right!" I called out. "We're laying down our weapons. Don't shoot!"

26

RUBEN QINLAO • CHRYSLER BUILDING, OLD NEW
YORK CITY, EARTH

The Grand Central Boys hadn't refused Ruben's deal.

There'd been no skulking around, no careful sneaking across the terri-
torial border at the L-Line. Ruben had simply led Strunk into GCB territory
until they'd been stopped. Then he'd ordered the enforcer to unroll Paré's
head from the dead man's poncho. The GCB patrol had been suitably
impressed. Their choices were simple, Ruben had said: hope for a payoff
from the Laskers for turning them in, or stick Paré's head on a pole and
march into the base of what remained of the Lafayette Pirates and annex
their territory to the Boys' own.

"Display a head, double your spread," Strunk said, laughing, to the
GCB patrol. "Advancement by decapitation is all the rage, now."

"Then, when all this is over and Taulke is back on top," Ruben had
added, "we'll bring you twice what the Laskers are offering."

The Boys hadn't just let them pass, they'd escorted Ruben and Strunk to
their home base at Grand Central Station. From there, Strunk's theory of an
old leg of the subway running beneath the Chrysler Building had proven
right. They'd followed the tunnel under torchlight, soon discovering faded,
cracked lettering that advertised "barber shops – telephones – restaurant –
specialty shops just ahead" and what must have been a popular destination
for the well-to-do in its day, the Chrysler Beauty Salon. An arrow painted

with seriffed elegance on the wall had even helpfully pointed the way. And now they stared from the shadows once more as two SSR troopers guarded a freight elevator located in the basement of the Chrysler Building itself. Sixty or seventy meters separated them across the abandoned subway platform.

"That's a lot of killing zone," Strunk remarked.

"But we need to move," Ruben said. "We have no idea what's happening with Tony. Cassandra could be putting him against a wall right now."

Impulse to action.

"Like we talked about?" Strunk said.

"Yeah." Ruben adjusted his marshal's cap. Strunk had lost his somewhere in the tunnels. Both men stood up and walked boldly forward, as they had in crossing the boundary between the two gangs' territories. And, as then, Ruben led the way.

Both Soldiers came to alert.

The trick, Strunk explained earlier, was to keep walking even when they ordered him to stop—but not to get killed. Success meant reaching can't-miss small arms' range by the time things got mortal.

One of the Soldiers whispered something, his attention diverted by opening comms on his sceye. The second unslung his automatic rifle.

"Hold up there," Soldier Two said. "This building is restricted to SSR only."

Ruben opened his hands near his hips to show they were empty. But he didn't stop walking forward.

"Orders from Central," he said in a raised voice so they could hear him clearly. He was careful to keep his hands open. Behind him, he could feel Strunk hunching, trying to hide the threat of his height and width. In other circumstances, it would have been amusing. "Gangs getting surly below. We're here for backup."

In a hoarse whisper, Strunk said, "Cover more ground."

Ruben increased his stride length but kept his pace.

"I said stop where you are!" Soldier Two pointed his rifle at Ruben. Soldier One finished his sceye conversation and whispered to the other.

"Slow it down," Strunk whispered.

Ruben made a show of slowing his pace, but his stride stayed long. He raised his hands over his head, the universal subliminal signal for *I'm not a threat*.

"Come on, Barry," Strunk said in a nasal stage whisper. "We ain't gettin' paid enough to get shot by the snakes."

"Stop, goddamnit!" Soldier Two raised his rifle to his shoulder. Soldier One unslung and raised his own weapon in one fluid motion.

Ruben stopped in his tracks, and Strunk did the same. The enforcer took two lateral paces to Ruben's right. He didn't raise his hands.

The charade of walking while talking had brought them within ten meters of the Soldiers.

"What the hell happened to you?" Soldier Two asked, nodding his rifle barrel at Strunk. Since Strunk had moved apart from Ruben, both guards could see the front of the big man's uniform. It was covered in Paré's blood.

"Told you," Ruben said, talking as much with his hands as his mouth. Their eyes went to him. "Gangs are stirred up. But they've got a few less members now." He laughed the knowing laugh of a man in a war zone, ego made fat on enemy kills.

Soldier One made an appreciative sound.

"How's Taulke?" Strunk asked. "Quaking in his float-chair?"

Soldier One lowered his rifle a tick. "That crazy motherfucker won't shut up. They have to tranq him, over and over. But he'll be shut up permanent soon enough."

"Yeah," Ruben said, lowering his hands.

"You boys need to turn around," Soldier Two said. "No marshals allowed. Sorry, but your reputation isn't exactly stellar for loyalties. There's a stairwell to the surface from Grand Central. You passed it coming here."

"Right," Strunk said in his affected whine. "I remember seeing that, Barry."

"Right," Ruben said. "Me, too."

"No hard feelings, fellas," Soldier One said. His rifle dropped to point at the floor. "We've got our orders."

"Sure, sure," Strunk said, "and no hard feelings at all. Barry?"

Ruben launched himself to the left, tumbling across the cold concrete. Soldier Two followed him with the barrel of his rifle but held fire. Soldier One opened his mouth.

Strunk drew two hand weapons from behind his back: an 11-millimeter and a stunner. They'd talked about this—would the SSR have MESH armor now or simply Kevlar? He fired both in rapid succession.

Crack! Crack!

Punk! Punk!

Both Soldiers fell. Soldier Two died immediately, a bullet in the brain. Soldier One collapsed, crying out from a wound to the groin. Strunk's bullet had found where the armor pieces met. As the enforcer approached, the trooper made a grab for his weapon, but Strunk kicked it away.

"Two choices," Strunk said. He placed a foot on the man's groin and pressed. "Quick or not-so-quick."

Soldier One cried out. Approaching, Ruben read the name stitched on the left breast of the man's uniform: *Weiss.*

Strunk pressed again.

"Strunk." Ruben's voice was less warning, more of a plea. "We need information."

"What do you want?" Weiss rasped.

"Taulke's location. Specifics."

"The twenty-first floor!"

Strunk adjusted his foot. Tears began forming in the corners of Weiss's eyes. "That was easy," Strunk said, unconvinced. "And a bit random."

"It is!" Weiss insisted. "That's the point!"

Ruben touched Strunk's arm and they shared a moment of silent debate. Strunk carried murder in his eyes. Weiss's fate was already written, and his pain meant less than nothing to Strunk. But he removed his foot, and the Soldier's relief blew out of him.

"Explain," Ruben said.

"Elinda expects a rescue attempt," Weiss explained. "So they picked a random floor for Taulke's bunker."

"Elinda?" Ruben said. "Elinda Kisaan?"

"Yeah. She's..." Grimacing, Weiss continued, "She's in charge of Taulke's security detail."

A warm feeling erupted behind Ruben's ribs, radiated through his core and out into his limbs. It burned hot. It was all he could do not to press his own foot into the trooper's groin.

"Where on the twenty-first floor?" he demanded.

"Don't know," Weiss said.

"All right, then," Strunk shrugged, aiming his 11-millimeter.

Terror lit Weiss's eyes. "No, wait—"

Crack!

The sharp report filled the subway tunnel.

"And before you ask," Strunk said, "yes, that was absolutely necessary."

Weiss's head lolled against his shoulder.

"I know," Ruben said. "I know it was."

"I said before that we needed to lose these uniforms," Strunk said. "Now we have something better. Help me strip these guys."

Ruben did so, his actions automatic, mechanical. His mind was elsewise occupied with images of Elinda Kisaan standing over Mai Pang's bloody corpse in the bedroom on Mars. The assassin who'd murdered his lover was here, guarding Tony Taulke.

"We'll send the vator up empty. That'll give them seventy-seven floors worth of possibilities to think about. Meanwhile, we'll go up the stairs, just one more sweep team, looking for the intruders."

Strunk motioned for Ruben to pick up one of the bodies. He hauled his own burden to the ancient railway channel, then dumped the deadweight onto the rusty track five feet below. "What are you smiling about?" he asked. "If you can even call that a smile."

Ruben dragged his own burden to the lip of the platform. He pushed the second trooper over with his toe. "Sometimes the universe surprises you, Strunk. On occasion, it even tilts toward justice."

Grunting, Strunk stood up straight and stretched. "Hasn't been my experience," he said, leading them back to the stairwell entrance. He opened the door and made way for Ruben.

The Regent of Mars led the way, saying, "I guess we'll see."

"It's like they patterned this place after Callisto," Strunk said as they climbed the stairs. Since leaving the abandoned subway, he'd kept up a mumbling commentary on the Chrysler Building's architectural style.

Everywhere arrows pointed upward. The coppery luster of the walls that was the design standard for the building extended even to the stairwells. The entire building seemed plated in copper, then painted with a bourbon-metallic sheen that invited natural sunlight to make it glow. "Which is funny, given they built this place a couple hundred years before anyone had even visited there."

Ruben ignored him, ignored the harried reports from SSR sweep teams looking for them, ignored the burning in his upper thighs from Earth gravity and twenty stories' worth of physical effort. Even freeing Tony had taken a back seat to settling accounts with Elinda Kisaan. A part of him knew it was dangerous to think that way. Knew the myopia of seeking personal revenge had every chance of absolutely compromising the mission. At least the voice in the back of his head that knew those things was gaining volume. The climb up the last ten flights or so had helped him focus it.

"Hold up, Boss Man," Strunk said. "We've been balls-to-the-wall, and we've been lucky and we're where we need to be. Now, a little caution is called for."

Ruben made a conscious effort to get his emotions under control. Strunk was right, of course. They *had* been lucky. Their infiltration masquerading as Soldiers had worked. Even the elevator with its mad dash to the top floor of the Chrysler Building had drawn resources and manpower out of their path. The one sweep team they'd met headed in the other direction from an upper floor had taken them at face value, their uniforms, Strunk's bravado, and the chaos of searching for two needles in a building-sized haystack weighing in their favor. It had all passed as a red blur to Ruben. But now, next to the door, in stark black and white—black, block numbers surrounded by a square of chipping white paint—read the floor designation: *21*.

"You got my back?" Strunk asked. "Cuz I'm less than confident. What-ever the hell's focused you like a goddamned laser—it feels dangerous. I need to know what it is."

Looking him in the eye because Strunk deserved that, Ruben said, "It's personal. The Kisaan clone, the one guarding Tony? We have a history."

"Do you, now." Strunk's tone held all the you're-just-now-telling-me-this? it could carry.

"She murdered my..." Not girlfriend, not yet. They hadn't quite formalized things that way, had they? They hadn't had the chance. "My friend, Mai. On Mars."

"Mai?" Strunk said. "Not Mai Pang, Tony's receptionist?"

Ruben's gaze answered for him.

"Shit."

"I thought you knew," Ruben said. "I mean, I assumed..."

"No, I mean ... I didn't know the woman beyond a howdy-do outside Tony's office. And, no offense, I don't really care that she's dead." Strunk raised a hand. "No disrespect. But brain cells need to be focused now."

A door slammed against a wall somewhere far above. The echo in the stairwell made it hard to gauge the distance. Another sweep team from the upper floors, headed down.

"This can't be personal, Boss Man," Strunk said quickly. "Killing is a cold business. It's gotta be. Emotion gets into it, and suddenly there are wildcards all over the table. We're here. Tony's here. This is for all the marbles, Qinlao."

There were boots marching down the stairs now.

"I'd just as soon not have to masquerade again," Strunk said. "Luck is a feckless bitch. These fellas coming, they might pay more attention."

"I'm good. I've got your back. Go, Strunk."

Gritting his teeth, Strunk opened the door, then covered the corridor with his stunner and 11-millimeter, ready to deal out two kinds of death, as he had earlier. "Empty as a hooker's sighs," he said. "Hurry up, now."

Once Ruben passed through, Strunk closed the door quietly, then held up a stern hand. The boots thumped past on the stairs beyond the door, continuing their sweep downward.

Strunk nodded. "Now we go."

27

ADRIANA RABH • ABOARD THE SUN TZU

"The admiral's orders were quite clear," said Captain Nuss.

"Fuck the admiral's orders!" Adriana shouted.

Onscreen, the battle over Earth played out like a sim-parlor joyride. It was bright and deadly and impersonal and distant. Crimson point defense rounds traced paths from counter-battery fire as starships engaged in close action.

"Mr. Shelby, pull us out another ten-thousand kilometers," Nuss ordered. It was all Adriana could do not to strangle him. "Pass the word to the *Sapphire of Sol* and *Venture Capital*, please."

Onscreen, a brace of nuclear missiles launched in echelon at the *Quantum Eagle*, a small Company light cruiser, from what had once been SynCorp Headquarters. The *Eagle* initiated evasive action. Chaff in the form of mini-drones expelled from the rear of the *Eagle*, their job to divert the missiles from their target. The cruiser followed up with PDRs, their fire tracing red dashes across the black fabric of space. One missile hit the chaff cloud and exploded. The other two passed around it, staying ahead of the tracking fire of the cruiser's PDRs. The *Eagle*'s engines burned like white fire as she attempted to outrace the missiles long enough to kill them before they killed her.

"No way they get out of there," Lieutenant Shelby said at the helm.

"Keep your thoughts to yourself, Mr. Shelby," Nuss said calmly.

"They got another one!" exulted another officer.

The flare onscreen testified to the value of PDR fire. A second ship, a frigate like the *Sun Tzu* named the *Templar's Gold*, swung between the *Eagle* and the third missile, concentrating its own PDR slugs on intervention. But the missile slipped past and under the *Gold*, still locked onto the *Eagle*.

"No, no, no," Shelby whispered.

"*Mister Shelby*," Nuss warned.

The missile impacted the *Eagle* in the aft-port quarter, detonating its nuclear payload in eerie silence. An orange-white firestorm enveloped the *Eagle*, momentarily overloading the *Sun Tzu's* forward screen. Pieces of the light cruiser began to separate slowly, spinning away. They were too far distant to see the bodies. Adriana closed her eyes.

The bridge crew of the *Sun Tzu* watched in silence as the conflict continued onscreen. Capital ships pounded one another at close range. Smaller ships offered support by concentrating their fire on drones and fighters, which swarmed the larger ships like angry hornets. The *Quantum Eagle's* death faded into sputtering fires, then became visual noise behind the rest of the battle.

"Captain Nuss," Adriana said, taut and brittle. "You will take the *Sun Tzu* and her escorts into action. You will support your Company's fleet in battle, or by the fucking Mother Universe, I'll—"

Nuss stood up from his command chair. Adriana thought he might actually take a swing at her.

Do it. Knock this old lady on her ass. Give me the cover of Company regs to twist your ballsack off, you—

"Admiral Galatz ordered us to stand off," Nuss said. For the thirteenth or fourteenth time, by her count. "We are to preserve your life at all costs, Regent. Perhaps had you not requested a berth on this ship, we could be doing our actual job."

"Fuck you," Adriana replied. "Your duty is to help win this battle."

"My duty," Nuss said, taking a step toward her, "is to follow orders." He returned to the captain's chair. "Question my duty again, and I'll have you removed from the bridge. I don't give a good goddamned what your position on the Company org chart is."

Adriana took a deep breath. Furtively and with a self-consciousness she wasn't used to feeling, she scanned the eyes of the bridge officers around her. Some seemed sympathetic to her desire to enter the fight, especially after what had happened to the *Eagle*. Most seemed shackled to tradition and loyalty to back their captain. They knew their duty, too.

"Captain, the *Arte della Lana* is moving to the *Sovereign*'s aid," Lieutenant Dhagari at tactical reported. "She's taking a pounding."

"Show me," Nuss said.

The camera view jerked hard across the starfield until Earth hung in the background. What looked like a stick with two mushroom heads, one at each end, stood in orbit over the planet—the former headquarters of the Syndicate Corporation and now the SSR's base of operations. In the foreground flew Galatz's *Sovereign*, now making its second attempt to close with the station. The enemy fleet, still crippled from its defeat over Pallas, was putting up a surprisingly vigorous defense. Every ship they had, including the old lightly armed *Pax Corporatum*, maneuvered to cut off the *Sovereign*'s attack run. Smaller Company ships, including the cruisers *Wall Street* and *Arte della Lana*, became blockers, attempting to wedge open the gap for the running back's power run up the middle. Several smaller ships engaged their opposites in the SSR fleet.

"This is our moment, Captain," Adriana said, attempting to sound rational and calm. Sage-like. "Admiral Galatz knows if we take out that station, we can win this thing. War is as much about morale as it is firepower."

"Please don't presume to school me in war, Regent," Nuss replied. "And nothing matters more than firepower. If he disables the station, it evens up the fight."

The *Sovereign* sped forward, a bull ignoring the pests trying to distract it. To Adriana, the PDR fire raging around her looked like a fireworks display ordered by Satan himself. Red and savage and unrelenting. The station launched another brace of missiles like the one that had killed the *Quantum Eagle*. The *Sovereign*, large and slow to turn, didn't bother trying to alter course, instead firing her own defensive missiles. This time, a captain's luck held. Each of the three missiles from the station plumed their payloads far enough away from the *Sovereign* that she sustained no damage.

Adriana began to think that maybe Galatz's stubborn strategy might just work. Then she saw the smaller SSR ship, a corvette, banking away from its one-on-one battle to aim straight at the *Sovereign*'s flight path.

"What's she doing?" Shelby asked.

Even Adriana knew the answer to that. "Sacrificing herself," she said under her breath.

The *Sovereign* had finally noticed the real danger. SynCorp's largest warship wasn't destined to die through overwhelming firepower. Her end would come at the hands of a seafaring battle tactic as old as seafaring itself. She launched a brace of nuclear missiles in a desperate attempt to stop the corvette aiming straight for her.

"Too close," Nuss said. "No time to lock on, no time to arm."

The missiles sped past the accelerating corvette. Red tracer fire from the *Sovereign*'s point defense cannons converged on the enemy ship. Someone magnified the forward screen. Adriana could almost feel the jolting thump of the tungsten-encased plastisteel slugs as they penetrated the corvette's hull. Maybe one would get lucky, create an explosion or ... but at that range, would that do more damage to the *Sovereign* than ramming her?

At the last moment, the *Sovereign* surrendered its mission to assault the station, attempting to accelerate away from the threat of the corvette. Too late. A collective groan passed around the *Sun Tzu*'s bridge as the smaller vessel plowed into the port side of the capital ship. Fire consumed the corvette, flaring with bright white destruction as it penetrated the hull of the pride of the SynCorp fleet.

"Holy Jesus," Shelby said. "Holy Christ on the cross."

The crew of the *Sun Tzu* went silent again save for the whirs and pings of the ship's systems. Not even Nuss raised his voice to rein in the helmsman's reaction.

The *Sovereign* continued on course, thrust forward by physics, but already beginning to list to starboard, redirected by the corvette's momentum. The battle onscreen seemed to relent in a kind of requisite respect for the sacrifice of one ship and the death throes of the other.

"Oh my God," said Dhagari behind Adriana. She turned to find the young woman shocked, her cheeks draining of blood. But she wasn't looking at the forward screen.

"What is it, Lieutenant?" Nuss said, eyes still captured by the inferno.

"Sensors..." The junior officer broke off, the words catching in her throat.

"Captain, we're receiving hails from the *Sapphire of Sol* and *Venture Capital* requesting the fleet captain's orders," First Officer Averson said.

"Lieutenant Dhagari," Nuss said, turning, "make your report."

For some reason, Dhagari looked at Adriana instead of her captain, though she addressed herself to him. "It's the Phantom Fleet, sir. It's here."

Adriana shared a look with Nuss. Someone needed to say something. Anything that wasn't mutinous or overly forlorn would do.

"Captain," Adriana said as evenly as she could, "the situation has changed. You must engage now."

But Nuss simply sat in the captain's chair in silence, staring at her. His eyes wanted answers. His eyes wanted orders.

"Captain!" Dhagari again. "Fast-movers coming in, fighters probing from the Phantom Fleet. Half a dozen, at least."

"Half a dozen," Nuss repeated.

Dhagari replaced the listing *Sovereign* on the forward screen with a tactical display of their position relative to the incoming ships. Center screen, the *Sun Tzu* held the far-right flank of Galatz's attack formation, well away from the battle. Between her position and the Moon, blips began to appear. Large triangles for ships. First one, then three, then six—the SSR's so-called Phantom Fleet. A vanguard of tiny triangles flew ahead of the main body. They were quickly approaching the *Sun Tzu*.

"Captain Nuss, your orders?" Commander Averson prompted. "I recommend engaging the fighters with missiles, sir, before they're in effective range. We can position the *Sapphire* and *Venture* to—"

"No," Nuss said, his voice oddly detached. Like he was reading from a textbook. "We need the missiles for the capital ships. I don't think we're going to have enough..."

"They're almost on top of us, sir!" Dhagari reported. She replaced the tactical image onscreen with a view of the attacking fighters. They broke formation in twos, preparing their attack runs.

"Point defense cannons online," Averson said. "Target the nearest fighters. Remember your training, people."

PDRs from the *Sun Tzu* marked a sharp line of fire toward the fighters. One fighter dived straight for the frigate, so quickly and with such fast breaks, the ship's cannons couldn't score a hit.

"No way that's manned," Shelby said. "The physics—"

"Focus, Mr. Shelby," Averson said with a nervous glance at Nuss, who sat inert. "Evasive action: pattern omega-four."

Two fighters exploded, targets of point defense rounds. But the fast one came around for another pass, aiming straight at the bridge.

"Brace for impact!" Dhagari yelled.

PDRs lanced out from the fighter's two bow-mounted cannons straight at the camera feeding the forward screen. Around Adriana, officers instinctively dove for cover. The fighter pulled up and away. The sensation of growing lighter bloomed in Adriana's belly, and she had the absurd flashback of hanging in the Tin Can in Jupiter's atmosphere. Had gravity failed?

The screams of panicky crew members surrounded her.

Averson shouted about containment.

Adriana's ears began to ache—her eardrums, expanding outward.

Hull breach, her old pilot's training told her. *We've been holed by the enemy.* Then, despite the pressurized pain increasing inside her skull, *That motherfucker holed the ship!*

"I said, get that goddamned containment online!" Averson shouted.

Even before he'd repeated the order, the swelling of her eardrums had begun to subside. Erkennen tech, sealing the ship from inside its own infrastructure. Her lungs began filling with air again.

Behind her, Dhagari was weeping. Adriana turned to see why.

Nuss's body sat slumped in his chair. Her stomach flip-flopped, and it had nothing to do with the stabilizing gravity. A point defense round had taken off his head. Gore painted the deck at Dhagari's feet.

"Where are those fighters?" Averson asked. His eyes, like everyone else's, were glued to the captain's headless corpse. "Dhagari! Plot their position and get me reports from the *Sapphire* and *Venture*."

Her voice shaking, she said, "Moved on, sir. Headed for the main battle. The corvettes are nicked but mostly unharmed."

"Helm, close up with the fleet." Averson's breathing was ragged. "Mr.

Shelby! Best possible speed to fold in with the fleet, if you please. Pass the word to our escorts."

"Aye, Commander ... aye, Captain, I mean."

"Belay that," Adriana said. Then, louder, "Belay that order!"

Averson turned to her. "Regent, I really must—"

"Look—onscreen," Adriana said.

Its view still focused on the approaching Phantom Fleet. Half a dozen ships, a motley assembly of cruisers and frigates and what looked like a converted freighter. It was a poor showing.

If there's no fleet to oppose it, it doesn't have to be that big.

"We can stop them," Adriana said. "Give our remaining ships a fighting chance against that station."

Averson closed his eyes, then opened them again. "We don't have enough firepower, Regent," he said, as if explaining to a child that water was wet. "Militarily, we should add our strength to the rest of the fleet and make a best, last stand."

"We have three ships," Adriana said. "Their formation is tight. Arrowhead, I believe you spacehoppers call it."

"The firepower is still—" Averson began.

"The only firepower we'll need is to get us inside their formation," Adriana insisted. Averson's eyes narrowed. She calculated her next words carefully. Negotiation was about being effective, not honorable. "Or are you a coward—like Nuss?"

There were gasps around the bridge. The whites of Averson's eyes flared. "You fucking ... you Alabastered Bitch. Captain Nuss gave his—"

"Yes, he did," she said. "And I'm grateful for his sacrifice. But his inability to see the bigger picture, to step into the gap, might have cost us this war. Or—gave us this opportunity? We can take advantage of it." She hadn't closed the deal. She could see it on Averson's face. "You have kids?" Adriana demanded, scanning the frightened eyes of the bridge crew. "You have loved ones you want to protect from that snake bitch? We can die making a difference, or we can die making a stand that's likely to fail, ensuring Cassandra's victory." To Averson, "Your call."

Averson's cheek flexed. Adriana could see his training, what he thought of as his duty, warring with the longshot possibility she'd hinted at. If they took this chance, this one chance, they might hand Galatz the reprieve he needed to turn the tide of battle.

"Lieutenant Dhagari," he said, "time to engage the second fleet?"

There was a quiet breath from tactical. "Ten minutes at hard burn, sir."

"Very well."

"Sir?" Dhagari said. "I don't want to die."

Adriana cleared her throat. "No one *wants* to die, Lieutenant. At best, we get to choose how we do it. And that's not nothing."

There was the sound of movement from the captain's chair. Averson, pulling Nuss's corpse from it. Carefully, reverently, he laid the captain's headless body on the deck.

"Have medical bring a stretcher," he ordered, staring at the blood-soaked leather. Turning to Adriana, he said, "You'll need a seat for the hard burn. We can clean—"

"I'm used to blood," she said, mounting the dais. Averson let her pass as she sat in the captain's chair. In truth, she was glad to sit down. Her knees and hips were threatening to collapse beneath her. "My comfort is less than secondary."

"Very well," he said. "Pass the word to the *Sapphire* and *Venture*. We hard burn to intercept those ships as soon as the captain's body is … stowed. And I'd … I'd speak with their captains in the privacy of my ready room."

"Aye, sir."

With the crew occupied by other things, Adriana reached into her right thigh pocket and withdrew one of Estevez's two remaining hypos. She placed it against her wrist where the officers of the *Sun Tzu* couldn't see.

Once more unto the breach, dear friends.

The soft *phish* forced Estevez's miracle microbes into her bloodstream.

28

RUBEN QINLAO • CHRYSLER BUILDING, OLD NEW YORK CITY, EARTH

Ruben led Strunk up the corridor. More of the upward arrows and bourbon-amber marble design lined the Chrysler Building's walls.

"Slower," Strunk said. "We're a patrol, not a rescue party."

They rounded a corner and spotted two Soldiers standing outside a suite door. Except for their presence, the suite was unremarkable—part of the plan of random anonymity Weiss had hinted at.

The comm chatter became excited. A patrol had found the men's bodies in the rail channel. The guards at the door to the suite were reacting, taking in the intel.

"It's now or never," Strunk growled, pulling his stunner-pistol combination.

Ruben was already moving. He reached the guards before they could react, thrusting his katara through the first man's throat. The second guard, hemmed in by the close quarters, struggled to raise his rifle. Strunk put his stunner against his unhelmeted head and fired.

Both men dropped.

Strunk held up a finger, then engaged comms.

"We've found the infiltrators," he said. "They're trying to escape through the tunnel into the subway."

Muting again, he said, "That should add some confusion." He knocked with a knuckle on the door. "Ma'am? Everything okay in there? We thought we heard some noise."

Ruben had a questioning look.

Proof of life, Strunk mouthed.

"Room is secure," a man's voice answered. "What was that noise?"

"At least two of them, then," Strunk whispered. "Kisaan and a guard or six."

"It's only going to get hotter up here," Ruben said.

"Yeah." Strunk made a motion for Ruben to give him space, then set his weight on his back heel and kicked in the door.

Ruben charged in, a pistol in one hand, his katara in the other. The room came alive. There were four SSR troopers, two squads of two each, and Elinda Kisaan, gazing out the window toward East River Bay. Tony Taulke wasn't there.

The Soldiers reacted, bringing their guns to bear on the entryway. Ruben dived and shoulder-rolled toward the nearest pair, used his momentum to stab his katara to the hilt through the first trooper's kidney. He yanked the blade free, keeping close in to prevent the others from having a clean shot.

Behind him, Strunk had followed up more slowly, letting the enemy focus on Ruben's fast-moving attack. Methodically, he fired each of his weapons together, a redundancy of deadly force.

Punk! Crack!

Punk! Crack!

One of the Soldiers from the other pair went down. The second leveled his rifle and sprayed the entryway with bullets. One, maybe two, took Strunk in the torso.

From the corner of his eye, Ruben saw Elinda Kisaan moving. But she wasn't attacking them—she'd sprinted for the bedroom in the adjoining suite.

The second Soldier of the two-man team he'd attacked slammed the butt of his rifle across Ruben's jaw, punishment for his distraction. Orange stars broke out in Ruben's vision, followed by the scarlet pain of the impact. He heard but couldn't see the sound of Kevlar and cloth and a plastisteel rifle body brushing together as the Soldier aimed.

Punk! Crack!

The blast from Strunk's two barrels. Despite his cloudy eyesight, Ruben saw the second Soldier fall backward. But he was cursing with venom, not screaming in pain. Ruben shook his head, trying to clear the crimson shadows from his vision. The trooper was on his ass but recovering, bringing his rifle around.

Ruben didn't think. He moved on instinct, throwing himself forward. It was clumsy and amateurish, but he got inside the Soldier's firing arc. Ruben stabbed the katara upward, only half-seeing his target—the man's Adam's apple. A burst of fire from the Soldier's rifle sprayed the walls and ceiling.

Bracka-bracka-bracka!

Blood poured from the wound. Ruben pulled the knife free and thrust in again. The rifle stopped firing.

Behind him, Strunk shouted, cursing in some unintelligible language or making sounds that weren't language at all. Fighting his urge to pursue Elinda Kisaan, Ruben turned and found the last of the four Soldiers atop Strunk, trying to force a blade of his own down into the enforcer's chest. Ruben rolled to his feet and dashed forward. He thrust his katara with both hands through the notch at the back of the Soldier's skull.

Strunk was breathing hard. Ruben rolled the trooper's corpse off him to find Strunk was shot in the stomach.

"Cheap-ass fucking armor!" Strunk yelled. Then, more soberly, "Thanks, Boss Man. I owe you—another one."

"We're not done here," Ruben said.

"I know." Strunk backed himself against the couch under the window, then pulled his attacker's rifle from the dead man's hands. "I'll guard the door."

Ruben stood and faced the door Elinda Kisaan had passed through. The room around them had become quiet in death, save for Strunk's murmured cursing at his wound.

"Come on, then!" Kisaan shouted from the bedroom. "A second chance for me to finish the contract."

Strunk reached a hand out. "A little caution, remember?"

The hand dropped away as Ruben stepped forward. Placing his back against the wall, he tried to follow Strunk's advice. He attempted to tamp down his rage at Elinda Kisaan.

His gun hand led as his eyes reconnoitered the bedroom. He hadn't needed Strunk's caution after all. Elinda Kisaan, hair tied back in the warrior's style—as it had been that night on Mars that seemed so long ago—stood in a battle stance. In each hand, she held a katara blade, one poised high for attack, the other low for defense. Tony Taulke sat in his maglev-chair near the window, eyes glazed with tranquilizers.

"No gravity control to help you this time," Elinda Kisaan said. Her eyes went to the pistol in his off hand. "Or would you prefer a coward's victory?"

"I'll get therapy after," Ruben said, aiming his pistol.

Kisaan's eyes widened.

Ruben pulled the trigger.

The hammer hit—but no report followed.

The weapon had jammed.

Kisaan's cheeks arced upward in a feral smile. Her hands worked the hilts of her katara blades, eager for blood. She advanced.

Ruben yanked twice on the slide, ejecting the bullet blocking the chamber—his last in the magazine. Without time to reload, Ruben flipped the pistol to hold it by the barrel. It was now a defensive weapon to counter Kisaan's second blade.

He moved quickly to meet her.

Their kataras clashed high, but her off-hand defensive blade had really been a feint. She brought it up and in, aiming for a kidney, but his pistol countered, the sharp ring of the knife's reinforced steel sliding along the meaner metal of the barrel. He could smell her raw, sour breath. A hungry smile warped her lips. Her eyes glowed with the sweet anticipation of killing him. They broke apart and began circling in the small space of the bedroom.

"You don't have the instinct, Qinlao," she said. "You're a rich kid who likes to get his hands dirty on the seedier side of the street. But you don't know its rules."

"You didn't have to kill her," Ruben said. "You murdered her for no reason."

"Wrong," Kisaan said, licking her lips. "I killed her because I wanted to."

The rage welled up in him, and Ruben charged again. This time he feinted with the knife, the more obvious weapon, and Kisaan countered, sparks jumping from the blades as they clashed. He brought the gun around wide, hoping to stay outside her peripheral vision, but Kisaan saw it coming and brought her second blade up. The clash bled the power from his strike. Kisaan chopped the blade down, carving him open. Ruben leapt backward, the pain searing and red across his left forearm.

"You see, this kind of wetwork isn't for you." Her smile blazed in her eyes.

His arm was painful but functional. He'd almost dropped the pistol. She was trying to get inside his head, he managed to think through the blistering pain.

"And speaking of wetwork, I was there for your big finish, Ruben. She squealed for me, too. Only difference? She wasn't faking it for Tony Taulke with me."

His vision clouded with red rage. He let it show. He wanted her to think she was succeeding in making him careless. He wanted her to get lazy and sloppy.

Ruben screamed the rage he'd held inside for weeks. It filled the room as he charged her again. His strikes came fast and furious, their combinations spoken with quiet proficiency in his sister Ming's determined voice. Strikes, efficient and without waste, not like in the martial arts vids. No flourishes, no broad swaths of air between impacts. Simple, straight, deadly strikes.

Metal rang, slid and scraped—knife to knife, knife to pistol barrel.

Kisaan's counterstrikes were mechanical and instinctive, not driven by strategy. Ruben drove her backward until her heels braced against the wall. Her own fury kindled in her eyes as her second knife at last worked past the grips of his pistol, slashing his arm again. Ruben cried out and his weapon clattered to the floor. The fear in her eyes changed to triumph, and she jerked the knife away to deliver the deathblow.

But Ruben performed a quick repost with his primary hand, twisting her knife out and away. In the moment before Kisaan powered her off hand up and into his gut, Ruben plunged his own katara down and into her heart.

Her blade reached his side but without any force. It dropped from her hand, clattering atop the pistol on the floor.

"That's for Mai, you fucking bitch," Ruben hissed. He twisted the knife and watched the light leave her eyes as she collapsed to the floor. He followed her down, reveling in her helplessness as her life ebbed away.

Ruben knelt and watched the blood pump out of her, burning the image of his lover's killer on the permanent record of his brain. Then he engaged the epsilon symbol on his sceye.

"Gregor, we've secured Tony," he said. "Though, for how long..." How long would it be till they were overrun by SSR troops? His gaze returned to Elinda Kisaan. Her blood had stopped pumping. Her eyes were flat and empty.

"That is fantastic news!" Gregor Erkennen said. "And we have finally regained control of CorpNet. We've got bots de-authorizing SSR control access systemwide. I'll see what I can do about diverting their command structure, too. Maybe buy you some time. Hold on, Ruben!"

Before Ruben could answer, the call dropped. Across the room, there was the silent whisper of a maglev-chair maneuvering.

"Well done, Ruben," Tony said, his voice still weak. "Well done."

Ruben turned his head to regard the man in the maglev-chair. Taulke looked very old in that moment.

"Your sister Ming would be proud of you," he said.

Ruben closed his eyes briefly, sighing. "Speaking of family, there's something you need to know, Tony. It's about your son."

Adriana Rabh • Aboard the *Sun Tzu*

The microbes sang in her veins.

The *Sun Tzu* shook and thrummed with enemy fire. The SSR ships kept coming on in their arrowhead formation, probably confident they could swat the frigate and her smaller escorts aside. What they didn't know was that the Company crews facing them had an edge—they knew exactly how they'd die and when. That tended to take the pressure off living.

"Sir," Dhagari said, "the Phantom Fleet is concentrating its formation tighter."

Good, Adriana thought, gripping the arms of the captain's chair. Her fingers hurt only a little. The enemy was doing exactly what they needed them to do. The tighter the target, the bigger the boom.

"Idiots," Averson said. "They're not a goddamned shield wall. This isn't the goddamned Middle Ages."

"Thank God for idiots," Adriana said. They exchanged a not-much-longer-now, solemn expression.

Point defense rounds peppered space on the forward screen like flocks of crimson crows whipped up by a hurricane. Missiles and counter-missiles flew until racks were empty, then reloaded again.

"Captain! It's the *Sovereign!*"

"What?"

Onscreen at extreme range, SynCorp's flagship for war was back in action. It resembled a wounded leviathan, a monster harpoon that had once been the enemy corvette still wedged amidships. Its escort vessels, including the *Templar's Gold*, were clearing the last of the SSR's First Fleet.

The comm channel crackled. "Nuss, what the hell are you doing?"

Galatz!

"Commander Averson here, sir. Captain Nuss is ... dead, sir."

There was an impact at the other end of the channel. "Short on time here, Commander. Turn those ships—"

"My orders, Matthias," Adriana said. "We're covering your ass."

"Regent? You have no..." Another blast. "Averson! Turn those—"

Adriana turned to find Averson with his finger pressing the comm button, severing the connection.

"We shouldn't be distracted now," he said. His voice became admiring, committed. "We really can win this thing. If we can keep these fuckers off Galatz's back."

She nodded, then was rocked hard against the captain's chair.

"Missile impact in the aft-port quarter!"

The lights snapped off, then returned with the red glare of emergency lighting.

"Status of the drive core?" Averson said.

They were almost there. Adriana imagined she could see the mirrored-

S emblem of the snake cult on the enemy ships ahead of them. All of them, firing desperately at the *Sun Tzu* and her escorts.

"Decks fourteen through twenty-eight are irradiated. We've lost—"

"*Status of the drive core!*" Averson shouted.

"Undamaged sir."

"Coming into range," Shelby said.

Averson pushed a button. "Averson to escorts—countdown to braking burn in ten, nine, eight..."

Adriana gripped the arms of the chair tighter, if that were possible. The ache from hanging on in Jupiter's atmosphere? Gone. A distant memory from another lifetime.

The *Sun Tzu* flipped and burned, followed onscreen by the *Venture* and *Sapphire* doing likewise. It was like watching a ballet of perfectly syncopated starships. By contrast, the formation of the Phantom Fleet began to fracture. Had one of them just strafed a friendly with PDRs?

"Countdown to detonation," Averson said. "Ten, nine..."

And here we are, Adriana thought. *No trumpets. No tears of the universe.*

"Six, five..."

Almost made it a whole century.

She shifted in the captain's chair, offering Nuss a brief regret for the slight she'd done him in front of his crew. Against her right thigh, the bulk of a final hypo pressed against the captain's chair.

"Two, one."

One extra life after all, Adriana mused. Then, "Fuck you, Cassandra."

The stars dimmed, overmatched by the synchronized detonation of three engine cores.

29

STACKS FISCHER, UN BUILDING, OLD NEW YORK CITY, EARTH

"Move out here and lay your other weapons on the ground," Cassandra ordered.

"My friend here needs medical attention," I said, stepping out from behind the column. I placed my revolver and stunner on the floor in front of me.

"Oh, I wouldn't think of letting her die," Cassandra said, "yet. That would be a waste of good PR." She motioned to the Kisaan clone, who mouthed orders into her sceye.

I looked around for evidence that I'd made the wrong decision. Daisy, bleeding out. Bekah, in mortal danger. Half a dozen Soldiers around us, their barrels pointed my way. If I'd gone for broke, if I'd implemented the backup plan now that Jericho had failed, I'd likely have killed Bekah. Cassandra held her like a shield. And maybe that's what I should've done. Maybe a bullet would have found the Snake Queen after all. But then I'd have no way to know that for sure because I'd be embracing Mother Universe myself, and Daisy Brace would follow on shortly thereafter. At least alive, we still had options.

Although, in that moment, they seemed pretty limited.

The clone's expression morphed from giving orders over CorpNet to receiving bad news. "Cassandra, it's..."

"Well?" Cassandra said, releasing Bekah. I could see red streaks on her neck from Cassandra's grip.

"It's Elinda ... our sister is dead."

"What about Taulke?" Cassandra demanded. "Status?"

The clone answered, "Unknown."

Cassandra's face clouded. "That is unfortunate," she said. "Our priority is to re-secure Taulke. You'll head up the detail personally, Elissa."

But the clone didn't move. Still processing her test-tube sibling's loss, I guess.

A medical team appeared to tend to Daisy. They knelt beside her, getting to work.

"So Tony's sprung, eh? Bad luck, that." I injected my tone full of cocky. The only weapons I had were words. "Add to that the fact that we know about your second fleet. Galatz is doing for them right now," I said, not knowing if it was really true. "Hell's come home, sweetheart."

Cassandra flashed me an indulgent smile. Like she was dealing with a child who, eventually, would understand the life lesson. Across the room a boy and his dog walked in. I recognized the kid from SSR propaganda. Cassandra's adopted son. Could the situation get any weirder?

"Trace, come in. I want you to see this," Cassandra said. "I want you to see—"

Bekah leapt forward, jamming the hypo against Cassandra's neck. I didn't move, couldn't move—I wanted to see the Wicked Witch melt into the floor. But Cassandra only scowled, turning and grabbing Bekah by the neck again. The Snake Queen walked forward, carrying Bekah's weight like it was nothing, and slammed her against the nearest column.

Unconscious, Bekah Franklin fell to the floor.

Trace Anderson, UN Building, Old New York City, Earth

She'd called him, and so he'd come. He and Bandit together, as always. They'd stayed in hiding when all the gunfire was happening, but now it was over. Cassandra had called him in to bear witness, she said. To see the Old World's final attempt at saving itself fail.

Now he watched as Cassandra collapsed. She began to crawl toward him as he stood beside the dais, waiting. But waiting for what? Her death, maybe. All this to be over? Something.

The old man she'd been talking to dropped to the floor and grabbed a gun. Elissa stood and blinked for a moment, then dived to the side as the old man fired.

Crack! Crack!

Bandit barked and barked. Soldiers raised their weapons at the old man, and all Trace saw was danger. Bandit was in danger. Someone might shoot him by accident. He grabbed the dog by the collar and pulled him behind the dais.

Bracka-bracka-bracka!

The room filled with rifle fire. Trace peeked out to see Cassandra still clawing her way across the floor toward him, agony stretching over her features. The old man had pulled back behind a column on the far side of the room. On the floor, one of the white-coated med-techs lay facedown over someone else, two bloody red holes in his back.

Bracka-bracka-bracka-bracka-bracka!

"Help me, Trace!"

Cassandra extended a hand, and out of instinct, he took it. He pulled her behind the dais with him, where she fell against it for support.

"Do you see?" she said, pain contorting her face. "Do you see how they fight the future? Such ... futility! This is why I must complete my work, Trace. We must breed this out of our species—this tendency toward violence."

Bracka-bracka-bracka!

Crack! Crack!

The gunfire went on, and he held Bandit close. Cassandra reached a hand out again. This time, Trace didn't take it. She was a murderer of mothers. Of all those bodies in the corpse pile he'd seen on CorpNet, fed by the reapers, buried by the bulldozers.

And now someone was murdering her.

Wasn't that what justice was?

Cassandra's arm flung out, cracking her hand against the base of the platform. It was as if she were losing control of her own muscles. Her eyes were closed, and he could see them darting back and forth behind the lids. Like a crackhead on Dreamscape. Or a computer, working a problem.

"Virus," she said aloud. Then her eyes flew open. "It's a virus!"

Stacks Fischer, UN Building, Old New York City, Earth

Jericho was working! Thank God and Bekah Franklin...

Cassandra crawled away to hide in the shadows. That seemed about right for a snake. If I'd had a clear shot, I'd have done for her right then.

Bekah was in the open and unconscious, and there were lots of bullets flying around. At least Daisy had the shield of a dead body slung across her. I had to move, and fast. The clone seemed to have lost her nerve. She hid behind her column while I scrambled across the floor, throwing shots behind me.

Crack! Crack!

Bracka-bracka-bracka!

Wild but persistent, the troopers were. I got to Bekah and pulled her behind the first column. Either the Soldiers across the room or the clone would get us. I had to do something to break the logjam.

One of the Soldiers got braver. He was young and stupid and made a dash across the open space headed my way. I took my time, released a breath, and shot him in the throat.

Crack! Crack!

Time to reload and no time to do it.

Punk-punk-punk!

The clone was back in the fight. I covered Bekah with my body. All three slugs from the clone's stunner punched my longcoat. It was like being kidney punched in the same spot, over and over. But at least I wasn't dead—and more to the point, Bekah was still breathing. I gritted my teeth as I shucked casings and put my hand in my pocket for more bullets.

And came up dry.

Then the Snake Queen slithered out from her hidey-hole. She was smiling.

"Did you really think your human minds could out-program me?" she said. Though her legs were unsteady, her golden eyes flashed, confident in victory. "Did you really think you could subvert the impetus of evolution with some ancient computer coding and the best tech magic Human-Alpha minds could conjure?"

She strode into the center of the room, and if I could have changed my nuts into bullets, I would've done it right there, and no hesitation. I just needed one more .38 slug and a half breath's worth of time.

"I've been too kind. I've been too merciful with Dreamscape," Cassandra said. Her words were arrogant, but underneath them, a volcano was ready to blow its top. "With a single thought, I can clear the way for the Human-Beta species. With a single command, I can end every human in Sol who isn't fit to evolve."

I could feel Bekah breathing beneath me, still alive. There was hope in that, but it felt false, misleading. Like if I believed in the hope, I'd just prove myself to be the biggest bumpkin at the turnip festival.

Around me, all I saw was defeat. Gregor Erkennen's genius, funneled through Daniel Tripp and Bekah Franklin, come to naught in Jericho's defeat. Daisy Brace, dying or dead. But I still had one thing to hold on to— the burning certainty I'd carried inside since learning Cassandra was the same Cassie Kisaan I'd failed to end thirty years earlier. I still knew I had to correct that mistake—solve my own, personal Hitler Paradox and save millions, billions even, by ending the Snake Queen's crazy ambitions.

My kingdom for a bullet!

Instead, one of the Soldiers came and stood over me, his rifle at the ready. All I could do was lie on top of Bekah Franklin, fooling myself that I was protecting her, while Cassandra the Snake Queen delivered her final monologue before the chorus comes out and urges the audience to think on thicker thoughts as they left the theatre. "Go forth, now, keen listeners, and thinketh upon the lessons we hereby teacheth thee."

Motherfucker...

"Cassandra," the clone said, coming out from cover. "The fleet..."

Cassandra's expression of triumph curdled. "Status!" she demanded.

"The fleet is ... lost."

"Which ... what are you talking about? Which fleet?"

The clone's eyes went vacant and slack.

Suddenly, I felt better.

"Both of them," she whispered.

"It won't matter," Cassandra said. A righteousness of her own, fueled by fury, maddened her words as she spoke. She turned to look at me, and my newfound hope evaporated.

Just a fucking rube, I thought. *That's what I am.*

"Dreamscape is our real weapon," Cassandra declared. "That's the engine driving the future now. I'm sending the signal…"

Trace Anderson, UN Building, Old New York City, Earth

Trace had followed Cassandra from their hiding place in a daze. He'd followed at a respectful distance as she'd made her way to the center of the room. Bandit as always padding by his side.

Her talk of kindness and mercy and the future—it was all just background noise. His eyes found the eyes of the old man on the floor. He stared up at Cassandra with a look that was hard to read. He didn't want to give up, Trace could see that much.

There was a gray lump on the floor. Elise Kisaan's head. A bullet must have knocked it off its pike. Trace hardly recognized the slack, bulging shape that had once been the head of Cassandra's own mother.

Elissa said something, her expression empty. She and Cassandra spoke while Trace stared at the head staring back at him with its rheumy, dead eyes. They seemed to weep skin. Huck Finn's words came into his head from that moment in the novel when he made the hardest decision of his life. The decision to do the right thing, no matter what.

All right, then, I'll go to hell.

The room blurred. Trace's heart thundered in his chest. Had been racing, anticipating, for a while. All the air seemed to rush from his lungs. He felt his determination gathering inside him.

"It won't matter," Cassandra said to Elissa, her back to Trace. She sounded angry and victorious at the same time. "Dreamscape is our weapon. That's the engine driving the future now. I'm sending the signal …"

"You murdered her!"

Trace rushed forward with the steak knife. Cassandra half-turned, but by the time she saw him coming, it was too late. Trace Anderson plunged the knife into her back, square and true and straight to the hilt.

"You murdered her!" Trace shouted again. He pulled the knife out and plunged it in again. There were tears, hot and flowing on his cheeks. Cassandra's hands came up, but there was little strength in them. Trace twisted the knife in anguish, screaming his anger and his grief and his desperate need to have his mother back.

Stacks Fischer, UN Building, Old New York City, Earth

Sometimes, life throws you a curve ball. Sometimes, it's even a gift.

I didn't know what motivated the kid to stick the snake, and I didn't care. Here was the reason I hadn't given up. Here was the opportunity I'd dared to hope for.

I got to my knees, sprung the blade from under my wrist, and hurled myself upward, stabbing the Soldier standing over me through the throat. I jerked the blade up and around and stepped back as let the blood splattered. I took the M24 from his hands as gravity took him down.

"You're murdering your own future, you stupid shit!" the clone shouted, moving toward the kid. "You're murdering all our future!"

My peripheral caught the other Soldiers, raising their rifles. I was faster. I went flat over the trooper's corpse, which was still twitching, and started spraying the room.

Bracka-bracka-bracka!

I was lucky and caught two with headshots. The rest dove for cover.

"You sonofabitch!"

The clone again, angling for the boy. I turned my rifle on her and heard a death knell only those who've experienced combat know to fear.

Click.

The clone smiled.

Crack!

Then again.

Crack!

Two shots, and the clone's body jerked. I traced the source and found Daisy Brace, her arm already failing, her pistol clattering to the floor. She collapsed again beneath her corpse-shield.

The clone walked another step or two, then forgot how. She fell, her mouth still working. Arguing with death, maybe.

I shucked the magazine and reloaded. There were Soldiers moaning and struggling around the room, but no one looked hungry for more bullets.

I made my way to where the Snake Queen lay, reclining in a pool of her own lifeblood. The boy stood nearby looking lost, like maybe he'd just been dropped on an alien world. When she'd slid to the floor, he'd held onto the knife. He held it, dripping, still.

"Turn away, kid," I said.

"You're too late," Cassandra gasped. "I sent the signal. The future is here. Now."

"Not for you," I said, placing the rifle against my shoulder. "Resurrect this."

Bracka-bracka-bracka!

It's always good to have a backup plan.

30

RUBEN QINLAO • UN BUILDING, OLD NEW YORK CITY, EARTH

"You're absolutely sure?" Ruben said. "The signal didn't go through?"

"Cassandra's was the first access we denied when we regained control of the subspace communications network," Gregor Erkennen said. "Plus—" He gestured offscreen, and Kwazi Jabari joined him in the shot. "—Mr. Jabari doesn't have the HLA mutation, and he's still alive and well. We'll let you know when we've verified that's the case systemwide."

"Thank you, Gregor," Tony Taulke said in their shared call.

"Of course." Gregor cleared his throat. "And Cassandra's remains? They've been secured?"

"I've got a cleaning team working on that now," Tony assured him. "It's being taken care of."

"I can't emphasize enough how important this is, Tony," Gregor said, his forehead wrinkling. He was a man with doubts, Ruben saw. A man worried about past mistakes. "You must account for every drop of blood, every hair... We let the tech get ahead of us once. *More* than once, as you know well know. Innovation without conscience, in the wrong hands—"

"Yes, Gregor, I'm well aware of what tech in the wrong hands can do," Tony said, gesturing at the maglev-chair. "I'll see that Cassandra's remains are ... properly stored."

"Masada Station is as secure a facility as you could hope for." Gregor's voice had turned hopeful. "I would be glad to—"

"I'll take it under advisement." Tony said. "But at the moment, I need to get ready for my speech."

Gregor regarded Tony and Ruben a moment, his eyes passing between them. "Very well," he said. "Best of luck with the speech, then. Das vadanya."

The call ended.

The room resumed its former state of controlled chaos. Bekah Franklin continued talking quietly to Benjy Anderson in one corner of the room. Nearer the double doors to the suite, like two bouncers who'd heard rumors that trouble might be brewing, Eugene Fischer and Richard Strunk sat conversing—which, for them, meant hardly talking at all.

A woman approached Tony. "May we continue, Mr. Taulke?"

"Sure, Kesh," he said.

Ruben watched as two other women descended again on Tony, resuming their preparation work for his broadcast. One worked on his face, the other his hair.

"More color," Kesh said.

"Have you met Marakesh?" Tony asked. Ruben shook his head. "She took over when Mai..." Tony, not known for his subtlety or sensitivity, stopped speaking. Marakesh stepped in to rescue him, and Ruben suspected that would be a regular job duty going forward.

"I'm so sorry for your loss, Regent Qinlao," she said. "Mr. Taulke mentioned that you two ... it was a horrible, horrible thing, what happened to Mai. This whole thing ... just horrible."

"Thanks," he said for something to say.

"Pop!"

With that one word, the self-entitled self-importance of one teen's attitude raised the hackles on Ruben's neck. A Pavlovian response if there ever was one. Right or wrong, he doubted he'd ever trust Tony's son to tell him how the Martian sky turns the color of butterscotch on a sunny day.

"Let me through, I told you!" Anthony Taulke III elbowed his way into the room.

Tony sent away the prep team for a second time and motioned his son forward. Marakesh made a huffing sound. Ruben gave them space, feeling almost like a voyeur at the father-son reunion. Then Matteo Lasker passed through the double doors and into the room. Ruben noted with amusement the wide berth Lasker gave Strunk.

Well, this should be interesting.

"Pop, how are you feeling?" Junior asked. "I mean, you look—"

"Like dried-out shit, I know," Tony said with a rueful smile. "But hey, I'm still here."

"Yeah," Junior said with a bright smile. "So glad!" He stepped over to Ruben, extending a hand. Surprised, Ruben accepted it without thinking. Junior's palm was slick and fishlike. "Thank you so much, Regent Qinlao, for helping to rescue my father. It's a debt neither I—nor the Syndicate Corporation—will ever be able to fully repay." Junior turned back to the suite's entrance. "You too, Mr. Strunk!"

Strunk smacked his lips and looked away.

Behind Junior, Lasker cleared his throat.

"Oh, Pop! You remember Matteo Lasker—Danny Lasker's dad?"

"Of course," Tony said. Though his tone was cordial, his expression was impassive. "How's the olive oil business, Matteo?"

Lasker stepped forward. He literally held his hat in his hand. It was all Ruben could do not to laugh out loud at the brazen hypocrisy.

"Well, things had fallen off a bit, Mr. Taulke," Lasker said, attempting a droll tone. He appeared flushed to Ruben, like he'd just climbed all thirty-nine stories of the UN Building to reach the penthouse suite. "But with you back in charge, I'm confident things will get back to normal soon enough."

"Are you?" Tony said. Ruben admired that Tony had the discipline not to look in his direction. "Well—faith is a good thing to have, I suppose."

Lasker half-chuckled. It was obvious and nervous.

"Olive oil?" Junior asked.

"Old industry joke," his father said without looking at him. "Matteo, I want to thank you for keeping my son safe during the ... event. It's good to know the Taulke Faction has such dependable allies during the worst of times."

Lasker shuffled his feet. "Of course, Mr. Taulke. We were glad to do our part." He clapped Junior on the shoulder. "Tony was very brave. And there's nothing more important to me than loyalty, Mr. Taulke."

From somewhere distant, Ruben heard Strunk coughing. It didn't sound injury related. It sounded decidedly like *Bullshit*.

Tony inclined his head in acknowledgment of Lasker's pledge of fealty. Then, he looked to Junior. "Yes, my son demonstrated his character in true Taulke fashion."

"A real chip off the old block," Lasker said.

Tony's calm smile returned. "Couldn't have said it better. Approach please, Matteo."

Lasker stepped closer. Tony motioned for him to lean down. Junior cocked an ear, but Tony's whisper was intimate and quiet. When the mob boss stood up straight, his posture had a quality of rigor mortis about it. And the color had drained from Matteo Lasker's face.

"Thank you for your time in coming today," Tony said in dismissal.

Lasker lingered a moment, then caught the clue and turned, walking stiffly from the room. Junior watched him go.

"And what shall I do with you?" Tony said.

Junior's look became open and wondering. "What do you mean, Pop?"

"Oh, just that," Tony began, "you deserve special recognition for all you did during the coup. Bravely smuggling yourself off the *Pax Corporatum*. Smart, leaving your mother behind like that—safer than on the run with you. She's fine, by the way." Tony Junior went to speak, but the elder Taulke cut him off, gesturing at Ruben. "Regent Qinlao tells me your counsel was invaluable in Darkside. And then, getting here and seeking out the Lasker Family for assistance—resourceful, too."

Junior glanced from his father to Ruben and back again. "Thanks," he said safely.

Tony beckoned as he had to Lasker. "Come closer, son. I can't get to my feet yet." He tapped the arm of the maglev-chair.

Anthony Taulke III moved forward and leaned down. Tony took his son's face in both hands and stared into his eyes, looking from one to the other.

"Uh," Junior said, "you're not gonna kiss me, are you? Not on the lips. Cuz, Pop ... people are watching."

Tony relaxed. Like he'd been holding in tension and then, all at once, had let it go.

"I was thinking about it, son," Tony said. "I surely was." He held Junior's face in his hands a moment longer. "But you're right. Decorum must be maintained." Tony released his son. But before Junior could stand upright, his father applied a friendly smack across the cheek with his open palm. "Now, give me some room. I have a broadcast to make."

Junior touched his cheek. "Sure, Pop. Can't wait. I, uh—I think I'll see what's up with Mr. Lasker. He didn't look so good."

As soon as Tony Junior stepped away, Marakesh was back with her entourage.

"More color, especially in his cheeks!"

Tony glanced sidelong at Ruben, careful not to move his head and disrupt the beauty team's ministrations. "I know what you're thinking, Ruben. But that kid's all I've got. You play the hand you're dealt."

"And keep your enemies close?"

Tony became pensive. "Tony Junior's not my enemy. Hell, even Lasker's not my enemy. You know what my enemy is?"

Ruben waited.

"Weakness." Tony shooed the prep team away. "Kesh, clear out the syco-phants behind me. I want the SynCorp seal over my head—so make sure the 'bot shoots me at an upward angle. Mid-chest up. Understood?"

"Yes, Mr. Taulke."

Nodding, he returned his attention to Ruben. "Weakness is my enemy. As long as I'm strong—or, at the very least, *perceived* strong—I'll survive. My son understands this."

"It's the law of the jungle," Ruben said.

"Yes, that's exactly what it is. All *successful* business embraces the law of the jungle. The fittest survives by killing and eating the weak. Because my son understands this simple fact, he'll keep SynCorp strong into the future."

"But he's—" Ruben began.

"An idiot? A self-interested, narcissistic playboy who's been spoiled his whole life?"

Again, Ruben stood by silently.

"So was I, once," Tony said. "He'll need regents like you, who can balance out his ... more selfish tendencies."

A flutter tickled Ruben's gut, working its way into his chest. "My sister said the same thing. More or less. There's the kind of leader who builds, and the kind who maintains."

"Two very different skill sets," Tony said. "Both very necessary to the Company's long-term success. What do you know of this Edith Birch that Adriana elevated to assume her faction's mantle?"

"Nothing," Ruben said. "But Adriana chose her, so..."

A look of disdain passed over Tony. He quickly reined it back inside. "That old woman delighted in vexing me when she was alive. Now she does it from beyond oblivion." He sighed. "Well, I guess we'll find out about Birch. Now, if you don't mind ... you're in my light."

Suppressing a smile, Ruben stepped away with the others. Tony was soon at the center of three spotlights, a camerabot shooting him from below.

"We've got the Company logo over your left shoulder, Mr. Taulke," someone said. "You're good to go in five, four, three, two..."

―――――――――

"Ladies and gentlemen and citizen-workers of the Syndicate Corporation— our long nightmare is now over. I know we're all tired, so I'll keep this short. I just want to mention a few brief items of business.

"Cassandra Kisaan is dead. The three traitors—Elise Kisaan's daughters Elaena, Elinda, and Elissa—are dead. The Soldiers of the Solar Revolution —the SSR—is now a disconnected series of terrorist cells. Their fleet is broken and adrift in space. In partnership with the Marshals Service, corporate security forces are rooting out the remaining traitors wherever they hide. It's only a matter of time before the last are captured or killed. At the end of this broadcast, you'll see a secure link to report them to SynCorp authorities. Working together, we can restore the peace we'd all enjoyed for so long under the Corporate Compact.

"Our victory has not come without a steep price. I cannot possibly name all your loved ones who sacrificed themselves in the Company's cause, but I want to take a moment and mention a few of those heroes. The stalwart resistance on Mars, led by Captain Medina Li, whom I'm singling out for commendation. On Callisto, the miners of Valhalla Station fought to the death to preserve Adriana Rabh's regency, eventually overthrowing Cassandra's occupation. Those deaths will not be forgotten. And it must be mentioned that Adriana Rabh and the gallant crews she inspired gave their lives in an act of bravery that ensured the victory of our fleet over the enemy. I've relied on her sage counsel since the earliest days of the Company, and so..."

Tony paused and swallowed. To the audience, he no doubt appeared overcome with emotion. To Ruben, he seemed exactly as he had before with Lasker and Tony Junior.

Measured. Calculating.

"And so, to honor her sacrifice, I will also honor her choice of Edith Birch of Valhalla Station to take over her regency. Regent Birch, I don't know much about you, but I know that your husband—God rest his soul—was a Jovian miner. I know you're an expert in managing money. I know you saved Adriana's life. And I know that if Adriana chose you to continue her work, you must be a singular talent indeed. Welcome to the Board of Directors of the Syndicate Corporation.

"To the Soldiers of the Solar Revolution still at large, I make a one-time offer of amnesty. Any crimes you might have committed while in the service of Cassandra—well, those will be adjudicated under corporate law. But as to the specific crime of corporate treason, I will extend the hand of clemency to you. Come home. Your Company needs you. Those of you who *don't* heed this call to peace..." Tony leaned forward. "We will hunt you down to the ends of the solar system.

"Ladies and gentlemen, citizen-workers—this is a new beginning for all of us. Miner, farmer, regent—however you serve SynCorp, today we embrace the notion that every worker, everywhere, matters. We embrace the never more-obvious truth that, without your help, we could never have staved off disaster and the deaths of millions lost to Dreamscape—perhaps even those *you* love most.

"One last thing, before I bid you all a good night of good rest, secure in the knowledge that all is as it should be."

Slowly, deliberately, Tony stood. He turned away from the camera to the corporate logo behind him and placed his right hand, balled into a fist, over his heart.

"I pledge allegiance to the star of the Syndicate Corporation of Sol." Around him, others in the room began to take up the pledge in a chorus. "And to the bylaws for which it stands; one compact under law; irrevocable; with service and security for all."

Silent and unmoving, Tony gazed reverently at SynCorp's logo—a five-pointed star, encircled by a band, with the solar system at its center and a letter representing each of the Five Factions in each of the star's fingers: Erkennen, Kisaan, Qinlao, and Rabh, with Taulke at the top, of course.

"And ... we're out!" the director said.

The room broke into applause. Tony caught himself, collapsing back into his maglev-chair. Marakesh and others surrounded him, congratulating him on the speech, assuring him that it had been the best he'd ever given. He accepted their praise cordially, until one by one they wandered away.

Only Ruben remained, looking on.

"Well," Tony said. "What did you think?"

Ruben lifted an appraising eyebrow. "Passionate. Earnest. Reassuring." He shrugged. "Good speech."

Tony smiled, spurring his chair forward toward the double doors. "I'm looking forward to a soft bed. Walk with me. You can be my bodyguard."

They passed the two deadliest men in the solar system, who quietly watched them exit the room together.

When they were alone in the hallway, Ruben began, "I wanted to ask..."

"Yes?"

"Lasker. What did you say to him? He left white as a bleached sheet."

Tony grunted. "A man who wants power all his life is like a hungry tiger. Ruthless. Ravenous. Then, when he gets it ... suddenly frightened, like a lamb."

Ruben didn't understand. After a respectable period of time, he expected to hear on CorpNet that Matteo Lasker had met his untimely demise in a purely accidental and not-at-all suspicious way. Likely at the surreptitious hands of Stacks Fischer. Tony was implying a different kind of future.

"Oh, I'm too tired for guessing games," Tony said at last. "I gave him Kisaan Faction."

Ruben didn't realize he'd stopped walking till Tony turned his chair around to face him.

"You gave ... Matteo Lasker ... Kisaan Faction?"

Tired and shrunken from fatigue, Tony's shrug appeared exaggerated. "Adriana inspired me, I suppose. The Company needs new blood. And Lasker rules New York's underworld, which makes him a master of distribution for Earth goods—including agriculture—across the system. He's as good a choice as any. All of Elise's direct heirs are ... demised. In business, we call that an *opportunity*."

"But, Tony, he conspired with your son to—"

Tony held up a finger. "Never speak of that again, Ruben."

"But..." Ruben paused, needing to make his point despite Tony's warning. "You can't *trust* Lasker."

"Not true. I can trust him as much as any man—any *human being*—to act in his own best interests. I just elevated him to one of the five most powerful positions in Sol."

Ruben considered that a moment. "And now he owes you."

Tony winked. "*Everything.*"

"And now he's more loyal to you than he is to Tony Junior."

Instead of answering, Tony turned his maglev-chair and continued on toward his bedroom suite. Ruben had to jog to catch up.

"And what about the vote?" Ruben asked. "What was the result?"

"Vote?" Tony said without looking backward. "What vote?"

EPILOGUE
STACKS FISCHER, UN BUILDING, OLD NEW YORK CITY, EARTH

Tony Taulke glided from the room, Ruben Qinlao at his side. The old and the new. Qinlao had certainly grown up from that shy, teenage boy I'd met hiding behind his sister's skirt.

Tony? Same as ever. A master manipulator of the camera and the spoken word. And, by proxy, the people watching and listening. Tony has always known the importance of stagecraft. The necessity of the show going the fuck on, no matter what. It's what made the people who didn't want to think for themselves confident in their decision—which is most people, really.

"They make a pair, huh?" Strunk said after the doors shut behind them. "About as opposite as two men can get."

I murmured something that might have been words. My eye had landed on another unlikely pair. Bekah Franklin and the kid that had done the deed, Benjy something. Bekah and Benjy. It was a CorpNet sitcom waiting to happen. The kid was shut down, not saying anything. He just kept petting his dog.

Bekah, on the other hand, kept trying to wedge in, make a connection. With Tony and Ruben gone, the hubbub in the room petered out. I might've heard her ask the kid if he'd ever been to Titan. And was that the slightest dawning of awareness, the smallest pushing back on the isolation he'd drawn around himself after sticking the Snake Queen? Maybe even a little excitement at the prospect of visiting that moon-sized amusement park at the end of the solar system?

"Do they take dogs?" he asked, clear as a bell.

He'd be all right. Maybe they'd be all right together.

I hate feeling sentimental. It's a distraction. Which, of course, got me immediately thinking about Daisy Brace. Still in danger in ICU but not dead, which is better than where she could have been.

Strunk stood up and grunted as he stretched his midsection.

"How's the gut?" I asked, thinking of Daisy still.

"On fire," he responded. "And shit."

"What?"

"I think I ripped my stitches." He probed daintily with his dick-thick fingers.

"Shit," I commiserated.

"Yeah." Then, "I thought you had a thing, Fischer."

"I do," I said. "But you won't get to see it."

"No," Strunk grumbled, "I mean—you machine-gunned Cassandra. And, not that I'm complaining—but I thought you didn't kill women. I'm curious…"

I grunted. "That thing wasn't a woman."

Strunk did a head waggle. "If you say so."

"I do."

Cassandra had been a thing, just like I said. A thing that needed killing. Simple as that.

I watched Strunk push around on his gut. Despite our shared profession—or maybe because of it—I didn't think much of Dick Strunk. He was a lumbering gorilla who thought with his fists. But after his work in Darkside and New York's subway, maybe he was wilier than that. I might have to revise my assessment. It pained me to do it, but I felt compelled to say what I said next.

"Thanks for taking care of Tony while I was occupied elsewhere. Keeping him alive, I mean."

Strunk stood still. Maybe it was to protect the stitches still in place.

"Yeah," he said. "Just doing my job."

That rankled a bit. "Actually, you were doing *my* job."

His slight smile hooked up at the corners. Through the pain he must be feeling, it looked painted on.

"For now," he said. "But you won't be around forever."

I started to revise my assessment right then. "You looking to climb the corporate ladder the old-fashioned way?"

Strunk raised a hand, proclaiming his innocent intentions. It had blood on it.

"Just career planning," he said.

"Uh-huh." I noticed he hadn't answered the question. "Maybe one day, Strunk. But not today."

He placed his hand against his gut again, applying pressure.

"Sure, Fischer," Strunk said. "Still—tomorrow never knows, eh?"

ACKNOWLEDGMENTS

As The SynCorp Saga's six-book series comes to a close, we'd like to take a moment and thank the folks who helped us make this series' last three novels the best they could be for you.

The cover is the first thing you see, so we start off with a nod to Tom Edwards's outstanding designs. They brought singular moments from each story alive. Tom really knows how to balance action and atmosphere. When you look at a Tom Edwards cover, you say, "Yeah, I want to know more about what's happening there." Learn more about his designs at http:// tomedwardsdesign.com/.

Our copy editor, Michelle Benoit, has worked with Chris for nearly 30 years at the Texas A&M Transportation Institute. We relied on her "eagle eyes" to find typographical errors, clarify confusing sentence structures, and point out plot holes to smooth the way for you to engage with the story. Michelle's willingness to argue with Chris over details of editorial precision are one of the things we like best about her.

Our beta readers across the series—Jason Anspach, Jon Frater, Arnold Poole, Alison Pourteau, and Janice Yaklin—saw the novels in their raw form and offered timely, insightful feedback. Beta readers are a great way to see "if the story works" while there's still time to fix the flaws, and these folks did a great job helping make the books better for you. Any remaining plot, character, or logistical errors are entirely our own.

And right behind them in the publishing process, we have to thank those dozens of folks from Chris's Review Crew who were willing to read advance review copies (ARCs) while the warts were still showing. ARC readers are the booster rockets for a solid book launch, and the Crew was fantastic at reading the books ahead of publication and getting their honest reviews up as soon as possible thereafter.

Jon Frater—the "Godfather of the SynCorp World"—has provided technical input on the SynCorp universe since before even the first series was born. You'll note our recognitions of him in the Frater Drive and the Frater Orbital Lanes in the story itself. Not only was he great at helping us figure out space physics (and turning a blind eye when we bent those rules a bit), but he also served as our expert on Judaism and New York City, of which he's a native. Thanks, Jon, for *never* saying "I'd love to, but I don't have time..."

E.E. Giorgi—a brilliant Sci-Fi author in her own right and genetics research scientist specializing in viral evolution—helped us map out Cassandra's master plan regarding the HLA-Delta gene. (There is, in fact, no -Delta version of the HLA gene complex.) Elena's brilliant command of the science helped make us look like we knew what we were talking about. She was fantastic at reading draft material and saying, "That's a great idea, but here's how it would really work..." in the most generous, diplomatic way possible.

Nick McLarty, cybersecurity expert, oversaw Cassandra's attack on Masada Station. Conversations with him regarding what cybersecurity might look like a century from now helped us translate "today's geeky stuff folks might be aware of" to "tomorrow's cool stuff we want to talk about."

Dr. Yvonne Baum consulted on Tony's condition following Elissa Kisaan's assassination attempt. She lent her considerable medical knowledge as a first opinion guiding Isaac Brackin's diagnosis and treatment of Tony in Darkside. Likewise, Bill Patterson—another great Sci-Fi writer and "science guy"—consulted on how to kick Cassandra out, once and for all, from the Masada mainframe.

To make the series as successful as possible we asked Nicholas Sansbury Smith—*New York Times* bestselling author of *Hell Divers* and other great science fiction series—to guide our marketing hand. Nick's wisdom helped us launch *Valhalla Station* strong, which was key to the novel's success. He's *still* taking our messages and answering our emails, which speaks volumes about his generosity and willingness to help his friends in the indie author community.

I'd be remiss if I didn't take a moment and thank Severn River Publishing for picking up the entire SynCorp Saga for republication. Andrew Watts, Amber Hudock, and everyone at SRP have been fantastic to work with and have created a publishing house that is every bit the definition of a "writer-friendly publisher." They've enabled our series to have a second life and helped us find all-new readers for a story we loved writing.

And finally, thank *you*, dear reader. For shelling out the cover price, sure, but more than that—thank you for your time reading these novels. Time is really the most precious gift anyone can give anyone else, and we appreciate you spending yours with us. Without you, books are just static collections of words. With you, they're adventures in the imaginations of others, waiting to be born.

Chris Pourteau & David Bruns

ABOUT THE AUTHORS

David Bruns is a former officer on a nuclear-powered submarine turned high-tech executive turned speculative-fiction writer. He mostly writes sci-fi/fantasy and military thrillers.

Chris Pourteau is a technical writer and editor by day, a writer of original fiction and editor of short story collections by night (or whenever else he can find the time).

Sign up for Bruns and Pourteau's newsletter at
severnriverbooks.com/series/the-syncorp-saga